# Danielle Steel

# TURNING POINT

MACMILLAN

First published 2019 by Delacorte Press
an imprint of Random House
a division of Penguin Random House LLC, New York.

First published in the UK 2019 by Macmillan
an imprint of Pan Macmillan
20 New Wharf Road, London N1 9RR
Associated companies throughout the world
www.panmacmillan.com

ISBN 978-1-5098-7763-8

Visit **www.panmacmillan.com** to read more about all our books
and to buy them. You will also find features, author interviews and
news of any author events, and you can sign up for e-newsletters
so that you're always first to hear about our new releases.

To my wonderful, much loved children,
Beatie, Trevor, Todd, Nicky, Samantha,
Victoria, Vanessa, Maxx, and Zara,

May your disasters and challenges
turn out to be Turning Points and blessings

May you be brave and wise, and fortunate,
surrounded by people who love
and support you,

and may your choices be the ones you want
and that bless you in the end.

I love you so much,

Mommy/D.S.

# TURNING POINT

# Chapter One

Bill Browning had been on duty in the emergency room at Zuckerberg San Francisco General Hospital and Trauma Center for five hours and had just finished surgery on his third gunshot wound of the day. This one was going to make it, the first one had too, but the second patient had died, a sixteen-year-old victim of gang wars in San Francisco, and the drug trade the gangs engaged in. It was Christmas Day and business as usual at San Francisco General. They got the roughest cases in the city, brought in by ambulance, by the police, by paramedics, or by helicopter from highway accidents or any major disaster in the area. They were set up for multi-casualty incidents, in the jargon of the trade. San Francisco General was the best hospital in the area for severe trauma cases. It was a public institution with the benefit of private funding, in partnership with the Department of Public Health and the medical school at the University of California, San Francisco. All the physicians who practiced there were UCSF faculty as well, which kept the standards high. It was a teaching hospital, and private donations had provided a new building that doubled the capacity of the trauma unit and the patients they could treat to three hundred. The old facility was still in use.

The original building was notoriously grim. Almost every door in the hospital was locked with electronic access codes, and it wasn't unheard of for injured victims from rival gangs to shoot each other in the emergency room once they were brought in, or pull guns on members of the staff and threaten them. There were metal detectors, but in spite of that, occasionally visitors were able to sneak weapons in. It was an added element at General that the medical personnel had to deal with, along with some of the worst emergencies and traumas in the city.

The care of trauma victims was their strong suit, and Bill Browning was the head of the trauma unit. He signed up for duty in the ER for most major holidays, since he had nothing else to do. It was his gift to his colleagues, allowing others to be home with their families. Holidays meant nothing to him when he didn't have his children with him. Now thirty-nine, Bill had specialized in trauma for his entire medical career. He was the senior doctor on staff on Christmas Day, and would be again on New Year's Eve. He only got to have his daughters for Christmas every other year, and this was the off year.

The nurses had decorated the emergency room and the visitors' waiting room in the old facility with tinsel and assorted holiday decorations, which no one seemed to notice. Their patients were usually too severely injured, and their families too distressed, to care about the slightly forlorn evidence of the holiday scattered around the unit. Patients with the flu, food poisoning, bronchitis, or a sprained ankle ordinarily went to other hospitals. Only the most severe injuries, and a steady flow of the homeless population who were injured or ill and brought in by the police, went to SF General. The work was challenging for the medical staff, and a valuable learning experience for UCSF students. Bill Browning had seen just about everything that humans could inflict on themselves and each other during his career as an ER and trauma doctor. Nothing shocked him anymore. But it still saddened him to see the victims of the gangs. Their deaths were so senseless, such a waste, and evidence of young lives gone wrong. He had signed the death certificate of a sixteen-year-old boy only two hours earlier.

He hadn't stopped moving or sat down in the five hours he had been on duty, since ten that morning. It was a hell of a way to spend Christmas, but his two little girls, Philippa, called Pip, and Alexandra, Alex, were in London, where they lived with their mother. They were nine and seven years old. Their mother, Athena, was British. She had left San Francisco when Alex was three weeks old, the earliest date their pediatrician would allow her to travel so far with a newborn. Athena couldn't wait to leave. The marriage had been dead long before that, although Bill had tried valiantly to hang on and convince her to keep trying, but their union had been doomed from the first.

Since the divorce, he had plunged himself into his work more than ever, and didn't see his girls nearly enough. He had them for a month in the summer, Christmas on alternate years, and whatever other time he could manage to fly to London for a few days. His ex-wife didn't like sending the girls to San Francisco to see him. They'd been divorced for six years, she had remarried a British lord a year later, and now had two-year-old twin boys. Her second husband, Rupert, was exactly who she should have married in the first place. Her family referred to Bill as "The American," and considered him her "youthful mistake."

Athena had been twenty-three when they met in New York. He'd been visiting his parents for a week during his residency. After medical school at Columbia, he'd done his internship and residency at Stanford, and stayed on in San Francisco afterward when he was offered a job at SF General. It wasn't cushy or glorious, but it was the right place for the trauma work he wanted to do. He had no desire to return to New York. He enjoyed the weather and the outdoor sports he could pursue in San Francisco in his time off, hiking, windsurfing, sailing year round. And he particularly liked the hospital where he worked, and the kind of patients they treated.

His parents were part of an elitist, snobbish social world that had always made him uncomfortable. He avoided it at all cost. While visiting them, under pressure he reluctantly agreed to join them at the party where he had met Athena. He was twenty-nine years old and dazzled by her. She was spectacularly beautiful, a little eccentric, outrageous, and a rebel. She had grown up in a sophisticated, glamorous, international jet-set world, and was visiting friends in New York.

Bill had fallen head over heels in love with her, and she had come to San Francisco a month later, to pursue their torrid affair. She stayed. He was working long shifts in his residency, and whenever he wasn't working, they spent most of their time in bed, or doing the sports he enjoyed and introduced to her. She thought their romance exciting and exotic. Bill was different from any man she'd ever known. He was straightforward, honest, hardworking, and modest. She was wild, sexy, and a rare bird for him. She'd gotten pregnant with Pip six months later, and they flew to London over a long weekend to explain the situation to her parents. Bill proposed, which he wanted to do eventually anyway. It was just sooner than he'd planned. They were married in a discreet ceremony, and neither family was thrilled with their decision. Her family thought him too dull. His family thought her too racy.

Pip was born six months later, and Bill bought a Victorian house in Noe Valley, where they could become a family and begin their life together. Her parents sent over a nanny from London so Athena didn't have to be tied down, and she went home to England frequently to see her sisters, parents, and friends, and then returned to Bill, their baby, and their San Francisco life, a little less enthusiastically each time. She felt like a fish out of water in sleepy San Francisco.

It had taken Athena all of five minutes to fall in love with Bill the night they met, and about a year to realize what she'd done, and how different they were. He was more of a detour than a destination in her life, and at the end of a year with him, she had begun to have serious doubts about the marriage. She was six months pregnant with Pip by then, and the baby brought them closer for a while. The life they shared was exactly what Bill wanted, a wife he loved and an adorable baby in a cozy little Victorian house in a family neighborhood. Athena was like an exotic bird trapped in a cage in a foreign land. It had taken her less than a year after Pip was born to fall out of love with him completely, and she got pregnant with Alex by accident after they got drunk at a party when Pip was fifteen months old. She spent most of the pregnancy commuting to London to see her old friends, and got increasingly depressed whenever she came back to Bill in San Francisco. His parents had never liked her, and were dismayed by what he'd gotten himself into, but he was still insisting that Athena would settle down and get used to married life. He had a long talk with her father, who suggested that Bill give up his career in medicine, move to England, and join him in the family shipping business if he wanted the marriage to work. Athena was never going to be a "California girl." The only one who refused to see it was Bill. Three weeks after Alex was born, Athena took the two girls to England and spent the summer in the south of France with her sisters and friends at her parents' summer home there. At the end of the summer she called to tell Bill she wasn't coming back and wanted a divorce. He was devastated and tried to talk her out of it, but she was already seeing Rupert by then, and Bill didn't have a chance. She and Rupert had had a summer fling in the south of France.

She and Rupert had grown up together. He was one of her own, and a British lord like her father. Rupert was as much a libertine and free spirit as she was, and her three years in California were over. She never came back. Bill lived in the house in Noe Valley until the divorce she filed was final, hoping she would change her mind. She didn't. Eventually he sold the pretty little house and moved to a small apartment on the Embarcadero, with a view of the bay and the Bay Bridge and a second bedroom for his girls when they would come to visit. The apartment was stark and barely furnished, and he was still living there five years later. He had never bothered to decorate it, except for the bare essentials from IKEA, including a pink bedroom set for the girls. The rest of the apartment looked as barren and empty as he felt.

When his daughters visited him now in the summer, they traveled most of the time. He took them to Lake Tahoe, camping in Yosemite, they went on road trips, he took them to Disneyland, and did all the things divorced fathers do, trying desperately to establish a bond with his children in too little time. They were as British as their mother and stepfather, and loved their little half brothers. Bill tried to plant the seed of their going to college in the States one day, which Pip was mildly interested in, but it was still nine years away. In the meantime, he had his month with them in the summer, an occasional weekend when he could fly to London to see them, and Christmas every other year. The rest of the time he had his work. He firmly believed that he didn't need more than that. There hadn't been an important woman in his life since Athena, and he was beginning to see now how unsuited they had been for each other. He told himself it no longer mattered, and insisted he wasn't bitter about the divorce. He hadn't been in love with her for several years. She had broken his heart when she left with their daughters. The loves of his life now were Pip and Alex. He readily admitted he was a workaholic, and saw no harm in that.

The absence of a wife or girlfriend gave Bill more time to devote to his work, and to his children when he saw them. He didn't want anyone interfering with his relationship with them, and a new woman might. He saw very little of his brother and parents in New York. They were part of a world he had never liked and had shunned since he'd entered medical school. His brother was an antitrust lawyer with political aspirations, married to an environmental attorney, involved in a multitude of causes. They had a booming social life. His parents were part of the old New York establishment, which had never interested him. He was happy with his much smaller life in San Francisco, spending time between the hospital where he worked and the outdoors. It was a choice he had made when he was young, and it still suited him.

He had hated people knowing who his family was when he was growing up, and he still didn't like it. His brother thrived on flaunting the family name and connections. They were very different men. Their parents regarded Bill as an outcast and renegade of sorts. His humble life and work mystified them. He could have had an illustrious career in medicine in New York, but he never wanted that. Caring for derelicts and patients with gunshot wounds that he saw almost daily in the trauma unit at SF General was exactly what he wanted to do. His family name meant nothing in the world he worked in, in San Francisco, and that suited him too. He had become something of a loner since the divorce. New nurses and female residents were always startled by how good-looking he was, but he paid no attention to them while on duty or off. He was all about his work and his two daughters. No one knew anything about his personal life, which was just what he wanted.

His romantic life had been sparse and sporadic since the divorce. There was the occasional superficial date, and nothing more. His one regret was that his parents barely knew his daughters. Athena had seen to that, and his parents had made no effort either. Their dislike for their ex-daughter-in-law had carried over to the children. They had tea with the girls in London, when they traveled, if they had time. But more often than not, they found making time to see the children inconvenient, or Athena made it difficult. Planning with her was never easy. She was as vague and unreliable as she had always been, so Pip and Alex had no real attachment to their American grandparents, only to their father, whom they saw too little of but enjoyed when they did. He called them several times a week, and tried to stay abreast of what they were doing. It wasn't easy maintaining a fully engaged relationship with children six thousand miles away. As girls from good families did in England, Pip would be going to boarding school in two years. She could hardly wait. Time and distance were not on Bill's side, and he did all he could to compensate for that. Whenever possible with his busy schedule, he flew to London for a long weekend to visit them. Although nowadays they were often occupied with their friends and finding the right time for them was getting harder every year.

Things got busier in the ER as the day wore on. Bill sent a heart attack to coronary ICU, an old man from the Tenderloin brought in by paramedics. He sent a homeless recent amputee, a drug addict with a fierce wound infection, to the surgical ward to be evaluated by the attending surgeon, and he moved a child suspected of meningitis to the pediatric ICU for a spinal tap. He called in a neurosurgeon for a woman in a coma from a brain injury she had sustained in a car accident. It was all in a day's work. He went from one exam room to the next, and stopped to chat with an elderly woman who had fallen down the stairs and was more shaken up than injured. Miraculously, she hadn't broken a hip, and he was warm and reassuring with her. The hospital had a fantastic elder care unit, the best in the city, and he referred patients there regularly. He had a kind, easy bedside manner that appeared casual to the patients, but wasn't, as he evaluated them carefully, looking for symptoms of hidden problems in addition to the obvious ones they had. The nurses all admired and respected him. He treated every patient with the utmost care and attention, no matter who they were. Unlike a lot of doctors, he didn't show off or have a big ego. He was a genuinely nice guy.

"Wowza . . . who's the handsome prince on duty today?" a relief nurse filling in on the holiday asked one of the regular nurses as Bill left an exam room and moved on to the next one. He had dark hair and warm chocolate-brown eyes, and looked athletic in the hospital scrubs he wore. His smile, as he talked to the ninety-year-old woman who had fallen, lit up the room. The relief nurse had been observing him closely, and commented afterward that he was a hunk.

"He's the head of trauma. He always works on holidays," the regular ER nurse told her. "Don't get too excited. I've worked here for ten years, and I've never heard of him dating anyone at work. He's a serious guy."

"Married?" the relief nurse quizzed her. He was too attractive to dismiss lightly.

"Divorced, I think. He must be to work the hours he does. He's just another workaholic. You have to be, around here. I think he has kids somewhere far away, Australia, New Zealand. I forget. That's why he works holidays."

"That means no girlfriend either," the nurse said hopefully.

"Or a very neglected one. The guys in trauma work crazy hours. You should find a nice dermatologist, they're never on call," the regular nurse teased her. "I worked with him on Christmas two years ago, and New Year's Eve. And he signs up for Thanksgiving every year."

"He probably just hasn't met the right woman," the relief nurse said. She was on a mission, which the staff nurse knew wouldn't get her far with Bill.

"Yeah. Whatever." They cleaned up the room and moved on to the next cubicle just as Bill was paged for another gunshot wound. It was an eighteen-year-old boy who died while Bill was examining him. The police had brought him in, and there was nothing Bill could do. He had almost bled to death by the time he arrived, shot in the stomach and chest. Bill looked grim as he walked to the nurses' station and filled out the paperwork. It was his second gunshot fatality of the day. The boy's family had been called but hadn't come in yet. It was going to be a hell of a Christmas for them. He glanced up and saw the police paramedic he had seen before. The medic knew what the paperwork meant, and shook his head.

"He was just a kid," he said. They'd arrived on the scene after the shooter had left.

"Most of them are," Bill said with a somber expression, as they paged him to go to another exam room. He walked away a minute later, and the police EMT called out to him, "Merry Christmas, Doc."

Bill waved, already halfway down the hall. "Yeah, you too." It reminded Bill to take a look at his watch. His girls were in Switzerland, at a chalet Rupert had rented for the holidays, in Gstaad. It was four o'clock in the afternoon in San Francisco, one in the morning in Switzerland. Pip and Alex would be asleep by then, after a busy Christmas Day with their mother and stepfather and half brothers. He had called them at midnight on Christmas Eve, nine A.M. on Christmas Day for them. In another eight hours he could call them again. It gave him something to cheer himself as he grabbed a chart, and walked into the next exam room. He could already tell it was going to be a long night. Talking to his daughters would be his reward at the end of it. He hadn't seen them since September, but he hoped he would soon. He lived from visit to visit, and for his work. It was the path he was on for now, and he had no regrets. As long as he had Pip and Alex and the trauma unit at SF General, it was enough.

Stephanie Lawrence had been up since six A.M. on Christmas morning when her two little boys, Ryan and Aden, four and six years old respectively, had charged into her bedroom and pounced on her and her husband in bed. Clearly the miniature cars and candy canes they'd put in the Christmas stockings in the boys' room hadn't distracted them for more than a few minutes. Ryan had the sticky candy all over his hands and face as he climbed into their bed, and Andy groaned, still half asleep.

They'd been up until three A.M., putting toys and the boys' new bicycles with training wheels together, most of which they'd bought online since Stephanie never had time to shop. The boys were desperate to go downstairs and see what Santa had left for them, as Andy opened one eye and looked at his wife.

"What time is it?" It was still dark and felt like the middle of the night.

"Ten after six," she said as she leaned over and kissed him. He put an arm around her, and then rolled over on his back, while the boys squealed with anticipation.

They lived in an old but comfortable house in the Upper Haight. They'd bought it before UCSF Hospital moved to Mission Bay. In its previous location, she'd only been a few blocks from work. Getting to the hospital's new facility took longer, but they loved the house, so they stayed despite the longer drive to work for her.

Stephanie worked at UCSF as a trauma doctor. It was one of the most important teaching hospitals in the city, on a par with Stanford Hospital, where she had gone to medical school. Andy was a freelance journalist and writer. He'd had a job at the *Chronicle,* the local newspaper, when they were first married, until she got pregnant with Aden during her residency at UCSF, and Andy had volunteered to become a stay-at-home dad, which was a huge sacrifice for him. His hope was to win a Pulitzer one day for his stories about urban crisis. His dreams had gotten somewhat obscured by his responsibilities as a father. But he wanted to support Stephanie's work. So his career was taking a back seat to hers. They had hired a part-time housekeeper so he could write a few hours a day. The arrangement had worked out well for the past six years, although as Stephanie's career advanced, she had less free time instead of more and he was always picking up the slack with the boys. He loved them, but had less time to write. She was working harder than ever, and her secret ambition, which only Andy knew, was to become head of the trauma department one day. She had done residencies in neurology and trauma, and was thirty-five years old. Andy was the same age.

He published articles in local and California newspapers and magazines. His career hadn't taken off as he had hoped it would. He talked about writing a novel one day, but hadn't yet, and Stephanie wasn't sure he would. He was a talented journalist but he wasn't as ambitious as she was. His time with their boys took away from his writing, and Stephanie felt guilty about it. They were both busy, and it was hard to find time for everything. She was frequently involved in hospital politics, which ate up her time. She was on call that day from noon on, and hoped she wouldn't have to go in. She wanted to spend the day with Andy and her boys.

They were both native San Franciscans, although they'd never met when they were kids. She'd grown up in Marin, with a doctor father, and gone to private schools. Marin Country Day, followed by Branson for high school, college at UC Berkeley, where she graduated early, medical school at Stanford, and her residency at UCSF. Andy had gone to public school and graduated as a journalism major from UCLA. They had met when he moved back to San Francisco and was working at the *Chronicle,* while she did her first residency. They'd been together for ten years, three before they married, and seven years since. Their marriage was solid, although he nagged her constantly to spend more time with the boys. As a busy physician in trauma, there was only so much she could do. The boys seemed to understand it better than their father, who constantly made comments about the important events she missed. She'd had to leave for an emergency in the middle of their recent Christmas school performance. A school bus got hit by a truck on the Golden Gate Bridge, and ten of the injured students were brought to UCSF. At least she'd seen Aden sing "Jingle Bells" onstage before she left. She was always being torn between her work, her husband, and her kids. Andy had never realized before just how busy she would be when her career took off. And she found all her roles harder to juggle than she'd expected.

She was respected, well liked, hardworking, a born leader, and had a golden reputation at work. She was diligent about being well versed in all the newest medical techniques, and worked longer hours than any of her colleagues in the department, despite the fact that she had young kids. She'd taken three weeks off when she had Aden, and two when she had Ryan. It was no secret that her career was her priority, but she loved Andy and the boys too, and did the best she could to spend time with them. There were never enough hours in the day, and more often than not, she came home after the boys were asleep. Andy never failed to tell her if they cried for her when he put them to bed. It was the only subject they fought over, the fact that in the last few years, he tried to make her feel guilty about how hard she worked. Her work was the bone of contention between them. Andy had begun to resent it. And they both knew it wasn't going to get better as her career grew.

Andy rolled out of bed first and put Ryan on his shoulders, Aden ran alongside, and Stephanie pulled on her bathrobe as she followed him downstairs. The boys let out a whoop the minute they saw the bicycles, and rode them around the living room until they nearly knocked over the tree.

"Slow down, guys!" Andy said, as they got off the bikes and opened their other gifts, while Stephanie took pictures and a video of them with her phone, and then went to make breakfast. The agreement she and Andy had made was that she cooked breakfast when she was home, and he did dinner every night. She made French toast, and set the plates down on the kitchen table just as they opened the last gifts. Then she called them in for breakfast.

The boys took their places at the table as Stephanie made coffee and handed a cup to Andy. Aden looked at her in surprise.

"No bacon, Mom?"

"Oops . . . sorry, I forgot." She made no move to correct her mistake, knowing that by the time she cooked it, they'd have left the table and would be back on their new bikes. She was well aware that Andy never forgot the bacon. The domestic arts were not her strong suit, but she had never pretended that they were. She was an outstanding doctor, but a very ordinary cook.

After breakfast, they went back to the living room, and Andy plugged in the lights on the tree. He had decorated it with Aden and Ryan. Stephanie had promised to be home for it, but had to stay late at work that night for a serious head injury. Andy had made gingerbread houses with them too, and she had come home for the tail end of that. She was constantly explaining to the boys that she had to work, and apologizing to them for the events she missed.

They'd had dinner at her parents' house in Marin the night before on Christmas Eve, with her sister and her children, and they were going to Andy's mother in Orinda, in the East Bay, that night. The boys were in high gear as they got on their bicycles again and rode around the living room, dangerously close to the tree. Stephanie put on some Christmas music from her computer. She and Andy were still exhausted after assembling everything the night before, and he had written letters to the boys from Santa, while she put out milk and cookies, and carrots for the reindeer, and took a bite of each of them. Between the two of them, they managed to get it all done.

Stephanie let them play with their new toys until lunchtime, and then helped them take all their gifts to their room. Andy showered and dressed while she watched the boys, and she smiled when she saw him in a black sweater and jeans with his sandy blond hair and blue eyes. He was a great-looking guy, and she had been the envy of her friends when she married him. He'd played football for a year at UCLA, but dropped off the team with a knee injury. He still had the same broad shoulders and slim waist, and tried to get to the gym every day when Aden and Ryan were in school. He kissed her and they went to their own room for a few minutes. So far the day had been a success, and the boys were thrilled with their gifts.

"My mom can't wait to see us tonight. I hope you don't get called in," Andy said, with a warning in his eyes.

"So do I." She had no choice. She'd had to sign up, they all had to be on call for some holidays every year. But with luck, the ER and trauma unit would be able to handle whatever came up without pulling her in. If they did call, though, there was nothing she could do about it. She had to go. She was planning to dress Aden and Ryan in the matching velvet suits her mother-in-law had bought them, with little red bow ties. She had promised Andy they would wear the Christmas suits from his mom.

Andy made sandwiches for lunch, and afterward, while the boys played in their room, Stephanie and Andy lay down on the bed together for half an hour, relaxing and talking, until the boys came in to see what they were doing. Andy offered to put a movie on for them, and was back a few minutes later, as Stephanie lay in her robe and dozed. It was nice not having to be anywhere or do anything for a few hours. She was going to wear a new black velvet dress that night too, but it was too early to dress. They were planning to leave the house at five, and get to his mother's home at six, leaving time for traffic on the bridge. Andy was an only child, and his widowed mother enjoyed seeing him and her grandchildren. Stephanie hadn't seen her in two months, since she'd been working on Thanksgiving, and Andy and the boys had gone to his mother's without her. Stephanie knew her mother-in-law never understood why she couldn't take off on major holidays. But she couldn't, especially since her dream was to be head of the department. There were sacrifices you had to make, and the competition for important jobs was fierce. There were lots of competent doctors at UCSF. She was one of them. But she was determined to rise to the top.

Stephanie dressed Ryan and Aden first, and left them with Andy when she went to shower and dress herself. She combed her long blond hair into a neat bun at the nape of her neck, and put on makeup, which she rarely had time to do. She put on heels and gold earrings, and smiled when she saw her husband in slacks and a blazer, and her sons in their black velvet suits.

She could feel her phone vibrating in her purse under her arm as she walked into the room, and prayed it wasn't the hospital. She took it out and looked, and saw the familiar 911 code, and the phone number of the trauma unit. She answered it immediately, as Andy watched her face intently and listened to her side of the conversation. She gave rapid instructions to call the neurosurgeon on duty, and said she'd be there in fifteen minutes. Andy's face fell. It was

Murphy's Law, the minute they tried to go somewhere when she was on call, the hospital pulled her in. He went to more than half their social engagements alone. He was used to it, but he didn't like it. And he knew his mother would be upset if Stephanie didn't show up on Christmas night. That was sacred to her, and to Andy too. He hated her working on the holidays.

"What am I supposed to tell my mother?" he asked, looking irritated, as though it was the first time it had happened and not the hundredth. Stephanie felt that he should be used to it by now, not take it personally, and be able to explain it to his mother without it being a drama.

"The truth always works, that I'm on call, and I had to go in. And please tell her I'm really sorry not to be there tonight." She meant it sincerely but was annoyed that Andy was making an issue of it in front of the boys, and that Aden and Ryan were picking up on the tension between their parents.

"She never understands why you sign up to be on call on days like this," he said, but he didn't add that he didn't either. "Why can't the people who don't have kids do it?"

"We all do it. It's expected in every department. And trauma and the ER are especially busy on nights like this." Her father was an obstetrician and her mother had never made a fuss about it. It seemed unfair to her that Andy did. She had understood it growing up. There were things her father inevitably missed when he was working, and no one complained. Why was it different for her?

She walked them to the car and strapped Ryan into his car seat, while Andy put Aden in his booster seat, for the drive to Orinda. Andy looked at her unhappily and didn't say a word, as she stood in front of the house while he pulled out of the driveway. She waved and then walked back into the house, took off the new black velvet dress and hung it up, put on jeans, a sweater, slipped her feet into clogs, and put on her white coat with her name embroidered on it. She put the nylon rope with her badge on it over her head, grabbed her purse, walked out to her car, and drove to the hospital in Mission Bay downtown. "Merry Christmas," she said out loud to herself. Her mind was already on her work, there was always something reassuring about it, knowing that this was what she did best. She loved her husband and children, but the hospital was where she belonged and felt most like herself.

Thomas Wylie stood with a cluster of women around him at the nurses' station desk of the emergency room at Alta Bates Summit Medical Center in Oakland, and a burst of laughter escaped from the women like balloons rising into the air. There were at least six of them standing there as he told one of his stories about when he had trained in Chicago, lived in Ireland for a year, or volunteered in Zimbabwe. He had a million stories to tell. He'd had a colorful life and a varied career, and the stories to go with it, half of which probably weren't true. But Tom Wylie knew how to make the nurses laugh. The rumor was that he had slept with half the female medical personnel in the hospital, which probably wasn't true either, but easy to believe. He had movie-star good looks, and at forty-three looked ten years younger than he was. There was a boyish quality about him. He'd gone to Yale as an undergraduate, medical school at the University of Chicago, done his residency at UCLA. He'd done some model-ing, in order to meet female models, and had wound up in Oakland randomly, when they needed more doctors for the trauma unit at Alta Bates and he applied and got the job. Alta Bates was the largest private medical center in the East Bay. He worked at the Summit campus in Oakland.

He liked to say that he was a nomad at heart, with no roots any-where, and never talked about his childhood. He was an artful seducer, and admitted that he'd never had a serious long-term rela-tionship, and didn't want one. If a woman got too serious about him, he was known to disappear immediately. He had no desire to get married. He was charming, supposedly fabulous in bed, and couldn't resist wooing almost every female who crossed his path. When the brief affair was over, he usually managed to stay friends with the women he'd slept with. He liked to say that they were his hobby—he collected them.

In spite of themselves, his male colleagues liked him too. He was outrageous and funny, and despite his casual style, he was an excel-lent doctor, and a good man to have around in a crisis. He took his medical career seriously, but nothing else. When it came to women, he was the class clown and Don Juan. He was a hard man to dislike, although some of the older, more conservative nurses disapproved of him, but most of the time he charmed them too. He was undeniably handsome and a practiced flirt.

Three of the nurses lingered after the others went back to work, and there was a momentary lull in the ER. Tom didn't mind working on Christmas Day, he usually did. He had nowhere else to spend it, and no family, so he signed up for all the major holidays and freed up the married doctors to stay home with their kids. It had been quiet in the ER for the last two hours.

"Everybody must be home opening presents," Tom said with a flirtatious glance at one of the younger nurses. "If you weren't so young and beautiful, I'd invite you to my place to play, but your father or boyfriend would probably shoot me," he teased her and she laughed. She was twenty-two and had just graduated from nursing school in June. Tom Wylie was attracted to women of every age. He thought they were all fair game, and his success rate was amazing.

The banter stopped immediately when an unconscious six-year-old boy was airlifted in from a car accident. His mother and sister had been killed and his father was in serious condition and was taken to surgery, while Tom headed up a trauma team to examine the boy. He called in a pediatric neurosurgeon immediately, and assisted at three hours of surgery. The child's condition remained critical but was stable after the surgery, and Tom advised the nurses' station that he would be spending the night at the hospital to keep an eye on the boy. He went upstairs to reassure the child's father, but discovered that he was still in surgery himself. Tom checked the little boy every fifteen minutes for the first hour, and then went to add some notes to the chart, and smiled at one of the older nurses at the desk when he did. She was used to his contradictory style of buffoon among the women, and serious, extremely attentive physician when needed by his patients.

"I think you should come home with me when we get off duty," he whispered to the nurse and she grinned at him.

"Just say the word, anytime," she whispered back, and he laughed and kissed her on the cheek.

"Thank God somebody still wants me around here," he said and turned his attention to the chart, relieved that he now felt fairly sure the boy would survive. The pediatric neurosurgeon had done his job well, to relieve pressure on the child's brain without doing additional damage, which was a delicate procedure.

Tom Wylie was a strange dichotomy of diligent medical practitioner alternating with Lothario. He was the handsome man that no woman would ever catch. His glib style got him all the women he wanted, but never a relationship that would last. Other than the funny stories, he never shared any personal information about his past. The women who had dated him knew as little about him as everyone else. He often said that marriage sounded like a nightmare to him, and that he much preferred life as a buffet, rather than a set menu every night. Some of the married doctors he worked with suspected that he might be right.

Most of his colleagues liked working with him, he lightened the mood of what was at times a very hard job, and his medical skills were impressive. And it was obvious from his dedication how much he loved the work he did.

Wendy Jones spent Christmas Eve and Day just as she had for the last six years, alone. It was part of the deal of loving a married man. She had known it would be like this when she fell in love with Jeffrey Hunter, renowned cardiac surgeon at Stanford University Medical

Center, where she worked in the trauma/surgical critical care program for adult and pediatric trauma patients. She'd met Jeff at the hospital, when one of his patients had come to the trauma center when she was on duty. She had fallen madly in love with Jeff from the first moment she saw him, and he had called her the next day. He was so brilliant that she found everything about him seductive, and was flattered when he called her.

She'd gone to lunch with him, hesitantly, even though she knew he was married. He said his marriage had been dead for years, and they were planning to separate. According to him, his wife, Jane, was fed up with being the wife of a surgeon, married to a man she never saw, who cared more about his work and patients than he did about her or their children. They had four kids, and Jeff admitted himself that he was an inattentive husband and father. His work was very demanding, and his specialty was heart transplants. He couldn't just drop everything and run to a school soccer game or a dinner party. His work was his priority. He said that he and his wife led separate lives, and he was planning to leave the marriage by the end of the year. Wendy had believed him, and in retrospect she thought he had believed himself. But six months into their relationship, his wife had convinced him that their children were still too young for them to divorce and they had come to a better understanding, so he stayed. And so had Wendy. From that moment on, she had known it wouldn't be easy.

Six years later, he was still married and his youngest child was eleven. The oldest had just left for college. He assured Wendy now that by the time his youngest son was in high school, he would feel comfortable leaving the family home. It was only three years away, but Wendy wondered if he would actually leave before his youngest was in college, or at all. She had promised herself she would end the affair a hundred times, but she never did. He always talked her into staying. His arguments were so convincing. And they loved each other.

They were well suited. They were both physicians and graduates of Harvard. Her work in trauma was almost as stressful and high pressured as his. The men she went out with before had complained about her dedication to her work. Jeff always understood. She had done her residency at Mass General, after getting her undergraduate degree and MD at Harvard, and been offered an outstanding job at Stanford, which was the same career path Jeff had chosen. Jeff's wife was the daughter of a highly respected surgeon, but she had said she didn't want to follow in her mother's footsteps with an absentee husband who was never around and hardly knew his own kids. And yet, it was exactly what she was doing, and had done since they married.

Wendy frequently wondered if he made the same empty promises to his wife as to her, but things never changed. He worked too hard and had too many patients to be more attentive than he was to either of them. His first responsibility was to his patients, more than to either of the women in his life. He spent weekends at home, and attempted to spend time with his children. He was with his family for holidays, and he spent Wednesday nights at Wendy's, when he had time and Wendy wasn't working herself. He spent an hour with her on his way home from time to time and would drop by without warning. She enjoyed the time with him, their discussions, and their sex life, which made her fall even more deeply in love with him, but for the past few years, he'd stopped mentioning marriage or leaving his wife. Wendy no longer broached the subject with him, and it was on holidays like Christmas that she realized how little she had with him. All she had were Wednesday nights, when they were both available, and an hour here and there. Jeff compartmentalized everything in his life, and he had put her in a little box, where he expected her to stay.

What she had noticed in recent years were the things she no longer did because she couldn't do them with him. The symphony, the opera, the ballet. What if he called and wanted to drop by? She didn't want to miss a visit by not being there. She loved museums, but had stopped going. And she no longer saw her girlfriends because they had husbands and children, and she was a married man's mistress and was ashamed.

For six years she had followed his rules. She was thirty-seven years old, she had her work, and one night a week with a man who belonged to someone else. Her work was fulfilling, but the rest of her life wasn't. Wendy felt like a car Jeff took out for special occasions, and left in the garage the rest of the time. She wanted to share so much more with him and couldn't. There were no weekends or holidays in her arrangement with him. And every year, on Christmas, she thought about what a fool she was, as the truth hit her squarely in the face, again. Even if she promised herself she'd leave him, she knew now she wouldn't. When the holidays were over, she'd go back to their weekly nights together, silently hoping something would change. She didn't want to rock the boat and lose him. She was living on crumbs, and pretending to herself it was a meal.

In Wendy's eyes, no one measured up to him, no one was as smart, as capable, or appealed to her as much. He was a trap she had fallen into and couldn't get out of, and didn't even want to. She'd had a text message from him the night before, on Christmas Eve, that said only, "Thinking of you, love, J." And now he was with his wife and children, while she sat alone in her house in Palo Alto, wondering what she was doing with him. Little by little, she had given everything up for him and now all she had was her career and a Wednesday night date.

She had been at the top of her medical school class at Harvard, and graduated cum laude, but what difference did it make? She was in good shape, a small, lithe, beautiful woman with dark hair and deep blue eyes. She had a successful career at Stanford, and every decision she made was influenced by her relationship with Jeff. She accepted no invitations in case he wanted to stop by on his way home without calling first, she didn't want to miss a minute with him. Their Wednesday nights were sacred to her, and Jeff tried to be reliable about them, as best he could. But she had to fit into the tiny little space allotted to her. Jeff always set firm boundaries, and everything was on his terms. He controlled his world and hers. She could never call or email him, and could only text him during office hours. She often wondered what would happen if she had an emergency and needed to get hold of him, but she never had. She hated herself for how willing she was to give up her life, and how little she expected in return.

She hadn't put up a Christmas tree this year. There was no point, he'd never see it and it would only make her sad. She tried to ignore the holiday entirely. He had given her a narrow diamond bangle bracelet from Cartier, which she was wearing, but she would have traded it and everything she had to spend Christmas with him. Her every thought was filled with him, and she kept imagining him with his wife and children while she sat alone. At thirty-seven, she knew that she was giving up her chance to have children, and now she could see herself still with him at forty-five or fifty. She knew that next year, on Christmas, everything would be the same. She was too hooked to leave him, and Jeff relied on it. The situation they had created worked perfectly for him, but a lot less well for her.

She was on call for Christmas Day and night, but her phone hadn't rung. Things were obviously quiet in the ER. No big trauma cases had come in, or they would have called her. She was listening to Christmas carols, which depressed her, and thinking of Jeff. Six years with Jeff lay behind her, and the future was a blur. And she knew, as she did every year, that nothing was going to change. Jeff had her exactly where he wanted her.

# Chapter Two

Tom Wylie was in the doctors' lounge at Alta Bates, having a cup of coffee and chatting with one of the anesthesiologists, when he saw flames shooting out of a building on the TV screen behind the other doctor's head. Someone had muted the TV, and he stared at the screen for a minute, wondering where the fire was, then a banner moved across the bottom, announcing the name of a hotel on Market Street in San Francisco. He picked up the remote on the table and turned the sound back on. The cameras showed Market Street closed to traffic, with fire trucks everywhere, hotel guests milling around in a cordoned area half a block away, and firefighters rushing past them into the hotel. The tall ladders had been set up against the building, and firemen were entering through windows on several floors. It was a five-alarm fire, and two hundred firefighters were on the scene. The reporter announced that several guests were being treated for smoke inhalation, and two firefighters had been injured. Due to their extensive conference rooms and grand ballroom for weddings, the reporter estimated that two thousand guests and several hundred employees were in the hotel. Both doctors stood and stared at the TV as the floor below the one on fire burst into flame and the windows exploded outward from the heat.

There was silence in the room for a minute, then Tom commented, "Looks like we might get a flood of customers tonight."

"They'll send them to SF General and Saint Francis's burn center first," the anesthesiologist responded, as they continued to watch the fire burning out of control on the news.

Several more doctors and some nurses wandered in to watch, as Tom tossed his paper cup into the wastebasket and went to check his young patient again. The boy was still heavily sedated but doing well, and Tom was pleased. He was back five minutes later. He looked at the fire again, and saw a line of ambulances arrive, paramedics rushing toward the scene to confer with the police.

"That's some hell of a fire," Tom said somberly as the announcer said it was believed that lights on some of the Christmas trees may have caused it, but arson had not been ruled out yet. Two floors of the enormous hotel were in flames. You could hear the explosions in the background, as the windows continued to blow out and the fire moved to other floors. The hotel had been evacuated immediately, and several additional units of firefighters were now on the scene.

The doctors from the ER were conferring, trying to guess if some of the injured would be sent to the East Bay, and the consensus was they'd be sending people to the city hospitals first, but it was a reasonable possibility that Alta Bates might get some victims of the blaze that night. Tom went to speak to the head nurse in the ER to have her check their burn supplies. He wanted everything ready to receive critically injured burn victims, who might even be sent over by helicopter. Anything was possible and he needed to be sure they were prepared. There was no joking around now.

It was five P.M., and the streets were already dark. Floodlights had been set up on Market Street, and they were shooting water from high-powered hoses into the hotel, with no effect on the blaze so far.

At San Francisco General, Bill Browning and his team were watching the same broadcast, and he dispatched everyone to check supplies, and had the nurses at the desk start texting all the physicians on call that night. He wanted their full complement of staff on-site to deal with all the injured and burn victims the police sent them. SF General was in the front lines, and in less than an hour, they were at full staff, and all the supplies were ready as the ER staff crowded around the TVs. The fire had gotten worse and six floors were involved now, ladders were set up all along the front of the hotel. Firefighters had come from Marin and the East Bay to join the forces in the city. All of Market Street had been closed off, the smoke from the fire hung heavily in the air, and the stunned hotel guests had been moved back a block. The reporter said you could feel the intense heat in the street.

"How many do you think we can handle?" Bill asked one of the doctors who had come in. They had two hundred and eighty-four beds with the new facility, and they weren't at capacity that night.

"Sixty easily. Close to a hundred if we have to." They had recently had training for terrorist attacks, which would serve them well in dealing with large numbers of victims. Bill went to call their contact at the police department, to give him an idea of how many people they could handle comfortably, and at what point to start sending them to UCSF.

"We're sending you twenty now, mostly older hotel guests suffering from smoke inhalation. We're treating minor injuries at an EMT station we set up. The Department of Emergency Management guys are here, they're doing triage right now. Get ready. We're going to have a busy night. They just sent a dozen firefighters to Saint Francis." Saint Francis had the best burn unit in the city, and Bill was sure they were prepared too.

Stephanie had just arrived at UCSF when the fire started, and after she saw the three patients they had called her in for, she joined the others at the TV. At five-thirty, they saw the first ambulances leave the scene.

The ambulances arrived at SF General ten minutes later, with the first smoke inhalation cases, and a pregnant woman Bill sent up to labor and delivery. She was having a panic attack and worried about her baby.

More ambulances showed up after the first ones, with minor injuries, including a broken leg that had happened when a hotel guest fell down the stairs during the evacuation. Eight badly burned firemen came in next, as Bill did triage at the ambulance entrance to the ER, and paramedics brought the injured in on gurneys, victims with soot on their faces and some of them still gasping from the smoke. They reached their limit faster than Bill had expected, and he called his police contact again, asking him to send the next group to UCSF, to give SF General a chance to organize their teams, and deal with the burn victims.

The ambulances went to UCSF after that, and Stephanie did triage along with two other trauma doctors. They had two heart attacks, more injured firemen, a number of children with their parents, and the fire hadn't been stopped yet. The damage was being estimated on TV at a hundred million dollars, including structural damage, and by then two of the firefighters had died on the scene, one of them a twenty-four-year-old rookie and the other a veteran fireman who had gotten trapped in the building. It was a scene of major carnage, and at the same time the victims were arriving at UCSF, the authorities started sending ambulances to Alta Bates, and another dozen victims to the Stanford trauma unit by helicopter. Wendy was waiting for them at Stanford, and their entire ER and trauma staff had been called in.

The news broadcasts said it was the worst fire in the history of the city since the 1906 earthquake, and by eight o'clock that night, the uninjured guests, who were now homeless, had been sent to other hotels in the city. Those who took them in were using their ballrooms and conference centers to set up food and cots for them, once they ran out of rooms. Everyone was rallying to help and do what they could. And the Emergency Operations Center, directed by the Department of Emergency Management, were working closely with the police and fire department.

It was two in the morning when the fire stopped growing, and was considered contained within the hotel, although it wasn't under full control yet. Every hospital had patients on gurneys in the halls, and additional nursing staff had been brought in to help. It was a disaster of major proportions. The mayor and governor were surveying the scene together, and planned to visit victims in the hospitals later that day.

By eight A.M., thirty-seven hotel guests had died from burns and smoke inhalation, as well as nine firemen who had been trapped. Another forty firemen and more than a hundred hotel guests had been injured. The evacuation had been properly handled, but panic had taken a heavy toll. Market Street looked like a bomb had hit it, and the fire had spread to a department store next door before it was brought under control.

Stephanie didn't make it home until two P.M. the day after the fire. Her white coat was black with ash and soot, and she looked exhausted when Andy saw her. He had watched the progress of the fire on TV all night, and Stephanie had sent him a text at two A.M. that their ER was being overrun. Every hospital in the city had been receiving victims of the fire, and even doctors not on call and from other departments had gone to help.

"How bad is it at UCSF?" Andy asked with interest, as she sat bone-tired in a chair, grateful that the boys were down for their naps. She was filthy and drained and hadn't slept all night.

"It's like a war." The hotel had virtually been destroyed, gutted by the fire. "It was like the terrorist drills they've been describing to us, only worse. The firefighters took the hardest hit." Firefighters had battled the blaze for fifteen hours, and many more would be on the scene in the coming days, making sure it was out, and they still didn't know if it had been arson or not. Stephanie hoped it wasn't, knowing that someone had set the fire intentionally would have been infinitely worse. She went to take a bath a few minutes later, and crawled into bed afterward, as Andy walked into their room and sat down on the bed. It reminded her of the dinner the night before. "How was your mom? With the fire, I would have had to go in anyway."

"She was upset, but she understands it's the nature of what you do. She just doesn't understand why you have to work on holidays," he said quietly.

"Because people get hurt even on Christmas," Stephanie said simply. "They called in everyone last night. We even delivered two babies in the ER. We couldn't get the women to labor and delivery in time." But the worst of it had been the burns, and she knew that several of those patients wouldn't survive. The firefighters had been incredibly brave.

Stephanie looked peaceful as she drifted off to sleep. The entire trauma unit and emergency room team had done a good job, and she was proud of them, and to have been a part of it.

Tom Wylie felt the same way at Alta Bates, and Bill Browning was still in the thick of it. He hadn't had time to call Pip and Alex at midnight as he'd meant to. They were still doing triage at General, and had gotten some homeless patients too. They had been asleep in doorways too close to the fire and been injured by falling debris. At Stanford, Wendy had her hands full as well. Jeff had come in at midnight to lend a hand, but all the cardiac patients had gone to SF General and UCSF to save time, and he left fairly quickly after talking to Wendy for a few minutes.

Tom Wylie got home at three P.M. His six-year-old patient who had had surgery the night before, after the car accident, was awake and doing well. And fresh teams had come in to deal with the victims of the fire, so he had finally gone back to his apartment. It was a depressing place, and looked better at night, lit with candles, than in broad daylight, which showed the threadbare furniture and the peeling paint. He had never spent much on rent and didn't really care about where he lived as long as the place had a comfortable king-size bed. He grabbed the remote and turned on the TV mostly out of habit. He liked hearing a voice in the apartment, and he expected to see more coverage of the fire. The DEM had done an amazing job on the scene and overseeing dispatch to the various hospitals, and were being highly praised by all. But instead of Market Street, Tom saw images of the Eiffel Tower and the Champs-Élysées in Paris. It was midnight on December 26 there, and a band that ran across the television screen read "Terrorism in Paris," as an American reporter described a scene of carnage on the Champs-Élysées. Four major luxury stores and two movie complexes that showed mostly American films in the original version had been taken over, with moviegoers and shoppers held hostage and gunned down, including children. A suicide bomber had blown up one of the stores, and another had entered the elevator at the Eiffel Tower, intending to blow it up, but had been killed before he could detonate the belt he wore and turn himself into a human bomb.

In all, one hundred and two people had been killed, and another fifty-three injured. It was the worst attack of its kind since the November attacks four years before. It was another massive assault on people going about their business, shopping the day after Christmas, taking advantage of sales, going to movies and having dinner on the famous Champs-Élysées. The motives were political, but however they justified it, innocents had been slaughtered, even young children. The attacks had occurred at six P.M., before the stores closed in Paris, and tears rolled down Tom's cheeks as he watched the scenes of destruction and mass murder, and the numbers of people injured as sirens screamed in the night. The ravages of the hotel fire seemed small compared to what Paris had just been through, again.

Incredible acts of heroism were described. There were videos from the cellphones of people who had been there, and sobbing interviews with the survivors. It was heartbreaking to see the effects of tragedy again, and impossible to understand. Listening to the stories, seeing the damage and loss of life, and hearing how many had died from gunfire or the detonated bombs, the only conclusion a sane person could come to was that the world had gone mad.

# Chapter Three

The cleanup after the hotel fire on Market Street was massive, and firefighters combed through the rubble for days, looking for clues to how the fire started. Foul play was eventually ruled out. Faulty wiring had caused it, and the fifteen-foot Christmas trees on every floor of the hotel had fed the blaze. Within a day or two, those with minor injuries left the hospitals where they'd been admitted. Others had to stay longer, and those with severe burns had a long road ahead of them. Three more of the firefighters and two elderly hotel guests died within days of the fire, and the death toll reached a total of fifty-one, with eighty-seven more people injured to varying degrees.

It took several days for the hospitals involved to calm down, and once the people with minor injuries had been released, they were left mostly with the burn victims to be treated. By New Year's Eve, each of the hospitals had almost returned to normal. Bill Browning and Tom Wylie were working again at SF General and Alta Bates. Wendy

Jones was on call at Stanford, and Stephanie Lawrence had the night off from UCSF, much to her husband's relief and her own. Both boys had come down with the flu the day before, and Stephanie didn't want to leave them with a sitter, so she and Andy stayed home on New Year's Eve. At least she wouldn't have to go to work that night. They opened a bottle of champagne after the boys were asleep, and watched old movies in bed. Stephanie had been working hard all week, and fell asleep at ten o'clock, while Andy saw the New Year in alone.

The savage attack in Paris took longer to clean up, and the country had been scarred again by tragic losses. Candles and flowers were left in vast profusion up and down the Champs-Élysées, and particularly in front of the stores and movie houses that had been affected. More than a hundred people had been killed. There was a special memorial mass at Notre Dame, and a vigil the night before. The images of the mourners on TV were heartbreaking, as people held up signs with the names of the victims whom they knew. It was nearly impossible to conceive of acts of a political nature carried out against innocent people going about their business on a Thursday night. It was an echo of what had happened before, but this time was infinitely worse with more people killed, and not just young people this time, but children too. The youngest victim of the attack was two years old. In some cases, entire families had been slaughtered.

It made no sense to Tom as he watched the coverage. In his mind, politics never justified the murder of people who had nothing to do with the issues. He had been watching CNN all week, and cried every time he saw an interview with someone who had survived the attack and described how the people around him had been assassinated. To

Tom, it seemed like a tragedy not just for Parisians, but for humanity and the entire world. It went against everything he believed and had dedicated his life to. He had spent twenty years putting wounded bodies back together, while others wanted to destroy them. He wished there were some way to help, but France was a long way away, and there was nothing he could do. It had depressed him profoundly, and he watched the latest stories emerging from the tragedy every day.

All the perpetrators had died with their victims. The whole thing seemed like a terrible waste, and he was overwhelmed by sadness every time he thought about it. The story had certainly eclipsed the hotel fire in San Francisco, which had genuinely been a regrettable accident. There was nothing accidental about the Paris attacks. They had been carefully planned, executed with precision, and entirely intentional. It made him think of the last time he'd been in Paris, while he was in medical school. He'd gone there for a summer break with two friends and fell in love with the city, and every girl he met.

The attacks worried Bill Browning too. If it could happen in Paris, it could happen in London, and he shuddered every time he thought of his daughters being potentially at risk. He called Athena to talk about it, and told her not to let their daughters go to movie theaters or big sports events for a while. She pooh-poohed it, and said that the British were much more careful about security than the French, and uttered some gibberish that you couldn't live in fear, and let terrorists win. And you had to go on with normal life and show them that you weren't afraid of them. Bill vehemently disagreed with her and said it was a good time to be cautious and not do anything foolish. He reminded her of the bombing of Harrod's, the London department store, years before, and more recent attacks. She brushed him off again and didn't want to hear it, which left him even more anxious after he'd hung up.

Government officials in France and every European country were assuring their citizens that secret service and intelligence operatives had tightened security considerably, but other politicians said that was simply not true. They didn't have the manpower to do that, and the public wasn't privy to the truth. Nowadays, it was in fact impossible to keep any nation entirely safe, even the United States, although the U.S. intelligence machine seemed to have much greater resources and manpower at its disposal than most countries, and more sophisticated high-tech methods to identify potential risks. But the crazies appeared to be ruling the world these days. There were plenty of people, even in the U.S., who were disgruntled, or disturbed, or certifiably insane, or had dangerous political affiliations, or some beef with the world, and killed other people in universities, schools, restaurants, on the street, or in government facilities, and even in churches. No one was exempt or entirely safe anywhere in the world anymore. It was unsettling to think about.

Tom Wylie was subdued all week after the Paris attacks. He was startled when the head of the hospital sent him an email the following week, requesting a meeting with him. Tom had met him, but had never been called to his office before. Tom wondered if some aspect of their rescue mission the night of the fire hadn't been carried out to the hospital director's satisfaction. It was the only reason he could think of for being called to his office, and he had a strong suspicion that he himself was in trouble. Or maybe the director had finally gotten word of Tom's womanizing. Or maybe some nurse had objected to his flirting and had complained. It was harmless and indiscriminate, and just a game he played to lighten the life-and-death tension of his work. It was difficult to believe that the head of the hospital hadn't heard of that before, and didn't know it was without malice or serious intent. Maybe he was going to issue a gentle warning, or possibly a not-so-gentle one, and a slap on the wrist. They couldn't stop him from sleeping with nurses in his spare time, but they could tell him to behave. No one had ever complained.

Tom walked into the hospital administrator's office looking humble, which he figured was the best way to go. He was all bluster and bravado when chatting up a flock of women, but getting called into the boss's office was no joke, and Tom looked solemn while he waited to be told what his crime had been, and what the punishment would be.

The director of the hospital rambled on for a few minutes and congratulated Tom again for his cool head and efficiency the night of the fire. Several of the people he'd helped had written letters of high praise for Tom's extreme competence and compassion that night. They were all heartfelt, and although Tom brushed it off casually, he was very touched by people's responses, and surprised to hear them.

He waited quietly for the director to get to the point. The director began speaking of the attacks on Paris, and then finally, twenty minutes after he had begun his deadly boring analysis of the political situation in Europe and the States, he told Tom that they had an extraordinary opportunity for him, and he hoped that Tom would be open to it. He said it had come in the form of an invitation, and Tom wasn't sure if that was good or bad.

"An invitation to what?" Tom blurted out, unable to stand the mystery and the wait any longer. The suspense was killing him. What invitation?

"As you may know, the cities of Paris and San Francisco partnered about fifteen years ago, and became sister cities officially. And rather than wait for our fearless leaders to solve the problem of future attacks and how to prevent and deal with them, which may not be possible anyway, the Department of Emergency Management here and its French counterpart under the umbrella of the Ministry of the Interior are proposing to send over four of our best trauma doctors to share with them how we respond to mass casualty incidents here. They're inviting four trauma doctors to France and will treat you royally for four weeks to have an information exchange. After a brief two-week hiatus, four of their emergency management doctors and officials would come here as the guests of our city, so we can show them the techniques we use. The only example of a large-scale public disaster we've had in San Francisco recently was the hotel fire, which was not an act of terrorism, but some of the same techniques were used to handle a large number of victims and coordinate several hospitals simultaneously.

"From all the reports I've seen, you did a heroic job of holding up our end that night, and I'd like to recommend you for this project, Tom. I think you'd be a great addition to the team from San Francisco, and there is always a lot to learn from pooling information. We're not exempt from terrorist attacks here either, or from crazed gunmen taking over a public place. Also, the earthquake risk we have here forces us to face some of these issues in case of a natural disaster. I think our French counterparts have something to learn from us too. And four weeks in Paris sounds like a plum assignment to me. What do you think?" Tom was beaming as he listened, and the nature of the project began to sink in. The chance to meet French women again and spread his talents internationally sounded like a fantastic opportunity to him.

"I think I can handle it," Tom said, smiling at him. "I think we'll all learn a lot from each other," particularly the French girls he was hoping to meet. The social aspects of the mission sounded even more exciting than the professional ones, now that he knew he wasn't in trouble with the big boss.

"We expect you to represent us in a dignified manner," the director said seriously, calling Tom to order, as though he could read his mind, so Tom wiped the lascivious smile off his face. "It's quite an honor for the mayor to allow us to present a candidate for the assignment. From what I understand, four hospitals have been selected, and we're very pleased to be one of them. A group of your peers seems to think you'd be the best man for the job. I understand that you have a cool head in a crisis, and with serious matters at hand, you're a great leader and never let your partners down. You are an excellent physician and up to date on state-of-the-art techniques." It was high praise from the administration and Tom beamed again.

"Thank you, sir. I won't let you down," he said.

"If I thought you would, I wouldn't be asking you to go. They want to get this project going quickly, after the recent attacks. You'll be leaving in two weeks, and staying in Paris for a month. Will that be a problem for you?" The director didn't know what kind of personal involvements Tom had that could stand in the way, but Tom assured him there were none.

"That works for me," Tom said soberly. The two men shook hands before Tom left the office. Tom couldn't believe his good fortune, to be sent to Paris on a mayor's commission, sponsored by the Department of Emergency Management and its French counterpart. All he knew was that three other San Francisco hospitals would be represented, with a doctor from each, but he had no idea who they were.

Tom went back to the trauma unit with a grin. He couldn't wipe the smile off his face, and he spun one of the older nurses around while she laughed in amazement, and kissed her firmly on the cheek.

"What happened to you?" she asked as he let her go.

"Six weeks from now, I'll be spinning you around and speaking to you in French," he said, looking delighted.

"That sounds dangerous," she said, laughing at him.

"Definitely, for the French women I meet. Paris, here I come!" he said cryptically, as he grabbed a chart and headed for an exam room while the nurse laughed and went back to work. He was a menace, but an endearing one, and a damn good doctor, she thought as she wondered what he'd meant.

At San Francisco General, Bill Browning had just heard the same speech from the head of the hospital, and Bill too was grinning from ear to ear. The intended mission sounded fascinating and like a great opportunity to share techniques and information, but all he could think of was that four weeks in Paris would give him four weekends to spend with his girls. He could visit them in London, or have Athena send them to Paris. Being able to spend time with them every week for a month was the best gift anyone could have given him, and he could hardly wait!

At Stanford, Wendy looked shocked for a minute, and mildly panicked. Four weeks was a long time, and she hadn't gone away for more than a few days in the last six years. She never wanted to miss a Wednesday night with Jeff. It made her uneasy to think of leaving him for that long. What if he forgot about her, or discovered that their Wednesday nights together weren't worth the trouble, or he fell in love with his wife again or, worse, somebody else? All Wendy could think about was "out of sight, out of mind," and she wasn't sure she wanted to go, or should. She was flattered to be invited, but her situation with Jeff was precarious, and being gone for four weeks sounded dangerous to her, in terms of their relationship. She almost turned it down, but then decided to wait and discuss it with him on Wednesday night, and see what he said. If he objected to her going to Paris, she would gracefully decline. She said she would give them an answer on Thursday, and the head of the Stanford Medical Center did all he could to encourage her to go. He said she would be a valuable member of the team, and a wonderful representative for Stanford.

There was going to be a reception hosted by the mayor at City Hall, when the French team came to town. It all sounded very appealing, and even exciting to Wendy, but not if she lost Jeff because of being away for four weeks. She realized, as she thought about it when she went back to her office in the trauma unit, that no matter how depressing the situation was at times, or how inadequate the arrangement, she wasn't ready to let him go. In fact, she was holding on to him for dear life.

The situation for Stephanie at UCSF was complicated too. She was stunned when they asked her to represent UCSF, and very flattered, and by the time they finished describing the assignment to her, she was ready to run home and pack her bags. Before she could stop herself, she said yes. But as she walked back to the trauma unit, she felt panic wash over her. What was she going to say to Andy? How could she justify leaving him and their two small sons for four weeks? Andy was going to have a fit, but this was another step toward her goal of becoming head of the unit one day. Being on the mayor's commission was an honor she didn't want to turn down, and she had already agreed. She had blurted out her positive answer before she had thought it through, but as reality hit her, she knew there was going to be trouble at home. What if he wouldn't let her go? She didn't want to miss it, but she didn't want to push Andy over the edge either.

She knew all of his complaints about her job, and he seemed to be getting more strident about it recently. Now she would have to tell him she was going to Paris for a month. She didn't know what to say, how to couch it in a palatable way. All she knew as she sat down at her desk in the trauma unit, staring into space, was that she wanted to go. More than anything in the world. It was a fabulous opportunity and she just couldn't pass it up. All she had to do was convince Andy of it too. That would be the hardest part.

# Chapter Four

Stephanie waited until she had a night off, wasn't on call, and didn't have to work late. She brought it up to Andy, as casually as possible, over a glass of wine, sitting by the fire, after they put the boys to bed. She had set the stage as carefully as she could, hoping for the optimum result.

"I got an amazing opportunity this week," she said as they sipped their wine. Andy was in a good mood. A California magazine had recently bought an article of his about conservation in Marin. He hadn't sold anything in a while. And he hadn't done one on the urban crisis in months. He was too busy with the boys to be diligent about his writing, which was frustrating for him. He wanted to advance his career too.

"What kind of opportunity?" He eyed her with suspicion. Announcements like that usually meant some extremely demanding project that would eat into her time with him and the kids. He knew her well.

"Apparently, the Department of Emergency Management is sponsoring an exchange through the mayor's office, with Paris as our sister city, to pool information and protocols about terrorist attacks. They're sending four doctors from San Francisco to Paris to work with their emergency services there, and then four French doctors will come here to learn what they can from us. It's a terrific idea."

"For how long?" Andy asked, frowning. He sensed immediately that there was more.

"A few weeks," she said vaguely, and then decided she'd better level with him. "A month," she added in a small voice.

"And you want to go?" He looked shocked.

"Actually, UCSF asked me to go as their representative. It's all trauma docs from the Bay Area. UCSF was invited to send the doctor of their choice, and I'm it. It's a big honor," she added, trying to convince him, and she could see it didn't.

"Jesus, Steph. You want to go away for a month?" He looked at her in astonishment. "What about your kids . . . and me? What are we supposed to do for a month?"

"You could come with me," she said, throwing it out there to pacify him. He looked upset.

"With two small kids, while you work all day and night with a bunch of French doctors and we never see you? That makes no sense, and the boys would go nuts in a hotel. They're better off here in school. But that's a long time for you to leave them. I'm beginning to feel like we're getting in your way. It didn't used to be like this. You balanced work and our family, but now, little by little your job is becoming your priority, and sometimes I feel like you forget about us entirely. I think you have some choices to make, Steph." He sounded harsh and angry, and her heart sank.

"What is that supposed to mean? Give up my family or my job? My father never did. He was a busy obstetrician, and sometimes he delivered babies almost every night for weeks. We hardly ever saw him, and nobody asked him to choose between his work and us. My mother made it work, for all of us."

"I'm trying to make it work too, but maybe the world isn't quite as fair as you think. I'm your husband, not an au pair. I want to work on my career too. This whole family is not just about supporting you. And now you want to go to Paris for a month. Where does that leave us, Steph? What am I supposed to think? What's your priority here? Work or us?" He couldn't see her giving up a month in Paris to stay home with them. And if she did, he knew she would feel cheated, and in some ways she wasn't wrong. It was a fabulous invitation for her. But it was going to come out of his hide whether she went or she didn't. The balance of responsibilities, and the way they'd agreed to divide them up, was beginning to weigh heavily on him. The deal they'd made to support her career came at a high price for him. And she never said it, but she thought medicine and saving lives were more important than writing, no matter how talented he was.

"Why does it have to be a choice?" She argued with him, but didn't want it to escalate into a fight. If it did, she knew they would both lose. And he had a point. Her career had become increasingly demanding in the last year. But he knew what she did when he married her. Hers wasn't a nine-to-five job, particularly in trauma, where they dealt with life-threatening emergencies every day. Sometimes she had to go in, even if she wasn't on call, because she was the best doctor for the job. But it was creating a lot of conflicts for them at home. "I'm torn about it too," she said in a gentle voice, trying to stay calm. "I hate leaving you and the boys, but I'd love to be part of this exchange. It's an honor to be asked, and I could learn so much. It could open doors for me at work," and close doors at home, if Andy resented it and held it against her. He had the power to hurt her severely, or even get tired of their life and have an affair, or leave her. He met lots of attractive young mothers every day, schoolteachers, and probably other women she knew nothing about, and he was great-looking and a nice guy. But in some ways, he was holding her back and making her feel guilty all the time. Things hadn't been as smooth between them for the past year, and she never had enough free time to make it up to him. He was angry almost all the time.

"I don't want to be the bad guy here," he said firmly, then finished his wine and stood up. Their cozy moment in front of the fire had come to a bad end. "I'm not going to deprive you of this and tell you that you can't go. You have to make up your own mind," but it was obvious from the way he said it that there would be a price to pay, possibly a big one, if she went. He was monumentally upset about the trip. "And when you're figuring it out," he said in an icy tone, "try to remember that you have a husband and two kids. Maybe married doctors with young children don't get to trot all over the world, going to monthlong conferences in other countries. There are sacrifices one has to make."

"I do," she said, sounding lame even to herself. "I give up plenty of stuff to do my job and be home with you as much as I can. It's a hard juggling act for me too," more than it was for him without a regular job. And this was the choice they'd made and agreed to when Aden was born. It was just harder than they'd expected six years later. Andy got angry now every time she had to go to work in the middle of the night, or came home hours late, or wasn't free to have dinner with their friends. But she made a good living, which they relied on. He didn't make enough to afford the kids' school, and the mortgage on the house, both of which she paid for. They never talked about it, but the reality was there. He had become a stay-at-home dad and kept trying to make his writing career a success, but hadn't made real money at it yet. She never complained about how little money he made. That wasn't the issue. The real issue was that she wanted the freedom to do her job, and enjoy the perks, without Andy and the kids holding her back.

"Maybe we should take a break when you come back," he suggested as he stood looking at her.

"Why? As my punishment if I go to Paris?" That seemed so unfair and the reaction seemed extreme to her.

"I'm not trying to punish you, Steph. But we need more balance in our marriage. We need more time together, and with the kids, if we want this to work."

"It's been working until now," she said, looking unhappy, and he did too.

"Not in a while," Andy said honestly. "At least not for me. I feel like your errand boy and babysitter. You're at work all the time. If you're not seeing patients, you're in meetings, or taking classes on new techniques."

"That's part of the deal, and what the hospital expects of me. I have to stay on top of new protocols, new surgical techniques, and new meds."

"Our kids are going to grow up before you know it, and you're going to miss it. You said that to me about your father when we met, that you hardly saw him when you were growing up. You can't get back the time you don't spend with the boys. All I know is that a month in Paris sounds like a long time to me, no matter how flattering the invitation is. You don't need to know how they deal with terrorism and trauma in France," he said practically. "You live and work here." He was right about that, but it sounded fascinating to her. For a minute she wished that he could go with her, but it made no sense. She knew he was right and she'd be busy all the time. He and the kids would be cooped up in the hotel, and the boys were too young to enjoy a month in a foreign city. They wouldn't even remember it.

"Do you want your mom to stay at the house with the boys, and you come with me?" she suggested as a peace offering, but he shook his head.

"They're too much for my mother to handle, she's seventy-four years old. And your mother wouldn't do it either. I don't want to leave them for a month," he said, sounding supercilious about it, and making her feel guilty again. He always did. "Let me know what you decide. It's up to you." She was almost waiting for him to add the famous words of Jiminy Cricket from *Pinocchio*, "and let your conscience be your guide." Why was everything in life a hard decision, involving so many sacrifices? Parenthood was harder than she had expected, and their marriage wasn't going as smoothly as it used to either. He was always pointing out to her where she fell short. He hung out with women who didn't work, the mothers he saw at the boys' school, and suddenly she had become a criminal in his eyes. He made her feel like an inadequate parent, and she wondered if it were true, and she was damaging her children forever. But if she backed down on her career or worked part time, she knew it would damage her and she would feel cheated. It really wasn't fair. He had nothing else to do, except write articles and essays that most of the time didn't sell. He had talent but getting freelance articles published wasn't easy.

She wanted to talk to someone about the trip, but didn't know who. She wasn't close to the other doctors at work, nor the mothers at the boys' school. She felt like a freak compared to them, and showed up in scrubs or surgical pajamas or her white doctor's coat every time they had an event at school, as though to show them she had an excuse for the times she wasn't there. And her mother was usually sympathetic to Andy, even though Stephanie's father had been at the hospital most of the time. Her mother excused it because he was a man. Her sister was even more extreme. She'd had a great job as a family law attorney, and given it up the first time she got pregnant. She had three children and spent all her time making bead jewelry with her daughters, papier-mâché Christmas decorations, perfect gingerbread houses for the school fair, and carpooling her girls to ballet. She thought Stephanie was dead wrong to maintain the pace she did, and continue working full time in the trauma unit. She had recently told Stephanie that she should be getting Aden onto a soccer team, signing him up for Little League, and checking out a Cub Scout troop. Stephanie didn't have the time, so Andy had promised to do it, but hadn't yet. Her sister had nothing else to do.

She felt as though her entire family was some kind of guilt factory, they were always picking on her. Her father thought they should have another child, he said her fertility was going to drop markedly in the near future, now that she was thirty-five. But a third child was the last thing Stephanie wanted, she could hardly take care of the two she had. Her baby-making days were over, and she wanted them to be. She loved the two boys she had, but couldn't have juggled one more. Andy had always said he wanted four, but Stephanie knew her limits, and two was all she could handle, with her job. Her sister's answer to everything was to tell her to quit. She could just imagine what Nicole would say if Stephanie told her she wanted to go to Paris for a month on a medical exchange.

She was looking troubled when the head of the trauma unit stopped to talk to her a few days later, and congratulated her on the trip to Paris. He had recommended her for the exchange. "You're lucky you've got a husband who'll pick up the slack for you with the kids while you're away," he said confidently, and Stephanie looked pained but didn't comment. "He's a good guy," he added.

"Yes, he is," Stephanie agreed softly, "but I feel guilty anyway. A month is a long time to be away from my kids."

"It'll fly by, you'll be so busy. And you'll come back with a wealth of information we can use here, especially with multiple casualty incidents, mass prophylaxis planning, and disaster preparedness. The French have been hit hard in the last five years and have probably learned a lot from it." San Francisco hadn't had any mass terrorist incidents, although other cities in the United States had, and no place was exempt anymore. Terrorism was a factor in everyone's life now, mostly from crazies in the States and political dissidents in Europe, but the end result was the same. Thousands of people injured and hundreds of people dead. All government agencies wanted to find ways to avoid the tragedies that were happening on campuses and in cities. It was man's cruelty to man at its worst. "I'm proud of you for going," the head of the unit said, tapping her on the shoulder. She realized after he left that this was not just about her and a trip to Paris. It was about what she would learn there and bring home to use for her patients' benefit, and to teach the other doctors. She was an ambassador on an important mission, and on her way home that night, she made the decision. She was going to Paris, whether Andy understood it or not.

She told him after dinner, when the boys were in bed, and he nodded, and made no comment. He went upstairs shortly after, took a shower, and went to bed, and he barely spoke to her for weeks afterward. She felt like a child abuser every time he looked at her, but she had made the decision and dug her heels in. On an intellectual level, and career-wise, she knew it was right. And five years from now, the boys wouldn't even remember that she'd gone. It wasn't going to scar them forever. They were four and six and they would miss her, but they'd forget about it as soon as she came home. It was Andy who would remember for longer.

When she told the boys a few days before she left, she promised to call them every day. Ryan cried for a few minutes when she explained it to them, and Aden looked sad for an instant and then said okay and went back to playing with his Legos. He was making a fort with his father. Andy hardly looked at her now that she'd decided to go to Paris. He never referred to it, or asked her when she was leaving. It had killed all but the most basic communication between them, exclusively about plans that involved their children. The romance or lust between them had been dead for months so nothing changed there. Her sister Nicole told her it was shocking, her mother didn't comment and stayed out of it, but had told Nicole it was a mistake. And Andy's mother told him how sorry she was that his wife was so selfish and gave so little thought to him and their boys. Stephanie knew she was definitely not a hero for leaving home, no matter how great the honor. And she hoped she wasn't making a huge error that would strain their marriage past breaking point, but she was going anyway. She would do her best to fix it when she got home.

Wendy told Jeff about the trip to Paris on their first Wednesday night together after she'd been asked. She waited until after dinner, which she'd prepared for him, and set on a candlelit table with a white linen tablecloth. She always went all out on their nights together, and bought a good bottle of wine since he was off call on Wednesday nights. She broached the subject carefully, not sure what he would say, and wondering if he would object to her being gone for so long. She expected him to be somewhat upset.

His eyes lit up the moment she told him about the exchange program organized by the DEM and endorsed by the mayor's office, and he smiled broadly at Wendy and touched her hand.

"That's fantastic! I'm so proud of you! What a wonderful opportunity. And Paris . . . you're going to have so much fun!" He assumed immediately that she was going and didn't pick up on the uncertainty in her voice and eyes.

"I wasn't sure . . . I thought that maybe you'd be bothered by it. I was thinking that maybe I could go for part of it, like a week or two, and not stay the whole time." It was a compromise she had thought of that week, but hadn't asked if they'd agree.

"Why would you do that? If the program they're planning is for an entire month, you should stay for the whole time. And why rush back to San Francisco when you can be in Paris?" He looked excited for her, and not upset at all.

"I don't like leaving you for a whole month," she said cautiously, but didn't explain why. That she didn't want to leave him alone with his wife for that long, without their Wednesday nights.

"I'll be gone for half of it anyway," he said matter-of-factly, and Wendy looked surprised. It was the first she had heard of it, as he smiled at her, looking relaxed. "The kids have their winter break then. Jane and I are taking them to Aspen. It's everyone's favorite vacation. They're all good skiers." Stephanie knew he was too. But she wasn't thinking about their skiing. She was bowled over that he was taking them on vacation, again, with his wife. They still went on vacation with their kids several times a year. He had even taken her to a medical conference the year before. Jeff said it was because it was in Miami and she had never been. But it didn't sit well with Wendy, and she knew that Aspen was a glamorous ski resort, and they would have a great time. She didn't like the sound of it at all. "When do you leave?" Jeff asked her more precisely.

"In slightly less than two weeks," she said. She had waited two days to tell him, until their Wednesday night tryst.

"That's perfect. We go to Aspen a week after that, we'll be there for two weeks, and you'll come home a week after we do. Perfect timing. We'll both be so busy we won't have time to miss each other while you're gone." Maybe he wouldn't, but Wendy missed him every day she didn't see him, and the thought that he'd be on a holiday with his wife made her feel sick.

"So you don't mind?" She wanted him to tell her he'd miss her while she was away, but he hadn't. He looked happy for her, and congratulated her with the last of the wine. "I can't wait to hear about it when you get back." He was at ease and pleased for her, and not worried in the least.

"I'll text you from there," she promised and he looked hesitant.

"Make sure you do it during office hours, and don't get confused with the time difference. You can't text me in Aspen, Jane will be around all the time." She wanted to cry as she listened to him. She felt infinitely inconsequential in his life. She was a pastime, a diversion, even though one of long standing. She was the Wednesday night spice in his life, and whether he admitted it to her or not, she could sense that his wife was still the main meal. She never wanted to admit it to herself, but now and then it hit her in the face, and it just had. It didn't bother Jeff at all that he wasn't going to see Wendy for a month, and rather than find a way to talk to her while she was gone, he didn't want her sending texts while he was on vacation with his wife and kids. It was a brutal reminder that Wendy had no role in his life.

Her fears were even greater now that he would detach from her, and get closer to his wife while Wendy was in France. It was an unhealthy relationship for her and always had been. It destroyed her sense of self-worth and she knew it. She didn't even want to go to Paris now, but she knew that she'd look like a loser to him and her boss if she didn't go. Her heart was in her socks as he talked to her about Paris, and suggested several restaurants where she should go. All she wanted now was to stay home with him, but he wouldn't be there anyway, and she would have been miserable if she'd been in San Francisco while he was on a two-week vacation with Jane and their kids in Aspen.

Things had suddenly come clear to her that whether or not Jeff saw her didn't seem of great importance to him. He enjoyed their Wednesday nights, and her company, but a month without her was no big deal to him, even though it was to her. And yet, whenever she had questioned the relationship and tried to get out of it in the past six years, he had talked her into staying. Was she merely a convenience to him, sex he had to make no effort for? Did he even love her? But even if he did, it felt like a dead end. Six years later, he was still going on vacations with his wife. It was obvious that there was no future in it for her, except as an affair he was having on the side, which was exactly who she'd never wanted to be in his life. She looked at herself in the mirror as she got ready for bed, and asked herself if that was what she wanted, someone who cared so little for her, and offered her no future. Year by year she was giving up the chance to have children. It was a high price to pay for sex every Wednesday night, no matter how handsome, impressive, and successful her lover was.

The next morning Jeff kissed her lightly on the lips before he left, thanked her for a wonderful evening, a good meal, and a great bottle of wine. He ran a hand across her bottom and said he'd see her sometime that week, if he had time to drop by. He knew she'd be waiting for him as she always did. They had one more Wednesday before she left for Paris, and she hated herself for making it so easy for him.

That morning, she told the head of the hospital that she would be going to Paris, to represent Stanford Medical Center's trauma unit in the exchange, and she walked back to her office with a heavy heart. There was no hiding from the fact of how little she meant to Jeff. The truth cut through her like a knife.

# Chapter Five

The four trauma doctors from San Francisco had been told to meet at the Starbucks in the international departure terminal at the airport, after they checked in. They were leaving on a Sunday.

Bill Browning was the first to arrive. He was an early riser and always punctual. He called Alex and Pip on the way to the airport. It was late afternoon for them and they had just come home from playing in the park. They knew he was going to be in Paris for a month, and he was taking the Eurostar to see them that weekend. In five days, he would be with them. He couldn't wait, and they sounded excited about seeing him too. Their mother had agreed to let him see them for four weekends in a row, and even send them to Paris for one of them, when she and Rupert were going to Spain for a few days. When he left Paris, Bill wouldn't see them again until the summer, so Athena agreed to accommodate him this time. The war between them was over and had been since she married Rupert, and Bill was a responsible, caring father, so she had no objection to his spending time with the children. It was almost as if their marriage had never happened. They no longer had anything in common, the only link between them was the girls.

He ordered a grande cappuccino, and stood watching for the others. He had looked all of them up on Google and had seen their pictures. Their credentials were impressive, they had all gone to important medical schools, and done their residencies at the best hospitals. They were equally matched in terms of their reputations and skills and where they practiced, at four of the finest medical centers in the Bay Area. There wasn't a weak link in the group. They were relatively close in age, with Stephanie being the youngest at thirty-five, and Tom Wylie the oldest at forty-three, and Wendy and Bill himself in between. Their profiles didn't say whether they were married or single, and it didn't matter to Bill. He noticed that Stephanie was very pretty with long blond hair and big blue eyes. She had a very American appearance, and a bright smile with perfect teeth. She looked like the girl next door, all grown up with a medical degree.

Wendy Jones appeared to be petite in the photograph, she had a smoldering sexy quality to her, blue eyes and hair as dark as his own. She was striking and beautiful, but he thought her eyes seemed sad. She wasn't smiling, and didn't look like a happy person. She seemed as though she had the cares of the world on her shoulders, but he was impressed that she had graduated cum laude from Harvard. He got the impression from her bio and photograph that she was one of those physicians who took herself very seriously. He'd done his residency at Stanford, where she worked now, so they had that in common.

Wendy arrived within five minutes of Bill. She didn't notice him at first, and was drinking a short nonfat latte with vanilla and cinnamon as she glanced around. Their eyes met and Bill smiled. She was as slim and petite as he had expected her to be, and appeared younger than thirty-seven. Her hair was long and she was wearing it in a neat ponytail. She was traveling in jeans, a black sweater, and a parka, and was carrying a tote bag full of medical journals she intended to catch up on during the flight. It was eleven hours to Paris, so she had her computer in the bag too. She didn't like to waste time being idle. Neither did Bill, but he wanted to watch a movie and catch up on his sleep. He had been on call for two nights in a row, and hadn't bothered to shave for the trip. His outfit was much the same as Wendy's, jeans, heavy black sweater, black down jacket, and running shoes. They looked like twins as they greeted each other and smiled.

"Exciting trip, isn't it?" he said warmly, nursing his cappuccino, and his smile lit up his eyes. "I'm really looking forward to it. I have two daughters in London, this gives me a chance to see them before the summer. Their mother's British so they live over there. I promised to take them to Euro Disney in Paris when they come to France." He chatted easily as they waited for the two others to arrive. "I've been trying to read up on the emergency services structure in France," he added. "It's incredibly confusing. They divide all their services by 'zone' geographically, at the local, department, and national level. It's all under the direction of the Ministry of the Interior. Our division of power is a lot simpler." She nodded and had been reading about it too.

\* \* \*

Stephanie had had a hard time leaving the boys. They hadn't been upset about her trip until then, but Andy looked so distressed that they picked up the signal from him, and started to cry before she left the house. She spent ten minutes trying to console them, although she was already late to meet the others before their flight.

Andy had hardly spoken to her since she told him she was going, and he was chilly when he said goodbye and she hugged him. He didn't kiss her, and stood in the doorway looking stone-faced with a crying child on either side of him. He didn't do anything to make the departure easier for her, and didn't console his sons until she left. He wanted his wife to see what it looked like when you abandoned your family for a month to run off to France, on a program he thought she never should have accepted as a married woman with two children. She had tried to reason with him again before she left, to no avail.

"I'm not going to join the Folies Bergère, for Chrissake. I'm going on a work mission with a bunch of doctors."

"You can do things like that when the kids are in college," he said sternly. He made it clear that he hadn't forgiven her for going, and she wondered if he ever would, but it was so unreasonable in her opinion that she didn't want to enter into his games, or argue the point with him again. The following weekend, he was planning to take the boys skiing in Tahoe, and putting them in ski school. She would have liked to go with them, but probably would have been on call anyway.

Stephanie was fifteen minutes late to meet her colleagues when she ran through the airport, her long blond hair flying, in running shoes and jeans, a pink sweater, and a fur jacket she was going to wear if they went out to dinner somewhere nice. Her parka was in her suitcase, and she'd been afraid to put her fur jacket in her checked luggage so she wore it. She was out of breath when she spotted Wendy and Bill outside Starbucks, and recognized them both immediately.

"I'm so sorry I'm late. My sons were crying when I left, I almost forgot my iPad." She looked stressed and didn't add that her husband was pissed at her for going.

Bill asked about her sons, and volunteered that he had two daughters in London, a little older than Aden and Ryan. It gave them something to talk about. Wendy said she had no children, but didn't say it was because she had been the mistress of a married man for six years, and still was, while her biological clock was ticking. She had wanted children when she was younger, but doubted now that she would ever have any. It had begun to feel like it was too late, and she didn't want a baby while Jeff was still with his wife, nor did he. He was careful to make sure that never happened, and so was she. It would have been a disaster, and he had made it clear that he expected her to have an abortion if she ever got pregnant.

They heard their flight called over the PA system, and walked slowly toward their gate, assuming that the fourth member of the group could get himself on the plane, since he was late. They wanted to board and settle in for the long flight, and just as they reached the gate and handed their boarding passes to the gate agent, Tom Wylie joined them. He was as fair as Stephanie and they looked like brother and sister. They were both tall and thin with long legs. He was wearing a navy turtleneck, jeans, a proper overcoat, and black suede loafers. He seemed sophisticated, and smiled at each of them as he apologized for being late.

"Overslept. Sorry. Late night." He grinned at them.

"Were you on call?" Bill asked sympathetically and Tom laughed.

"Not really," he said in an undervoice. "I had a date. A new nurse in the ER." He looked so wicked when he said it that Bill laughed, as they followed Stephanie and Wendy onto the plane and found their seats. Their seat assignments were in pairs on either side of the aisle, and they automatically sat with the two men on one side, and the two women on the other. They were chatting comfortably with each other before the plane took off. Tom asked Bill his marital status, was delighted to hear he was divorced, and told him that he had the names of several nightclubs, and they should go out together some night. Bill laughed at the suggestion.

"That's not really my thing. I go to bed early and I'm an early riser, and I'm planning to see my daughters on the weekends."

"There will be no early nights in Paris!" Tom said with the voice of authority and Bill laughed again. Clearly, Tom was planning a busy nightlife while they were there. He wasn't going to waste a single moment.

"Maybe one of the French doctors will join you for a night on the town," Bill suggested. They were going to be meeting their French counterparts in two days, but had read nothing about them yet. The DEM in San Francisco had been more organized about sharing information. They had a schedule of their first day of meetings, and a list of the names of the participants, but after that they would be in the hands of the French authorities that handled emergency services.

They'd also been given access information for their apartments. They each had an apartment in the same building, in the Seventh Arrondissement. The apartments were supposedly small but functional in one of the government buildings. Many of the buildings had been homes two hundred years before, and in recent years were purchased by the government and broken into offices and small apartments. At least they'd be together at the same address. As the two men compared information about the respective hospitals where they worked, the two women were getting acquainted. Tom was shocked at the security measures Bill had to deal with at SF General, and the number of shootings that occurred in the hospital itself, sometimes right in the emergency room. An intern had recently been grazed by a stray bullet. But Bill had nothing but good things to say about working there and how the hospital was run. He said the new modern facility that had been added a few years before was amazing. And the diverse nature of the patients was inevitable in a public hospital, and interesting for the medical staff.

"It's much more civilized at Alta Bates," Tom informed him, "though not as exciting." They talked about the recent fire, and the last act of terrorism in Paris. Bill and Tom each purchased a breakfast roll, and a flight attendant poured them each a cup of coffee.

"Do you have children?" Stephanie asked Wendy, who regretfully shook her head.

"I'm not married. And it's a little late for that now, although I have a lot of friends in their forties having first babies," Wendy said quietly.

"Boyfriend?" Stephanie asked bravely. They were going to be seeing each other every day, and she wanted to know more about her. Wendy hesitated before she answered.

"More or less," she responded vaguely, which told Stephanie the relationship was less than perfect. Wendy didn't offer the information that he was married. "We see each other once a week. We're both busy. He's a cardiac surgeon at Stanford."

"That must be easier in some ways," Stephanie said wistfully. "At least he understands what the work pressures on you are like. My husband is a freelance writer, and he takes it personally every time I have to go in to work at night. We fight constantly about how much time I can spend with our kids. He works from home, so he's with them a lot. I'm always feeling guilty, and the boys were crying when I left this morning. It's so difficult always being pulled between your family and your job. I feel like I never give enough to either one, and someone is always pissed. I think if I had known that, I'd have waited to have kids. Your friends having them in their forties are a lot smarter. I was still a resident when I got pregnant with my first one. It's been insane ever since. I just hope I still have a husband when I get home from this trip. He is *not* happy about my spending a month in Paris. What about your boyfriend?"

"He thought it was a great idea," Wendy said, smiling at her. She liked Stephanie, she was friendly and direct and open. "A little too much so," Wendy added. "He's going skiing for two weeks while I'm away. It feels weird not seeing him for a month, but we don't see much of each other anyway. His specialty is transplants so he works even more than I do."

"I feel so lucky that we got sent on this mission. I'm fascinated to hear how they do things differently from us. Do you speak French?" Stephanie asked her.

"Only what I learned in high school. I've forgotten all of it. I'm not sure I can get past 'bonjour.'"

"I took Spanish, so you're in better shape than I am. I think all the doctors we'll be dealing with speak English. At least I hope so." They were like two girls going off to college and sharing what they knew about the school.

Wendy got to work on her computer after they took off, and Stephanie watched a movie. The men had breakfast and talked for a long time, and then watched movies too. And eventually they all fell asleep and slept for several hours. They had another meal before they landed, and were glued to the windows as they flew over the city on a cold winter day, and then landed at Charles de Gaulle airport at six A.M. local time on Monday. It was seven in the morning local time when they left the airport with their bags, found the van and driver who had come for them, and were driven into the city as the sun came up. They were all wide awake and had slept well on the flight. Stephanie texted Andy that she had landed safely and he didn't respond. It was ten P.M. for him by then and she knew the boys would be asleep and he might be too.

They drove through the city, and the driver took them down the Champs-Élysées so they could see it. There were barricades where the bombs had gone off, and riot police in combat gear and soldiers with machine guns patrolling the street. They crossed the Pont Alexandre III onto the Left Bank with the Seine beneath them, and the Bateaux Mouches tied up at the dock, which reminded Bill that he wanted to take his daughters for a ride on one of them to see the sights. Then they drove down the Boulevard St. Germain to the rue du Cherche Midi, to the address they'd been given. The concierge was sweeping the street, and they used the access code to enter the building.

There was an ancient elevator that looked like an open birdcage big enough for two people. All four of their apartments were on the third floor, French style, which would have been fourth in the States. They decided to walk up the stairs, which slanted severely, rather than trust the elevator, and they each had a set of keys for their apartments.

As they opened their doors, they could see little bits and pieces of what must have been beautiful rooms a long time before, but had been chopped up into tiny apartments. The apartments were almost identical, with wooden floors that were original to the two-hundred-year-old building. Wendy's had a small marble fireplace, and there was one wall with beautiful moldings, the other walls had been put up more recently, and there were elegant windows. Each apartment had a small bedroom, a tiny bathroom with an old-fashioned bathtub, a toilet, sink, and a bidet, and each kitchen had a small two-burner stove, a narrow refrigerator, a sink, a minuscule oven, and a kitchen table for two that dropped down from the wall like an ironing board. They looked like student apartments. When you looked out the window, you saw the streets of Paris and in the distance the Eiffel Tower, which had recently been saved before a bomb could go off in the last terrorist attack. Paris had been a city under fire for several years now, but France had lived through worse before, during the German occupation in the Second World War. The current attacks were more insidious and of a different nature, but the Parisians were banding together to defend their homes and their city. Wendy noticed that there was a French flag at almost every window on their street.

The doctors left each other to unpack, set up their computers, and get organized for a full day of meetings the next day. They all wanted to explore the neighborhood, buy some groceries, and check out the restaurants where they might want to have dinner. They decided to meet that night at the Café Flore, which wasn't far away. It was a famous old writers' bar, one of the oldest in Paris.

Wendy and Stephanie agreed to go out walking together in a few hours. Bill had emails to answer, he wanted to call his daughters that afternoon, and Tom wanted to check out the nearest bars, so he'd know where to go after dinner, hopefully to pick up women. He didn't conceal how he intended to spend his evenings, and he was still trying to enlist Bill as a cruising partner but hadn't convinced him yet. Tom had mischief in mind and made no bones about it. He could hardly wait to get started and had a pickup phrase book in his pocket and an app on his phone to translate whatever he wanted to say. He could have been offensive, but he wasn't, and both Wendy and Stephanie found him funny, since he didn't try to hit on them. He wasn't obnoxious, he was just exuberant, like an overgrown high school kid or a college boy away from parental supervision for the first time. He had been that way all his life.

The two women bought cheese, pâté, a baguette, and some fruit that afternoon at a nearby grocery store, and a bottle of wine for each of them. They bought another bottle for the two men, and then wandered back to the apartment building, and were going to meet at eight for dinner. Wendy said she'd text Bill and Tom to meet them downstairs, and they set out together a few minutes before eight. They had a delicious meal of bistro food at the Café Flore and talked about where they'd been that day. They had all gone out and done some exploring and loved their lively St. Germain neighborhood. It was full of activity, people, stores, bars, restaurants, galleries, and things to see.

They went back to their apartments at eleven. Even Tom looked tired by then, and decided to wait a day before beginning his pursuit of Parisian women. They were all being picked up at nine the next morning, to be taken to the offices of the emergency services. They had a day of introductory meetings and orientation scheduled, and would be meeting their French counterparts.

They each settled into their beds that night with a sigh, thinking with pleasure of their first day in Paris. Stephanie called Andy again, but he didn't answer. It was three in the afternoon for him, and he was probably busy with the boys. It was midnight by then. She sent them a text and said she'd try them later, and as soon as she sent the text, she fell sound asleep. The others were asleep by then too. All four of the American trauma doctors had enjoyed their first day, and couldn't wait to see what was in store for them. They were becoming friends and for the first time in years, they felt like students on an adventure, and it was all going to begin the next day.

# Chapter Six

The van picked them up on time, and traffic was heavy, but the ride to the office they'd been assigned to gave them a chance to look around and see other parts of the city. The office was in the Eighth Arrondissement, and it was a combined office of the COZ, the Centre Opérationnel de Zone, the operations center for the Paris zone. It was under the direction of the Ministry of the Interior, and the COZ was in charge of an arm of emergency services called CODIS, the departmental center for fire and rescue operations. The division of power was very different than in the United States.

A dozen people were waiting for them when they arrived. The four Americans felt like the new kids in school, and weren't even sure if their counterparts spoke English, although they assumed they did.

The office that was used for conferences was once again in a very old building that looked like it had previously been a home. There were chandeliers and marble stairs and fireplaces, a large reception area, and everyone shook hands as soon as they walked in. After a few minutes they were led to a large conference room with a long table, where they all took their places, and there was a folder at each seat. Wendy checked hers and found that their schedule for the first week was in it, and some articles in English about the most recent acts of terrorism and which agencies had handled various aspects of them. And there was a brief description of some of the most important hospitals in the city, which the group would visit: the Pitié-Salpêtrière, Pompidou, Bichat, Cochin, Hôtel-Dieu, and Necker for children. Some of the hospitals sounded like the medical centers they worked in, particularly Bill at SF General. All of the materials had been printed in English and were informative and easy to understand. In addition, there was a chart showing the hierarchy of French emergency services, from the president to the minister of the interior, the COZ, CODIS, the SAMU medical teams, COGIC, the mayor, and the police. As they read the material, all four Americans were trying to guess who were the four doctors they'd been assigned to, and who would be coming to San Francisco in six weeks for a month's stay, just as the four Americans were doing now.

Everyone introduced themselves by name as they went around the table. An older man in a suit and tie from a supervisory government agency said that he was sure they were eager to meet the four colleagues they would be working closely with, and he introduced them in greater detail first, as to their credentials, and then let each of them speak for themselves. Two pretty young women served coffee to those who wanted it, and Tom looked at them carefully for a minute with a smile, and then turned his attention to the woman who stood up first.

"My name is Marie-Laure Prunier," she said in excellent English, with a French accent. "I'm in charge of this office of the COZ, the center of operations for the Paris zone. We have two hundred and sixteen geographical regions and two hundred and twelve metropolitan regions in France. The minister of the interior and the chief of police are my bosses. At the COZ, we coordinate information from all emergency services twenty-four/seven. I'm a physician, but I'm not in private practice anymore. I work exclusively for the center of operations for emergency services in this zone. We try to plan where we will achieve the best medical care in future disasters, and how best to avoid them. I am on-site and work closely with the police when an attack occurs. We do not always deal with terrorist attacks. It can be a fire, a gas explosion, a train collision, a plane crash, a bombing. If there is an emergency situation in Paris, we are there, and my job is to be there too." She smiled pleasantly. "Our specialty is crisis management. I received my medical training at the Faculté de Médecine here in Paris, I'm thirty-three years old, divorced, and have three children. My medical specialty is neurology and emergency medicine, like you, and I have additional training in surgery. I am a pediatric neurosurgeon by training. In France, all specialists deal with trauma in their particular area of expertise. But our 'emergency medicine' resembles your specialty in trauma. I work here now, planning how to save injured children, or overseeing rescue operations, or even ways to prevent an attack. I have been instrumental in setting up the White Plan, which is a means of handling catastrophic events with large numbers of casualties. I'm a civil servant, and at night, I can go home to my children." Several people in the room smiled and she and Stephanie exchanged a warm look.

Marie-Laure had a desk job, which was much easier to manage for a divorced woman with three children.

Gabriel Marchand was the second person at the table to stand up. He looked like a banker except his graying hair was too long for him to be one. He had a powerful frame and was a tall man with wide shoulders. He exuded energy as he greeted each of their American visitors. "Like Marie-Laure, I'm also a doctor, a cardiologist. I work for the Assistance Publique, the public health services, which is a government position. I see patients occasionally, but not very often. I am a fonctionnaire, what you call a civil servant, and like Marie-Laure, we try to devise systems that will keep our citizens safe in case of an emergency. I am forty-three years old, I have four children, and I am very excited to come to San Francisco," he said, smiling at them, and then sat down. There was something very strong about him, as though he was accustomed to commanding. He was almost military in his bearing and his style, and all four Americans correctly suspected that he had a high-ranking position in public health.

The next person to stand up was a tall willowy woman with a spectacular figure, long blond hair, and a dazzling smile. In a seemingly effortless way, she was noticeably sexy. She spoke English with a British accent, from where she had learned it. "My name is Valérie Florin. I'm a physician, a psychiatrist. I have a private practice of patients whom I see regularly here in Paris. I also devise the programs for victims of traumatic events, with ongoing follow-up care, for what you call post-traumatic stress. Our programs begin immediately after hostage situations and the kind of violence we've seen recently. We set up therapy programs on-site, as the event is happening, for victims, parents, and spouses. I work closely with the police in the negotiation with hostage takers. I am a consultant with the COZ and the author of three books." And then she grinned. "I am forty-two, unmarried and I prefer it that way, and have no children. My patients are my children, and fortunately none of them live with me." Everyone laughed at that, and she sat down gracefully. She was one of the most striking women any of the Americans had ever seen, she was gracious, sexy, poised, calm, and totally French, despite her near-perfect English. Tom Wylie was staring at her, and looked like he wanted to crawl across the conference table and grab her. Valérie seemed totally uninterested in him, ignored him, and focused on the others, which drove him crazy. He was unable to catch her eye, and she glanced right through him as though he wasn't there.

The last member of the team they would be working with was Paul Martin, he looked about eighteen, tall, gangly, awkward with a shock of uncombed hair. He was thirty-four years old, single, had worked for the COZ for a year. He was an emergency doctor and a surgeon, and had worked for Doctors Without Borders for three years in Africa, and loved it. He had come to Paris to learn more about violence in the cities, which he said was much more savage than what he'd seen in Africa. Paul was full of life and very excited about everything he said. He exuded youthful zeal, energy, and idealism, and spoke as though he had just been shot out of a cannon, as he ran a hand through his already disheveled hair. He sounded extremely bright and excited about the work he was doing, and what he had learned at the COZ, COGIC, and CODIS so far.

The others at the table introduced themselves and were part of the administration of the various branches that provided emergency services. They took a break after that, so people could talk to each other and get acquainted. Marie-Laure, the head of the office, explained that they would be visiting the hospitals where victims were sent in an emergency. They would also be meeting members of the government and the police. They would be speaking to the SWAT teams that handled hostage situations, and also participate in a drill for a terrorist attack. It was going to be a fascinating four weeks, without a dull moment. As the various people milled around the conference room, Tom Wylie made a beeline for Valérie Florin, and looked like he wanted to gobble her up. More than anything he seemed like an excited schoolboy, and she was visibly amused.

"Dr. Wylie?" She had correctly guessed which one he was.

"I'd love to spend some time talking to you, maybe we could have dinner sometime." He was hopeful and starstruck and she laughed.

"I don't think so. But you are all invited to my apartment for dinner tomorrow night, at nine o'clock." The time was very French and later than they were used to. "Casual, in jeans, nothing fancy. *Hachis parmentier,* which is one of the few things I know how to cook." She said it to their four American counterparts and her three French colleagues, all of whom were delighted. She gave them each her address on the rue du Bac, which was fairly close to where they were staying, within walking distance, on the Left Bank.

For the rest of the day, they were barraged with pamphlets, information, statistics, newspaper and magazine articles, and several books in English. They were all exhausted by the end of the day. Marie-Laure went home to her children, and Valérie hurried off to see patients. It felt good to walk into the cold night air at seven o'clock after being cooped up all day.

"No one said there would be homework," Tom Wylie complained, and his fellow Americans laughed at him and teased him about how he was going to chase women, if he had homework to do. But they were all looking forward to dinner at Valérie's the next evening.

Bill and Tom rented bikes from a Vélib' stand to go back to the apartment, and Stephanie and Wendy took the Metro, figured it out, and chatted on the way. It had been a very interesting day, and more serious and intense than they had expected. When they got back to their building, they all went to their apartments to relax. The two men then went to a bistro down the street for dinner, and both women said they were too tired to go out. Stephanie wanted to wash her hair and call her children, and she had to stay up until midnight to do it, to catch them after school. But she reached them this time, and they talked to her for ten minutes and then handed the phone to their father. Stephanie told him all about it, and how interesting it was. He mellowed for a few minutes and told her he missed her. She missed them too after she hung up. She had some of the cheese and pâté from the day before, and poured herself half a glass of wine. It felt very grown up being in Paris without her children or Andy. The Eiffel Tower was sparkling as she looked out the window, sipping her wine. She was thinking about Marie-Laure and wanted to get to know her better. And Valérie was fascinating.

Wendy was thinking about them in her room too, and she thought the men in the group were interesting also. Paul Martin was a little firebrand, and she had thought Gabriel from the public health department very intelligent and articulate. It was going to be a very interesting month, and she was glad she had come. They all were so far.

\* \* \*

The next day, they participated in a drill that had been set up for them. It was a simulated terrorist attack, using the White Plan to determine triage of the victims. A deserted school was used, with actors, to demonstrate an attack on a school and how it would be handled. And afterward, they were given a tour of Necker Hospital for children, and the care that would be administered there, and by whom.

Valérie had reenacted a hostage negotiation in the morning's drill, and both the military and SWAT teams were on the scene, shooting blanks. It had been stressful even though they knew it wasn't real. And Bill said afterward that they should do something similar in San Francisco. They all agreed.

At the end of the day, they went back to their apartments, and changed for the dinner at Valérie's. Bill got them all to ride the public rental bikes to her place. It was fun. Wendy said she hadn't ridden a bike in years, and they were all in good spirits when they got to Valérie's apartment. They had to walk through a courtyard to get to it, and it had a lovely garden, with a view of the Eiffel Tower. Her apartment was in a wing of an old *hôtel particulier,* a previously private home, and was filled with interesting objects from her travels, beautiful textiles and fabrics, a canopied bed she'd had sent back to Paris from India. There were cushions on the floor and comfortable couches, with candles on all the tables. She set the dinner out as a buffet, and they helped themselves to the delicious duck and mashed potato dish with shaved black truffles on top, a big salad, and excellent wines. Gabriel and Bill engaged in a serious conversation about public health, while Tom volunteered to help Valérie in the crowded kitchen, but she quickly sent him back to the others. After his conversation with Bill, Gabriel sat down next to Stephanie, and Bill next to Wendy. Gabriel appeared to be fascinated by Stephanie and asked her endless questions about herself while sitting close to her on a loveseat that was barely big enough for both of them.

There was something wonderfully intimate and cozy about Valérie's apartment and it made everyone want to stay forever, relax, and be among good friends. It felt that way as they chatted and opened up to each other. Stephanie admitted to Gabriel that she had felt very guilty leaving her children, but she knew this was an important trip for her so she came.

"How did your husband feel about it?" Gabriel asked her in a gentle voice. He was a huge teddy bear of a man, and she could easily imagine feeling safe in his arms.

"He wasn't pleased about it. In fact, he was still angry when I left," she said honestly.

"Is he a physician?"

She shook her head. "He's a freelance writer."

"It's very difficult being married to someone who's not in medicine. Most of the time, they don't understand the demands a medical career makes on us. It destroyed my marriage too."

"Mine isn't destroyed yet," she corrected his impression, to be fair to Andy. But they hadn't been doing well for the past year, and the trip to Paris was the icing on the cake.

"My wife and I began going our separate ways five years ago. It was just too difficult arguing with her all the time, about the children, about dinner parties I couldn't go to, about her parents. I was never where she wanted me to be. In truth, I have very little spare time, and what I do have, I spend with my children." She understood perfectly what he was describing and she was living it herself.

"You're divorced?" Stephanie asked, curious about him. He seemed like such a nice man, and he appeared to have gone through the same things she had, with his wife. It sounded like the marriage was over.

"Not yet. We've discussed it many times. The animus of the marriage is dead. The disposal of the paperwork and the property are details. We have an arrangement that works for us both," he said in a smooth, matter-of-fact way.

"That sounds complicated," Stephanie said, frowning. "Divorce is very clear. You're married or you're not."

"Americans make it very simple. The paperwork and division of property is more complicated here. Sometimes it's just easier to lead separate lives. The address is just an administrative detail. And you wait to divorce until you meet someone you want to marry. Otherwise, why go through all that pain and expense if you don't want to marry again?" It was one way to look at it, but not hers. "My wife and I both agree that we're free."

"That must be awkward for the people you go out with, and for your kids," she said practically.

"Most of their friends' parents are in the same situation. It's not unusual here."

Stephanie nodded. She couldn't imagine wanting an "arrangement" with Andy. If their marriage broke down, she would want a divorce. It seemed cleaner. But Gabriel didn't seem sneaky or dishonest, just French. They talked about many subjects and agreed on almost all of them. He explained to her about the French public health system, and social security, which paid all medical expenses for everyone. All you needed was a green credit card, a Carte Vitale, and you could have any procedure you wanted or needed, for a minimal amount or even for free. Surgeries which cost a fortune in the States cost very little or nothing at all in France.

They discussed the high cost of medical care in the States, and then talked about their children. He had married young, and his four children were in their teens. She was amazed by how comfortable she felt with him, and the others seemed equally so in the nest Valérie provided. She was a wonderful hostess. The atmosphere was intimate and warm and sexy, like Valérie herself. Tom was following her around like a puppy while she continued to ignore him, but every now and then she would smile at him, and he looked like he was going to melt. Bill and Wendy noticed and laughed at how besotted he was. Valérie only appeared amused, and treated him like a silly child. His Don Juan act had dissolved like ice cream in the summer sun.

She had bought a delicious apple tart for dessert, which she served with vanilla ice cream, and café filtre. No one made a move to leave until after one A.M., and it was nearly two when they finally made it out the door. The whole group left together, after thanking Valérie profusely. Gabriel offered to drive Stephanie home. He said it was too cold for her to go back on the bike. He offered the others a lift too, and they declined, but Stephanie gratefully accepted the ride with him. When they reached her building, he gazed deep into her eyes and didn't speak for a minute.

"I've never met a woman like you, Stephanie. You're so honest and strong and brave. I wish I had met you a long time ago." A chill ran down her spine as he said it, and she felt a powerful attraction to him, which she hadn't felt in years for anyone. They had both had a fair amount of wine and she wondered if it was due to that. "When we left the office yesterday, I couldn't wait to see you again. The night was too long without you." It was a very romantic thing to say and she didn't know how to respond. She was a married woman, and she didn't have an "arrangement" with Andy, unlike Gabriel and his wife. And she'd only known him for two days. He seemed very intense. "I think destiny brought us together." She wondered if that was true. He kissed her fingertips, which sent an electric thrill through her, and she got out of his car as the others arrived and parked the rental bikes in the stand in front of their building. A minute later Gabriel drove away with a last heated look at her and a wave.

No one commented on how attentive he'd been to her as they walked upstairs. They didn't know her well enough to say anything, but they had noticed. And once in her apartment, she thought about him. There was something so incredibly attractive about him. She tried not to think about it and called her boys as soon as she took off her coat. They were with the housekeeper, who had picked them up at school. She said Andy was out. He had an appointment that afternoon, which he hadn't told her about the night before. She wondered where he was.

When she hung up after talking to the boys, she thought of Gabriel again, even though she didn't want to. No matter what his arrangement was, he was a married man, and she was a married woman. She reminded herself of it again as she fell asleep, and thoughts of him filled her mind. She remembered the feel of his lips on her fingertips. She tried to make herself think of Andy, but she couldn't and didn't want to. All she could think of was Gabriel, and all she wanted was to see him again. The morning couldn't come soon enough.

# Chapter Seven

For the rest of the week, they toured the hospitals with the best emergency services. They met other doctors and government officials, went to lectures and meetings, visited the different facilities and offices, and met with police and the SAMU, which were teams of doctors who treated victims on the street, right where they were injured. As a rule, SAMU didn't move patients until they were stable. The doctors saw videos of recent attacks and how the SWAT teams handled them, pointing out where mistakes were made and where the operation had gone smoothly.

There was a constant flood of information, which the American team tried to absorb attentively and discuss with their French counterparts to better understand how the systems worked in France. They worked well together as they got to know each other, and their respective strengths provided similarities and contrasts and posed some interesting questions they sought answers for. The mesh of the group was perfect, and by the end of the week all eight of them had bonded and were a cohesive group.

They had the weekend off, which everyone needed. They were exhausted from all the facts and details and new material they had studied.

Tom invited Valérie for dinner, and she flirted with him as she declined, which tantalized him unbearably. She was seeing patients on Saturday, and driving to Normandy on Sunday to see her mother. She didn't tell him what she was doing in the evening, but said she was busy. She did it so charmingly that it drove him insane. He wanted her so badly he could taste it, and he stared at her during most of their meetings.

Gabriel always seated himself next to Stephanie and spoke to her in whispers, but she didn't mind it. She loved being near him, and couldn't pull herself away from him. She had agreed to have dinner with him on Friday night. And Valérie had whispered a warning to her, as they left one of the hospitals they visited.

"Don't forget he's a married man, and he's French," she said softly, which startled Stephanie. She knew that about him, but was telling herself they could be friends. But he didn't act like that was all he wanted, and their mutual attraction was a powerful magnetic force.

She and Wendy were going to the Louvre together on Saturday, and planning to have lunch afterward, and they wanted to go to the Galeries Lafayette to do some shopping. They were going to have a girls' day, and they both wanted to catch up on their reading on Sunday. Stephanie liked having a woman friend in the group, and Wendy enjoyed it too. She had stopped seeing everyone for the last few years, and lost touch with her women friends, so she'd be available anytime Jeff wanted to drop by. And suddenly she was free, and had someone to do things with again. Marie-Laure had invited them both over for tea on Sunday to meet her children. The two youngest were close in age to Aden and Ryan, also boys, and her oldest son was eleven. They were very young, and they rarely saw their father. It was all on Marie-Laure's shoulders, as she had explained to them one day over lunch. Her husband had left her when her youngest was born, five years before. She managed on her own, with babysitters, which Stephanie thought was heroic. When her husband left her, she'd had an infant, and a three- and a six-year-old.

Bill was catching the Eurostar at six o'clock on Friday night to see his daughters in London. He had booked two connecting rooms at Claridge's, and he was picking them up that night. He was beside himself at the prospect when he left by cab for the train station. He ran into Wendy as he was leaving the building, and she wished him a good weekend and a great time with his girls. She was on her way to the little food store nearby, so she could have dinner in her apartment. She said she was exhausted after their busy week. So was Bill, but he was revitalized at the idea of seeing his daughters.

And Tom had convinced Paul Martin, the young French doctor from the COZ, to go barhopping with him to meet women. They had a plan and Paul was picking Tom up at nine. Tom had a list of bars he'd been given and wanted to try, and Paul was young and game for anything. He thought Tom was a lot of fun.

Gabriel picked Stephanie up at eight-thirty in his car, and drove her to a small, cozy restaurant in her neighborhood where they could talk quietly. Gabriel lived in Neuilly, a residential neighborhood full of families and some very pretty houses, and he looked very pleased to be having dinner with her. She told herself it wasn't a date, and they were just colleagues getting to know each other and becoming friends, but he was warm and supportive, and enthusiastic about everything she said, which was exciting for her.

They shared a passion for medicine, and he understood everything about her work. It was impossible not to be drawn to him, and he seemed so much more mature than Andy, who was always complaining about something, pouting, ignoring her, trying to make her feel guilty, angry at her, or acting hurt. It was so tedious to listen to. She always had to be justifying herself, and it made all their exchanges so unsexy. It was just one long battle. Being with Gabriel was so much easier, and the attraction between them was undeniable. She was trying to resist it, but it was hard. She had an enormous crush on him, was physically attracted to him, and he looked as though he was totally swept off his feet by her. She had never felt like this about any man since she had married Andy.

She hadn't come to Paris to have an affair. What's more, however he described it, Gabriel was a married man. But by the end of dinner, as they sat across the table from each other, they were holding hands. They'd both been drinking wine, but not enough to account for how she was feeling, or how attracted they were to each other. He told her he had never felt this way about any other woman. He readily admitted that he had been unfaithful to his wife, and didn't view it that way given the lack of emotion between them. But he said the other women had never meant anything to him, and he thought Stephanie the most enchanting woman he had ever met. He couldn't keep his eyes off her, or his hands, and when they left the restaurant, he kissed her, and for an instant she melted into his arms. Her own willingness to do so shocked her, and they had just met.

There were tears in her eyes when she pulled away from him. "Gabriel . . . we can't . . . I'm married. A lot more so than you are. I have a husband and two children waiting for me at home."

"And you're unhappy with him. You've said it in a thousand ways. He doesn't understand you. He's jealous of your work. He makes you feel guilty. You constantly feel torn between him and your career. You can't live like that forever. He's holding you back." What Gabriel was saying was true, but they were married and had two little boys, and in some ways, she knew Andy was right, she didn't spend enough time with their sons. And she had left them to come to Paris for a month, and she felt guilty about that too. It was the age-old battle between family and career. She wanted both, and the career path was an easier one for her. Now she was kissing a man she barely knew and felt fatally attracted to.

"I'm not unhappy enough to leave him," she said honestly. Or she never had been until now. But what if Gabriel was right, and Andy was the wrong man, or they had outgrown each other? Their life together seemed so dreary to her now. His writing career had stalled, and she sensed that Andy blamed her, or was jealous of the fact that her career was going well. But she worked harder than he did, and was more determined to succeed than he was. Stephanie was more ambitious, and Andy was more of an artist. She used to find it charming, but she no longer did. Gabriel was a powerful man in a powerful position, it made him infinitely more attractive to her than Andy with no real job, and nothing but dreams about his writing. She felt guilty for everything she was thinking. Gabriel was temptation personified, and she was having trouble resisting. That had never happened to her before, but she had never met a man like him.

"Let's not waste what's been given to us, Stephanie," he said gently. "Something like this doesn't happen more than once in a lifetime, for soul mates to meet. What if we were meant to be together? We will regret it forever if we don't follow our hearts." There was more than her heart involved, and he knew it too. It was a powerful physical attraction that had hit her like a tidal wave. She had come to Paris to work, and was being swept away by a handsome Frenchman. She felt like this was a movie, and she was afraid of how it would end. She couldn't ignore the fact that he was married too. They had the potential to create a huge mess if they gave in to what they were feeling. She had been sensible and responsible all her life. And suddenly she didn't want to be. She was doing everything she could to resist him.

"We don't have to make any decisions," he said in a voice that was smooth as silk. "This is only the beginning. You'll be here for a month, let's see where this goes. We have time. And I'm coming to San Francisco for a month. By then we'll know what we should do." What he said almost sounded sensible if she was willing to get out of her marriage, but that was a huge decision. She couldn't do that for a man she had known for five minutes. But he was right, in the next two months, they would know if it was real or an illusion. The prospect was exciting and terrifying, and while she thought about it, he kissed her again.

He drove her home after that and walked her to her door. He stood smiling at her for a minute, and gently touched her lips with his own, but didn't ask to come in.

"Thank you for dinner," she said, looking confused. She had never been as tempted in her life to do something so utterly crazy.

"I'll call you tomorrow," he said gently, and watched her go inside.

When she got into her apartment, she sat down on her bed with a dazed look, and tears slid slowly down her cheeks. She didn't know if she was happy or sad. She missed Andy, and the boys, and their safe, familiar world. But she wanted to be in Gabriel's arms and to let him kiss her again. She had no idea what to do and just sat there and cried.

When Bill got to St. Pancras Station, he took a taxi to Athena and Rupert's house on Belgrave Square. He had the cab wait for him while he rang the doorbell, and Athena answered it with a look of surprise, as though he were the Ghost of Christmas Past.

"Oh right, I forgot . . . I thought you said tomorrow morning." She was as beautiful as ever, with a halo of blond hair around her exquisite face. He always forgot how stunning she was, until he saw her again. She had hardly changed in the years he had known her, and she smiled as their daughters came bounding down the stairs and screamed with delight when they saw their father and threw themselves into his arms. Bill beamed as he held them for a minute, and Athena told him to come in, while she helped the girls finish packing their bags. She glanced at him again over her shoulder with a look he remembered only too well, as she walked up the stairs. It was the look that had torn his heart out a thousand times. She was a beautiful woman, but she was never meant to be his. She waved him toward the library while he waited for them, and he wandered around the room, admiring the paintings and the books. The house was magnificent, and Rupert had spoiled her. It was a far cry from their cozy little Victorian in Noe Valley, or his stark apartment now.

Bill knew he would never have provided a home like this for her, although he could have one day. But this wasn't how he wanted to live. It reminded him of his parents' townhouse in New York, or his brother's apartment on Fifth Avenue. He was different from them, and always had been. There was something missing in him. He had no desire to live in luxury or show off. He loved his work at SF General, the real people he worked with, and the outdoors. Athena's parents had been right. He would never have been able to keep her for long. He had been the wrong man. He had suited her for a minute in her rebellious days as a twenty-three-year-old. She had now become everything she'd grown up with, and he never wanted. He wouldn't have chosen to live this way, even for her. It woke him up to the fact that the years he had mourned her had been wasted. He would never have fallen in love with her if he met her now, no matter how beautiful she was. She was someone to admire, like a magnificent piece of art, but not to have.

She came back down the stairs with Pip and Alex five minutes later, carrying the bags they were taking to the hotel. They were excited to be going with him, and Athena smiled at him again.

"I'm sorry to get here so late," he said to her as the girls circled them like puppies.

"It's fine, Rupert is hunting in Scotland this weekend. I always eat late. What are you doing in Paris?"

"Attending a conference on terrorism and emergency services, to compare with ours in the States." She made a face and laughed. She had never liked his specialty, and he remembered his father-in-law's suggestion that he give up medicine and come to work for him. That had never been an option for him, not even to keep her.

"It sounds dreadful," she said and laughed, and they looked at each other for a moment, wondering how they had ever gotten married. But he was glad that they had, with Pip and Alex as the result.

"It's actually very interesting. You would hate it." He laughed, relieved. He finally felt free of her. It had taken years. The girls were anxious to leave then, and Athena looked at him in that enchanting way of hers that used to make his heart pound, but it no longer did, which was a comfort now.

"Have a wonderful weekend," she said and kissed the girls.

"We will," he said as he smiled at his daughters. "I'll bring them home on Sunday afternoon. I'm catching a four o'clock train back to Paris. And I'll be here again next weekend. The weekend after, I'd like them to come to Paris." He had emailed it all to her, but she was never good at making plans, or remembering them when she did. She lived in a world all her own.

"See you next weekend, then. I'll be out on Sunday when you bring them home." She waved as they hurried down the stairs to the taxi waiting at the curb, and he caught a last glimpse of her as she closed the door. She was the woman he had loved so passionately, and mourned for so long. It was a relief to realize that he no longer loved her, and that seeing her no longer hurt. There was a wonderful feeling of freedom to it, as he put an arm around each of his girls, and they sped toward the hotel, talking about everything they were going to do over the weekend. His time with his daughters was what he lived for. It was perfect. He was happy as they walked into the hotel. There wasn't a woman in the world who could make him feel that way.

After a big breakfast at the hotel the next morning, Bill took Pip and Alex to the Science Museum. He always tried to do something educational with them, instead of just indulging them, although he did that too. Pip begged him to take them to Harrods, and they went after lunch. She loved to shop for clothes. They visited the Tower of London, which he had done with them a dozen times, but they always enjoyed it. They got back to the hotel in time for tea, with watercress, cucumber, and egg salad sandwiches, and scones with clotted cream and jam. They watched movies in his room afterward, and had hamburgers from room service for dinner.

On Sunday, they went for a walk in Hyde Park, and then he took them to their favorite pizza restaurant for lunch. He got them back to Athena's just after three o'clock. The nanny opened the door, with the twins standing next to her. They were very handsome little boys, and looked just like Rupert. The girls threw their arms around Bill's neck and held him tight, and thanked him for a wonderful weekend. He was planning to take them to the theater next time. The concierge at Claridge's was trying to get tickets to something suitable for them.

He kissed them both goodbye, and said he'd be back on Friday. They were going to go to Euro Disney when they came to France. Since he didn't have a home in London, they stayed busy and kept moving, doing everything he could think of to entertain them. It made his visits extra special. He did the same with them in San Francisco, mostly with outdoor activities, like walks on Stinson Beach, short hikes on Mount Tam, and trips to Lake Tahoe. They were never bored when they were with him. The previous Easter he had taken them to Rome and Venice, and they'd ridden in a gondola. He had already promised them a ride up the Eiffel Tower when they came to Paris.

He was quiet on the train ride back to Paris, thinking about them. They were growing up as typical British children. Pip liked saying she was half American but Alex was still too young to care about it. It always made him sad to leave them, but less so than usual this time, since he knew he would be seeing them on Friday, and for two more weekends after that. He had paid an additional amount on the airline ticket he'd been given, and was going home through London, so he could spend the last weekend with them. Seeing them now would make the wait more bearable until they came to San Francisco in the summer to spend a month with him.

He looked peaceful and happy as he walked into the building on the rue du Cherche-Midi, and saw Wendy parking a bike in the Vélib' stand. He waited for her to catch up to him so they could walk upstairs together. The elevator had been out of order all week.

"How was your weekend?" she asked him pleasantly. She could see that he was relaxed and in good spirits. He always was when he'd spent time with his daughters.

"It was perfect." He beamed at her. "We ran around all weekend. They're coming here in two weeks. I'd love for you to meet them." She was touched that he would ask, and smiled as they stopped in front of her door.

"I'd like that very much," and then she thought of something. "I bought a roast chicken this morning. They only had a whole one, and it's too much for me to eat. Have you had dinner?"

"No." He smiled at her. "And to be honest, I'm starving. I was going to walk down the street to the bistro after I drop off my bag in the apartment. I meant to eat on the train but I fell asleep. My daughters wore me out."

"Why don't you come over in five minutes? I'll get dinner organized." He left her to drop off his bag, and was back five minutes later. She had put the chicken on a platter on the small dining table, with a slab of pâté, some cheese, and she was making a salad. She set a fresh baguette on the table. "I've fallen in love with the food hall at Le Bon Marché. Valérie told me about it. It's fantastic. I'm going to get fat here, I've been living on pâté and truffled cheese," she said guiltily, but she was tiny.

"I don't think you have to worry about that." He helped himself to some of the pâté, a chicken leg, and the salad, then she handed him a bottle of red wine to open. They sat down to the simple meal, which was delicious. It was a perfect end to the weekend. "What did you do this weekend?" he asked her.

"Stephanie and I went to the Louvre yesterday, and did some shopping. I went to Notre Dame today. There's so much I want to do here. There's a Picasso exhibit at Le Petit Palais I want to see too. I never get to museums in San Francisco. I'm too lazy to go into the city on the weekend. I just hang around at my house in Palo Alto."

"I take it you live alone?" He was curious about her. He knew she wasn't married and didn't have children, but he figured there had to be someone. She was very attractive and she hadn't looked at any of the men in the group with any particular interest. She hesitated in answer to his question. "No boyfriend?" That surprised him, she was a very pretty woman.

"There's someone, but it's complicated. We don't see a lot of each other. I don't really have time to with work anyway. He's a cardiac surgeon. He's busy. What about you?" She was equally curious about him. He was very reserved, and hadn't said much about his personal life, except that he had two daughters in London.

"I live alone, and I'm happy that way," he said easily, helping himself to some of the cheese and the baguette. "We lead a crazy life with the work we do," he said, using the same excuse she had, and then decided to be honest with her. "My wife left seven years ago with the kids, to go back to England. It blew the lid off my life, and I spent about five years being angry and bitter. I saw her the other night when I picked up the kids, and I suddenly realized that I don't hate her anymore. I'm not angry or bitter, and when I looked at her, I think I saw for the first time how completely different we are. There's no way it could ever have worked. I just didn't see it then. She hated California, and eventually San Francisco, for all the reasons I love it. After that she got to hate me for taking her there. She's remarried and has two more kids. We were young when we met ten years ago, but the truth is I have absolutely nothing in common with her, and never did. I was a momentary lapse for her. And if I met her today, I wouldn't talk to her for five minutes. I have nothing to say to her, except about our children. She's living the life that I left New York to get away from.

"She was like a flower dying of thirst in San Francisco. All she wanted to do was go home, and I became her jailer. She hated me for keeping her there. I would have had to give up practicing medicine to go back to England with her, as her father suggested. That was never an option for me. I would have drowned there, and died of boredom. I was devastated when she left and took my girls. I stayed angry for years. And suddenly when I saw her the other night, I realized the war was over. I don't know when it happened, but the steam is gone and everything else went with it. I don't even know her. I never did. It was a fantastic feeling of freedom. It takes a lot of energy to stay mad at someone. Now I can use that for something else. She got over me a long time ago. It took me years longer. I would have been miserable if I'd stayed married to her. It took me all this time to figure that out. I never had room for anyone else while I was furious at her. It nearly killed me when she took the girls and left."

"It's funny," Wendy said thoughtfully. "I think I've been hanging on to something that should have died a long time ago too. It should never have happened either. I think I had to come here to realize it. It's amazing how long you can hang on to a mistake. I'm going to try and deal with it when I go back. I've wasted six years on a relationship that's never going to work or go anywhere. I didn't want to see that." And she had given up so much to be with Jeff, her friends, all the pastimes she enjoyed, her dreams, and a big piece of herself.

"It takes a lot of courage to let go," he said simply, and she nodded. She liked talking to him. He was a sensible, down-to-earth person. She would have liked to get to know him better and be friends with him. She hadn't even had room in her life for friends for years.

"Gabriel seems very taken with Stephanie," she commented. They had all noticed it. "I wonder where that's going to lead."

"Into deep water if she's not careful. They're both married. That seems dangerous to me. And complicated when she goes back. It's easy to forget that when you're far from home and real life," Bill said wisely.

"I like our group," Wendy said, at ease with him. "And I like the French docs too. I wasn't going to come on this trip. I'm glad I did." She smiled at him.

"Me too. I leapt at it, as an excuse to see my girls for four weekends. But it's been really interesting so far." They agreed that they'd both been impressed by the emergency services drill that had been organized for them.

"I wonder what they have in store for us this week," she said. They would get their schedule on Monday.

"A lot more hospital visits. How do you like working at Stanford?" he asked her, since he'd done his residency there.

"I love it. SF General must be a tough place to work."

"It's fantastic. It suits me. I love the cases we get, as long as I don't get shot in the process." He grinned at her. "It's probably the only trauma unit in the city where patients shoot each other in the ER."

"I can live without that," Wendy said, horrified by the thought. They talked about work for a while. They both loved working at teaching hospitals, and he was on the faculty at UCSF, like the rest of the staff at SF General. Then he got up, and thanked her for dinner. It had been a nice end to the weekend for both of them.

"See you tomorrow," he said easily. They both felt as though they'd made a friend, and Bill hoped to see her again when they got back to San Francisco. There was no pressure, no romance, no agenda. It would be nice to have a female friend for a change. They worked in a rough-and-ready world, which ate up one's personal life, if you let it. It sounded like she needed to broaden her horizons too. It was easy to let your life shrink to the size of the trauma unit. It was a hazard of the kind of work they did. They went home too exhausted and emotionally drained to do much else. He always marveled at the doctors he knew who went home and managed to give more to their spouses and children. Some days he was too empty after work to even talk to another human being. You gave everything you had to give at work, and the people at home felt cheated. He'd seen it happen a lot in trauma work. There were easier specialties, but Bill knew they would have bored him. He loved what he did.

He went back to his apartment next door to hers, and was glad he'd had dinner with her. They were the gladiators of their profession, and they worked under constant pressure. A split second could make the difference between saving a life and losing a patient.

Wendy was thinking about him as she washed the dishes and put them away in the tiny kitchen. The apartments weren't fancy but had everything they needed. She felt like a student being there, going to their meetings every day. And she liked what they were learning from their French partners. There were some new techniques and equipment they didn't use in the States yet, and a different attitude about terrorism and trauma due to their more frequent incidents and present risks.

She admired Valérie too, and her take on the psychological aspects of the world they lived in. She wanted to get to know her better. Wendy had enjoyed everyone she'd met in the program so far. She would have liked to tell Jeff about it, but contact with him was taboo.

She knew he had left for Aspen that weekend with his wife and children, and what she had said to Bill was true. All hope for a future with Jeff had gone out of the relationship while she wasn't looking. She knew now she'd never have more with him than their stolen Wednesday nights. She was angry at herself for settling for so little, but she didn't know if she had the guts to leave him. She was so used to building her life around him and putting everything else on hold, even though she saw so little of him. Thinking about him with Jane in Aspen still made her sad. His wife had everything Wendy wanted and would never have. She was giving the relationship serious thought while she was in Paris.

It also occurred to her that most people in trauma and ER work didn't seem to have stable home lives. She, Tom, and Bill didn't have partners, and it sounded like Stephanie's marriage was shaky. On the French side, Gabriel's life wasn't solid either, and Marie-Laure, Valérie, and Paul were alone too. They gave everything they had to their jobs. They had nothing left when they came home at night. At least Bill seemed to have a good relationship with his kids, when he saw them. But Stephanie had admitted to her how torn she was between her work and her family, and how guilty she felt because of it. Wendy wondered if she had a better life after all. Maybe if she were married to Jeff, they'd have nothing to give each other either. Jeff's priority was his work, just as hers was. How much room did that leave for a relationship or another person? Maybe not enough.

It was a concept she wanted to explore with the others. They were all warriors in a cold, lonely world, fighting for each life they saved, more than in other specialties. Wendy had been challenged by the severity of the injuries they dealt with during her residency, and loved the work, but she hadn't understood the high price they themselves paid until later. And few of their patients made full recoveries, which was disheartening. Most were just too damaged. Even when they saved patients, quality of life afterward was an issue, especially with head injuries. It was serious business. But she still loved being pushed to the maximum of her abilities, and the successes they had. They all did, which was why they stayed in it. She couldn't imagine doing any other kind of work, and Bill had said the same during dinner. It was a victory every time they saved a life.

Wendy wasn't even sure she wanted children anymore. She had given up the idea a few years before, because of the Jeff situation, but maybe having them wouldn't have been right for her anyway. She wondered if you needed a nonmedical partner to have a family and do it successfully. Bill had admitted that his ex-wife was a good mother to their daughters. And he spent less than two months with them every year, although he would have seen more of them if they'd lived in San Francisco. He seemed like a good dad to Wendy.

There was a lot to think about when she went to bed that night. Then her mind drifted to Jeff again, in Aspen with Jane, and her heart sank as it always did when she imagined them together. She had become the willing outcast in his life, the dark secret. It was a role she didn't want to play anymore, and she was sure of that now. She hadn't told Bill her boyfriend was married because she was ashamed of it. All she had to do now was tell Jeff. That was the hard part. And then walk away, which was going to be the hardest part of all.

# Chapter Eight

Feeling very Parisian, the four Americans rode rented Vélib'
bikes to their COZ meeting on Monday morning, to start their second informative week. Wendy and Stephanie complained that they
weren't wearing helmets, and Tom and Bill brushed it off, as they
watched for cars and motorbikes in the erratic traffic patterns.

"It would be embarrassing if we end up brain damaged while on
our mission here," Stephanie grumbled, pedaling as fast as the men
with her long legs. Wendy had to work harder to keep up, and Bill
occasionally slowed down for her to make sure she didn't get lost on
the way.

"No one on bicycles wears helmets here," Tom reminded Stephanie. "Pretend you're French." The traffic was insane, particularly at
that hour of the morning, but despite Stephanie's concerns, they got
to the office safely in time for the meeting, as the others filed in.
Wendy had already said she would go home on the Metro at the end
of the day, and Marie-Laure came over to talk to the two women to

ask how the weekend was. She said two of her children had been sick and she had been stuck at home. They told her about shopping at the Galeries Lafayette and their visit to the Louvre.

"Maybe you should visit some of the smaller boutiques," Marie-Laure suggested. "We get a lot of threats on the department stores now. I don't feel comfortable shopping there myself." It had occurred to Wendy, but Stephanie had insisted they'd be okay, and the bargains were great. There were sales everywhere, and they had both gotten some things they loved. Stephanie was wearing a new red V-neck sweater, which Gabriel noticed immediately when he arrived. He smiled at her, dropped his briefcase next to a chair, and walked over to her with the same intense expression that had haunted her all weekend. He kissed her on both cheeks, and just standing next to him gave her the same thrill as when he'd kissed her. Everyone in the room was aware of their mutual attraction, which Stephanie found embarrassing, but he didn't mind at all.

Valérie was the last to come in, and smiled with a particularly wry glance at Tom, who felt weak at the sight of her.

"I had a very hard day yesterday, thanks to you," he scolded her as she approached, and she was puzzled. "Paul and I visited every bar in St. Germain on Friday and Saturday night. I had a splitting headache all day. If you'd had dinner with me, I wouldn't have been forced to check out every bar on the Left Bank, where I was shamelessly overserved by evil waiters." They had progressed from red wine to tequila shots to scotch, and most of Saturday night was a blur when he woke up on Sunday.

"So that was my fault?" she asked, amused. Paul looked rough too. Neither of them had shaved before the morning meeting, but both were handsome men and could get away with it, and it was the current trend in Paris as well as the States. Bill had shaved and looked fresh and relaxed after his weekend with his children. His activities had been more wholesome than theirs.

Paul had wound up going home with some Brazilian girl from the last bar, which he barely remembered. She was an exotic dancer the bar had hired with a samba troupe for the evening. Tom had a vague recollection of dancing on the bar with a half-naked girl wearing a G-string made of feathers. He was sure they'd had fun, what he recalled of it, and had found the G-string in the pocket of his jacket when he woke up in his apartment on Sunday morning. He wasn't sure if the girl had been there or not, but kept the G-string as a souvenir of a very entertaining evening in Paris. He had other mementos like it at home.

"It sounds like you deserve the headache you got," Valérie commented, and the others laughed as they sat down at the conference table and got down to business, looking at the schedule for the week. Gabriel sat next to Stephanie and whispered to her occasionally as they studied statistics and descriptions of the hospitals they'd be visiting. They went over a lot of paperwork, and Valérie handed out a synopsis of their post-trauma programs, how they were run, and how quickly they were set up after the incident. The systems in place sounded very efficient, and they had a two-year follow-up program with free therapy for as long as it was needed, and it could be extended on request.

They left with an armload of paperwork at the end of the day. Stephanie already had a stack of papers on her desk at the apartment at the end of the first week, and so did the others. She and Wendy went back to the Left Bank by Metro, and the boys rode home on the Vélib' bicycles. The four of them had dinner together at the closest bistro to the apartment, and made it an early night. Tom still looked a little rough and suggested he might have a brain tumor as they all laughed at him. Bill thought it might be the tequila shots he had imbibed heavily on both weekend nights. Tom told them about the feathered G-string he'd found in his pocket and they laughed. He was running true to form, and hitting his stride in Paris.

Gabriel had wanted to have dinner with Stephanie that night, but she declined and said she wanted to have dinner with her team. He called her three times during the meal and sent her several texts. He was continuing to pursue her at the same intense pace, and Stephanie was half uncomfortable and half excited by it. No one had ever courted her so avidly, but she didn't want to stop it either, and was feeling confused about him.

"What are you going to do?" Wendy whispered after one of his texts. Stephanie looked flushed and mildly embarrassed.

"Nothing. I'm married," she said with determination, but she sounded like she was trying to convince herself. Other than his dogged pursuit of her, he seemed like a sane person. He was incredibly smart and fatally attractive. He was a hard man to brush off, and she didn't want to, which was what scared her about him. He had a powerful effect on her, almost like a drug.

"Your being married doesn't seem to slow him down," Wendy suggested cautiously. "I'm sure you can handle it, and you'll know what you want to do, but be careful of married men. They're probably not much different here than in the States. That's a hard game to win," she said wistfully, thinking of Jeff. "Sooner or later everyone gets hurt. I don't know many stories of married men leaving their wives for another woman. I actually don't know any. It just doesn't seem to happen. They're comfortable where they are, and the two women wind up complementing each other, which just makes the guy's marriage work better."

"You sound like you've been there," Stephanie said gently, and saw the look on Wendy's face as she nodded but didn't explain. There was nothing unusual about her story, except that it was happening to her.

"Just be careful. And don't throw your life out the window for him yet." Stephanie nodded. She barely knew Gabriel, it had only been a week since they met, although he made it feel like she'd known him for years.

She talked to her children that night before she went to bed. Andy sounded tired and sad when they talked for a few minutes afterward. He didn't ask what she was doing and didn't seem to care. He wasn't interested in the medical details of what she was learning, only in the fact that she wasn't there. It made it hard to share her activities with him, and she could hardly tell him about Gabriel. But he had become a big part of the experience in Paris for her, and she couldn't share that with Andy either. There was nothing left for them to talk about except the kids, which happened to them at home too. Whatever interests they had shared before seemed to have disappeared. Seven years of marriage was beginning to feel like the Sahara Desert, which she had admitted to Gabriel over dinner. He said he had experienced the same thing, and only their children had kept him and his wife together. But his children were older and he had less reason to hang on now. Ryan and Aden were four and six, and needed them both, or so Stephanie thought. And she couldn't manage them alone with her work. But it seemed like a poor reason to stay married. Even Andy had suggested they take a break, before she left, which had sounded extreme to her at the time but less so now that she had met Gabriel. Maybe it was what she needed. Time away from Andy to figure things out when she went back. Or maybe the time in Paris would do that. She had never felt so torn and confused in her life. Gabriel had already upset the apple cart in a major way, and it had only been a week.

She set her alarm for seven o'clock, and it was cold and rainy when she woke up. They all took the Metro together to their meeting. At ten o'clock, both the French and American teams were going to visit one of the major public health hospitals, where trauma victims were taken after mass casualty incidents like the recent attacks. All their intake and triage procedures had been changed in the last four years to keep up with public events. Their systems were working, but Gabriel explained that they still needed improvement, and they were working on it diligently. He hoped to pick up some new ideas in the States.

They all rode in a van to the hospital they were visiting, talking animatedly about recent studies and actual events. It was a subject they were all passionate about. Tom walked into the building with Valérie, while Bill discussed some of their procedures at SF General with Gabriel.

They started their tour of the hospital promptly, and noticed that some things were vastly different from how they were done in the States, others seemed more efficient here. Their street triage was very different, and they frequently treated victims right at the scene before moving them, getting them stable where they lay, which wasn't done in the States. It wasn't possible in either place if the dangers were still present and the area was under fire or at risk of a bombing. The street treatment model was more adapted to single nonviolent incidents than to terrorist attacks.

They had just finished touring the surgical floor shortly before noon, and were talking with admiration about the state-of-the-art equipment, when Marie-Laure got a call on her cellphone and moved away from the group to speak to the caller in terse rapid French. Stephanie saw Gabriel react immediately to what he overheard, and walk over to Marie-Laure, frowning. She ended the call and conferred seriously with Gabriel and then they returned to the others, who sensed that something was wrong from the look on their faces.

"We have a situation," Marie-Laure said quietly, "at a school. It just started twenty minutes ago. I don't have all the details. We're not sure yet if there is one shooter or several. There are hostages, and already a number of victims, both children and teachers. The police are there. I have to go immediately. It's up to you whether or not you want to come." She looked tense and they could see that her mind was racing. Her cellphone was ringing again as they followed her rapidly to the elevator. All four members of the American team wanted to go with her. This was what they had come to learn about, but they had hoped to study past events, not new ones.

The fact that it was a school made the situation even worse. Marie-Laure didn't know how many victims there were, but had been told that there were several. There was no metal detector at the entrance to the school, and the shooter had a sack full of weapons, and used a Kalashnikov automatic weapon when he began shooting. Guns weren't easily obtainable in France, but the bad guys always seemed to have them, and this one was no different. The police hadn't contacted the hostage taker yet, and their information on-site told them that the hostages, possibly several hundred, some adults but mostly students, were being held in the school gym, and the police were hearing gunfire from the street. Two teachers inside the building had contacted the police and said there was only one shooter that they could see.

Within minutes all eight of them were in the van with Gabriel at the wheel. He stepped on the gas, took backstreets, ran through red lights, went well over the speed limit as Marie-Laure spoke to her police contact on her cellphone. Valérie listened carefully, and translated for the others. They made it to the school in just under ten minutes. It was a *lycée,* a public school in a good residential neighborhood, with students from five to eighteen years of age. It was in an area where there had never been any trouble, and there wasn't expected to be. It was the first incident of its kind and precisely what the government had dreaded, an attack on a school or any facility for young children. They had just been told at the hospital they visited that one of the weaknesses in their current systems was inadequate pediatric surgical equipment should an attack occur involving large numbers of young victims. Pediatric surgical instruments were in short supply, and they were planning to correct that soon. Maybe not soon enough now.

They jumped out of the van when Gabriel stopped it and drove onto the sidewalk where the police lines were, half a block from the school. Two men in CRS riot gear, with helmets and bulletproof shields, approached them immediately and Marie-Laure showed them her badge and accounted for the others. Valérie and Paul had their own ID badges, and Gabriel had a high government clearance and a card that showed it, so he didn't need a badge. Marie-Laure explained the presence of the Americans, who all had their passports on them, and that all four were physicians who specialized in trauma of the nature they were facing at the school.

The riot police allowed them to go behind police lines and they could plainly hear gunfire from the Kalashnikov the hostage taker was using. Two teachers had escaped, with six kindergarten students, moments before, and the terrified children were pale and wide-eyed as they were led away by police. The two teachers told police what they knew as SWAT teams began to arrive and CRS riot police in full armor circled the area.

The teachers explained that the gunman had shot into several classrooms before anyone could warn the teachers, so the rooms weren't locked according to their emergency procedures. Most of the teachers were women, he was heavily armed, and no one had tried to tackle him or stop him, for fear of being shot. He had ordered everyone into the gym at gunpoint and got on the PA system. It was the time of the daily assembly for the middle and upper school, which he seemed to know, so most of the students and teachers were there, and he demanded that the younger students be brought in so they could watch their classmates and teachers get punished. No one had known then for certain if he was alone or not, but it seemed that way. The police had to assume there might be others. But no one had been seen except the single shooter so far.

One of the teachers estimated that at least thirty people had been shot before he reached the gym, and they had managed to escape with the six kindergarten students through the kitchen, which they said was a viable escape route. The workers from the kitchen were already hiding in a back alley, and police were dispatched to find them as they heard another round of shots from inside. There had been many so far.

Marie-Laure and Gabriel joined the conversation with the teachers and asked additional questions as the other six stood to one side, not wanting to interfere with the tense exchange. Both teachers were women, and shaking from the shocking experience they'd just been through. One of them said that two of her kindergarteners had been shot and were dead when they left the classroom. She cried as she reported it to the police and the other teacher put an arm around her, as Valérie came to stand beside her and speak gently to her. The police allowed Valérie to lead the two teachers away at a short distance, so they would remain available for further information, but for now they had told the police enough to be extremely helpful.

One SWAT team was deployed to the back of the school, and the homes around the perimeter were evacuated so neighboring residents wouldn't get shot by random bullets when the SWAT teams stormed the school. The question was when that would happen, and how. They didn't want to wait too long, or go in before they were fully prepared. And inevitably, there would be casualties when they went in. At the request of the police, Marie-Laure, Gabriel, and Paul walked to a police bus parked half a block away and got in to confer with the senior officer in charge. Bruno Perliot was the captain coordinating the SWAT teams and responsible for police response. They were planning their entry attack as the others waited outside, cringing every time they heard gunshots again.

"We don't know why he's in there," Perliot said with a calm voice and angry eyes. This was exactly the kind of situation they had feared for years, involving a building full of children. They had just learned that there were six hundred and twenty children in the school, and approximately eighty adult staff who worked there.

There were at least a dozen senior police officers on the bus, which served as tactical headquarters for what they were going to do. There were squadrons of riot police and SWAT teams in the street around them, waiting for the order to go in, but no one wanted to sacrifice safety for speed, nor to wait too long. Whatever they did would have a downside. And they had no idea why the shooter was there, if his motives were political or religious, or if he was a random lunatic on a mission of some kind.

"I want to know who this bastard is," Captain Perliot said through clenched teeth as two policemen in combat gear stepped onto the bus with an older woman. She identified herself as the school librarian. She had climbed out a basement window where she was putting books in a storeroom when the attack began. She had heard the ranting of the gunman on the PA system and before she left, she had looked for some of the children to take with her. She had approached the gym and said that the doors to the gym were locked, and she thought everyone was trapped in there with him. She said some students and teachers might be hiding, but she had escaped without finding any.

"I think I know who he is," she said, her voice shaking. "He was talking about his wife, and said everyone had to pay for killing her. The administration reduced the staff three years ago, and about twenty teachers were let go. If he is who I think he is, his wife was one of them, Élodie Blanchet. She taught history and Spanish. She was a lovely woman. Six months later, she discovered that she had breast cancer, she had surgery and treatments. I visited her in the hospital when I heard about it. She died about a year ago. She told me when I saw her that her husband was very unstable, and he was convinced that she got cancer from losing her job. They were separated when she died. They had a daughter who is fourteen or fifteen now, and lives with Élodie's mother. We all went to the funeral. Her husband was there, but he didn't talk to any of us from the lycée. The whole story is very sad. I think he had a history of mental problems and lost his job because of it. That's all I know about him." She was certain it was him from his ranting over the PA, and he had mentioned Élodie by name.

Captain Perliot asked his name and she said it was François Blanchet. The librarian had heard him speaking of his wife on the PA system and then gunshots and people screaming afterward.

Two policemen got on their cellphones immediately, to the intelligence unit, to get everything they could on François Blanchet. Five minutes later, police intelligence called back. He was forty-nine years old, had a psychiatric discharge from the army, so he knew weapons, and was an unemployed engineer by profession. He lived in a rough part of Paris, and was on welfare. The whereabouts of his daughter were unknown. Ten minutes after that, they had a cellphone number, and, holding his hand up for silence, the captain called him. Marie-Laure sent a policeman to find Valérie, and she came back to the bus at a dead run before the call connected, and stood an arm's length away from the captain. The call was being recorded.

There was no answer at first as the gunfire continued from inside the building, and then it stopped and François Blanchet answered.

Bruno Perliot spoke to Blanchet in a calm, even voice and said that they wanted to have a conversation with him, and wanted him to come outside.

"You must think I'm stupid. And then what? You shoot me on the way out? Don't try to come in here," he warned him. "If you do, half the children will be dead before you shoot open the doors."

"Let's talk about this. I'm sorry about your wife. That was a terrible thing to happen," Bruno said in the most soothing voice Stephanie had ever heard. They had been invited to join the French team on the bus, and told where to stand so they wouldn't get in the way.

"They killed her!" François Blanchet exploded into the phone, and then started to sob. "They killed her. She got sick almost immediately after they fired her. She was so beautiful, and so sweet, and a good teacher. They made her sick. She would never have gotten cancer if they didn't fire her. She was never sick a day in her life. They were too cheap to pay her, so they killed her."

"I'm sure they're very sorry now," Bruno Perliot said smoothly, but the gunman got irritated immediately.

"I will make them sorry for every day she suffered, and every minute she's been dead. I loved her so much," he said, sobbing again. "She was such a good person."

"That's what I've heard." As Perliot spoke to the shooter, SWAT teams were exploring the building for points of entry, had found two they wanted to use, and were entering through the basement. "François, I don't think she would want you to hurt the children. She loved them." The captain was stalling him, trying to buy time, while they frantically planned their entry into the school.

"I know she did. And they fired her anyway, and killed her. Now my daughter has no mother and I have no wife." He cried audibly for a few minutes, and then a volley of shots rang out again.

News of the school hostage situation had leaked out by then, and the TV news trucks had arrived on the scene, with reporters everywhere being told by police to stand back. The press were waiting for the dramatic scenes at the end, but there was nothing for them to show now. A small cluster of parents was standing in the street, clutching each other and crying, waiting for news of their children. Someone had called them, most of the parents didn't know yet. A special area had been cordoned off for them, with two policemen in charge. Valérie had gone out to see the parents briefly, and was back on the bus minutes later, in time to listen to the call with the hostage taker. She was standing by with an intent expression, listening to every word he said. The captain was handling it masterfully. Ideally, they would have liked the gunman to give himself up, but the likelihood of that happening was slim to none. He had already gone too far. As they watched, both Stephanie and Bill were thinking of their children, and how they would feel if this happened to them. Their hearts went out to the agonized parents, as one of the riot police handed out police armbands to the four Americans, to identify them as part of the official police operation if things got crazy and rough later on. They slipped them on over their jackets as the drama continued to play out. It had just been on the news that a crazed gunman was shooting children and teachers at the *lycée,* in retaliation for the death of his wife. The police knew that more frantic parents would begin to arrive.

Five minutes later, one of the policemen approached the captain and whispered that Blanchet's daughter was calling in on the main police line, or someone who had claimed to be her. She said her name was Solange Blanchet. The captain pointed to Valérie to take the call, which she did, on a phone someone handed her, and she walked away a little distance so as not to interfere with the captain's conversation with the gunman.

Solange said that the hostage taker was her father, and he was very sick. He had been that way since her mother got cancer. She hadn't seen him since the funeral and didn't know where he'd been, but she told Valérie that they had to take him to a hospital and not kill him, just stop him from hurting the children at the *lycée*. She was crying and sounded desperate.

"How fast can you get here?" Valérie asked her.

"I don't know. Fifteen minutes. My grandmother can drive me."

"It would help if you could talk to your father," Valérie said on her own initiative, but she had done things like it before, sometimes with success. It brought a sick shooter's mind back to reality to speak to his child, or wife, or mother. Sometimes they could do the job better. Valérie knew it would be traumatic for the girl, and she would deal with that later, but for now it was all they had. Bruno was establishing a rapport with Blanchet, but they could already sense that he wasn't going to be able to convince him to put down his gun and come out. And shots continued to pepper the conversation. They could hear the screams from inside the gym. Sometimes he shot in the air to demand silence, and at other times he was shooting victims.

Students who had them were using cellphones to call out of the building by then, lying under the chairs from the assembly. They weren't supposed to use cellphones in school, but some had them in their pockets, and the police were talking to them, as the students answered in whispers. They said that at least fifty students were dead in the gym, a lot of teachers, and they didn't know how many were in the halls, and Blanchet was still shooting. One of the teachers in the gym said that he had a sack of loaded Kalashnikovs, and was using them. Blanchet had told them he had enough ammunition to kill them all.

There was no doubt in anyone's mind that they had to go in. The question was when. There were snipers poised to shoot through the windows, but they didn't have a clear shot at him because the windows were too high. Ladders had been set up along the side of the building, but they were waiting for the order to open fire, and the SWAT teams already in the basement had been told not to advance farther, but to be ready at a second's notice. Their best marksmen were already in the building. And there were at least two hundred police in various uniforms on the street. Ambulances had arrived, and teams of doctors and paramedics were standing by.

Valérie handed the captain a note that Blanchet's daughter would be there in fifteen minutes. She had already left her school, and her grandmother was on the way to her. Bruno decided to wait until she got to them. What he didn't want was another hundred victims while the SWAT teams entered the room and took him down. If they could get him to give up peacefully, it was worth the wait. And meanwhile they were still studying the best access to the building and the gym.

Bruno went on talking to Blanchet, while he sobbed about his wife, but he had stopped shooting for a few minutes. And it seemed like an eternity until a slim young girl with her blond hair in a braid climbed onto the bus looking terrified. Her maternal grandmother, with whom she lived, was waiting outside. Solange was fifteen, had already lost her mother, and now her father had gone insane and was killing children. She wanted to help the police, and Valérie explained to her in a quiet corner what they wanted her to say. Just hearing Solange's voice might subdue him, and bring him back to earth, before more people got hurt. They handed her a phone connected to the same line the captain was on, so he didn't have to give his up and he could listen to the conversation.

"Papa," she said softly, in a tremulous voice, her eyes brimming with tears, "Maman wouldn't want you to do this. You have to stop now. I love you. Maman loved you." She and her father were both sobbing as she spoke.

"They killed her, Solange. You don't understand, you were too young. She got cancer because of them. They deserve to die for it."

"I don't want you to die too . . . or the children . . ." she begged him.

"It's the only way they'll pay attention. There was no other way. I'm avenging your mother," he said, sounding aggressive again. "It's only right. And the children didn't suffer. I shot them in the head." Everyone on the bus felt sick as they listened, and Solange choked on a sob. Even she understood that her father was never going to come out of this alive. The police wouldn't let that happen. All they could hope was that no more children would die, but François Blanchet was a marked man. And he knew it too. "I want you to go home now, Solange," he said firmly, for an instant sounding like any parent of a teenage girl. "You shouldn't be here, you should be in school."

"I wanted to be here with you. Can I come in and see you, Papa?" It might be her last chance to see him alive.

123

"No, go back to school. Maman wouldn't want you here."

"I love you, Papa."

"I love you too. I have to work now, go home," he said sternly. Valérie was both listening to the conversation and texting her assistants to send in the post-trauma teams. Some had already come, but she had a feeling they had underestimated the numbers of victims.

The captain was shaking his head as he listened to the exchange between father and daughter. Blanchet wasn't coming out, and he sounded like he was about to continue his rampage when he said he had work to do. Captain Perliot indicated to Valérie to take Solange off the bus and she escorted her outside. Once the girl was gone, he gave the order in code to go in. The plan was set. Four teams were going to attack simultaneously to break down the gym doors and free the hostages. Marksmen were already halfway up the ladders, poised just below the windows to shoot Blanchet as quickly as they could. Everything was in place and waiting. They had been there for less than two hours, but it felt like two hundred years. And Bruno Perliot wouldn't have felt responsible going in any sooner. He wanted everything perfectly set up for the best protection he could get for the students, and so the SWAT teams could act as quickly as possible.

He gave the final code word with a grim expression, which went through the earpiece of every member of the SWAT teams, and within a split second, the marksmen were up the ladders, the doors exploded into the gym, windows were shattered, bullets flew, children were screaming and François Blanchet lay dead on the stage with six bullets in his head and four in his chest, which had come from all directions. Police and SWAT teams were running and carrying injured children out of the building to paramedics and ambulances, and another detail of police had the grim task of counting the bodies as they moved systematically through the school, also making sure that Blanchet had committed the assault alone, which appeared to be the case.

Outside, parents were frantic and sobbing, rushing toward ambulances trying to identify their children, and the police couldn't stop them. Children were clutched, others were missing, people were shouting, and Solange stood sobbing in her grandmother's arms. She was the daughter of a murderer and her father's death had been confirmed. Both her parents were dead now, and her father was a monster.

It was a scene of slaughter and desperation, terror and tragedy that tore at the most hardened policeman's heart. Some of the parents tried to rush into the building and were stopped. Unharmed children were brought out in groups by the SWAT teams, looking dazed, some screaming, some carried. Valérie was among the first in line to see them as they went by, speaking a word here and there, and she looked up to see a burly member of one of the SWAT teams carrying a five-year-old covered in blood, and she saw someone run past her like a shot. It was Tom Wylie, who took the child in his arms, and ran toward the nearest medical truck. He could see that the child was dying. She had been shot in the chest and was bleeding out. In minutes she'd be dead. A doctor on the scene joined him, saw that Tom knew what he was doing and had noticed his police armband, and together they got an IV line into her, administered a transfusion, and applied pressure to the wound to stop the bleeding. Tom signed to him that he would go with the ambulance, and the doctor nodded and shouted to the ambulance driver to get to Necker Hospital as fast as he could. The ambulance doors closed and they were gone. The child's parents had never even seen her, although a lone photographer had caught the moment when Tom ran up and took her to save her.

Tom talked to her in English all the way to the hospital, as her eyes fluttered, her pulse was thready but she was alive. Two paramedics had ridden with him. The three worked on the child together in perfect unison to keep pressure on the wound. Tom was covered in blood and when they got to the hospital she was still alive. A team from the trauma unit rushed her away and Tom prayed they could save her. She was too young to die. He rode back in the ambulance with the EMTs, and when he got to the school, Wendy was on her knees on the concrete holding a boy whose arm had been nearly shot off and who was in shock. He was an upper class student and bigger than she was, and she helped get him on a gurney and they rushed him away.

Bill and Stephanie were bent over a ten-year-old boy who had just died. Paul was carrying injured children from the building along with the police, and Marie-Laure and Gabriel were helping to get the walking injured into ambulances quickly as Valérie moved among the parents, consoling, hugging, reassuring, helping them find their children. The children who had not been injured were already on buses to be taken to another school where the post-trauma teams were waiting for them, they would spend several hours being counseled and debriefed, then be reunited with their parents.

Valérie suggested to Solange's grandmother that they remove her from the scene quickly, before the reporters spotted her and surrounded her. They drove away a few minutes later. She had given the grandmother her card, and asked her to call later, and bring Solange to see her in the morning. Solange's grandmother promised she would.

Once the injured had all been sent to hospitals, the body count began in earnest, and the bodies were removed from the school, as policemen and workers sobbed at what they saw. Some children had been shot in the head, as the gunman had said, but many weren't and had bled to death in classrooms and in the halls, or in the gym. The final count was horrifying, the worst mass slaughter in Paris ever. A hundred and twenty-nine students had been killed, and thirty-two teachers. A total of one hundred and sixty-one people, a quarter of the population of the school, and more would die in the hours to come. More than fifty children had been injured and even lost limbs due to the assault weapons he used. A single man had done this with a sack of fully loaded automatic weapons, shooting them relentlessly for two hours. He was unpredictable and deranged, no one could have foreseen it. It was a tragedy of mass proportions.

When all of the children and teachers were gone, Marie-Laure suggested that they all go back to her place. Her children were in school and the combined team needed a place to gather and mourn, catch their breath, and cry over the senselessness of it all. They climbed into the van, filthy, bloodstained, and exhausted. Stephanie and Wendy were crying. Tom didn't even know the name of the child he had tried to save. Valérie had gone on to the other school to meet with parents and students, and teachers and their families, in the post-trauma operation. But the rest of their team was in the van going to Marie-Laure's, and Bruno Perliot, the captain in charge, had told her he would be in touch later. There would be countless debriefings, press conferences, and meetings in the coming days to analyze what had happened, what had gone wrong, if anything, and what could have been handled differently. They had lost too many lives, but they all agreed there was nothing they would have changed. It had been conducted with the precision of a Swiss clock. But one mad gunman with a sack full of weapons had beaten them soundly and stolen a hundred and sixty-one souls.

They spent two hours at Marie-Laure's and then went back to their apartments while she went to join Valérie to see how things were going with the post-trauma counseling. They had a huge number of parents and families to console, of the fallen teachers as well. It was overwhelming, but had been handled with the utmost professionalism. The four American trauma doctors had immense respect for what they'd seen.

Andy had called Stephanie on her cell the minute he had seen it on the news. He'd been up late watching TV, and demanded she come home. He said there was no reason for her to be there, and she belonged with her children, not risking her life in France.

"I was never at risk," she said calmly, in a sad voice. "We weren't in the school. And there is every reason for me to be here. We have a lot to learn from them, and information to share. I'm here because of situations like this in both our countries."

"Get your ass home, dammit!" he shouted at her out of his own fears.

"I love you, but I'm staying," she said quietly, and he hung up on her a minute later. She could hear how frightened he had been for her.

Jeff called Wendy when she was on her way home in the van. She was surprised to hear from him, although she knew he stayed up late. "Are you all right?" he asked in a matter-of-fact voice, as though she were a colleague or an old friend, and she suspected that Jane might be near him, from the impersonal tone.

"I'm fine, but it was heartbreaking," she said, breaking down.

"I'm sure it was," he said quietly. "I was concerned about you. I just wanted to check in. I'm glad you're okay. See you when you get back." And with that he hung up, and she was left starving for more, and some tenderness and comfort. It would have been nice to hear the words "I love you." But that wasn't Jeff. He hadn't said those words to her in a long time, maybe because he didn't love her anymore, or didn't think he had to say them. Or maybe he thought he wasn't cheating on his wife if he didn't say he loved her.

Bill had overheard the conversation, and looked over at her. He could see how disappointed she was. "Surgeons are like that. All heart," he commented and she smiled. She didn't want to say that his wife was probably with him.

They were all shattered when they got home, and wished that there was more they could do for the injured. Tom wanted to go to the school where Valérie's trauma teams were working, but he didn't want to intrude. Instead he knocked on Bill's door with a bottle of scotch, and they had a drink together, and Stephanie joined them a few minutes later.

"I could use some of that," she said. Tom poured her a drink, and Bill knocked on Wendy's door to invite her to join them and she had some too. It had been a smooth operation in many ways, but a hell of a day. And parents would be mourning their children. Bill turned on CNN on the TV and the reporter said there would be a candlelit vigil at Notre Dame that night at 9 P.M., to honor the victims. The four of them agreed to go. And in their own way, they were each glad they had been there to do what they could. It seemed so little with so many children dead, but this was what they had chosen to dedicate their lives to. And all four of them knew that they'd been right to come to France. This was confirmation of it. They were meant to be here, and this grueling, agonizing job was what they'd been born to do, even if it broke their hearts.

# Chapter Nine

The team from San Francisco met in the hallway outside their apartments, dressed in warm clothes, at a quarter to nine that night. Stephanie and Wendy were wearing wool beanies, and they'd called a cab to take them to Notre Dame. They had to stop a few blocks away and walked from there. The area was filled with silent people, carrying candles and flowers, walking solemnly toward the cathedral. Their eyes met and then they looked at the army of strangers who had come to mourn the students, young lives cut too short, and the teachers, many of whom were young as well. It was a way of facing it together with people they didn't even know. They felt a powerful bond, deploring the madness of one lone gunman who had changed so many lives forever, on a mission of revenge spawned in his twisted mind. There was no way to understand it. No one did. He had killed so many.

The school had been shut down, and on the news they had said that it would not reopen until the next semester. The students would be dispersed to other *lycées* in the area and the teachers put on leave, after being severely traumatized. New tighter security measures would be put in place in all the schools, too late for those who had died and been injured that day. Two more of the injured children had died since the shooting, which brought the death toll to a hundred and sixty-three, more victims than in the November shootings four years before. That tragedy had been carefully planned and executed. This incident had been haphazard, and carried out impulsively, by a man misguidedly mourning his wife and blaming the school for her death. He had made students and teachers alike pay for it. They all knew that his orphaned daughter would never be the same again.

There had been a photograph of Solange in the newspaper that night, as she mounted the steps of the police bus to talk to her father on the phone, but her back was turned and you couldn't see her face. She looked like any schoolgirl with her backpack and her hair in a braid. If the press chose to single her out, they would be punishing her too.

Gabriel somehow managed to find Stephanie in the crowd outside Notre Dame, which was nearly impossible, but he had combed the crowd until he found her. Thousands of people had lit their candles and left small bunches of flowers on the steps of the church. A priest on the balcony said a blessing over them, as the bells tolled one hundred and sixty-three times, ringing in everyone's heads and reverberating in their hearts. Gabriel said nothing to Stephanie when he found her, he stood next to her with an arm around her shoulders, and the other holding the candle he had brought.

Marie-Laure and Paul were there as well, and found them by calling Wendy's cellphone. It felt good to be together, they stayed until eleven o'clock, and then went home. Tom left them afterward and went to find Valérie at the school where she was working, counseling families before they went home, and speaking quietly and respectfully to groups of parents about what to expect from their children and how to help them in the coming days. There would be nightmares and tears, panic attacks and night terrors as the reality of what they'd been through settled in and had to be processed. The meetings with parents and children were poignant and heart-wrenching, and what the children had been through showed on their faces as they clung to their parents, or threw themselves into their arms, seeking some semblance of safety. But Valérie knew it would be a long time before any of them felt safe again. They would relive the horror of that day for years.

Tom waited for Valérie to take a break, and they went to get a cup of coffee at a station that had been set up for everyone, and there was food for those who wanted it. Some of the children weren't even able to talk, and Valérie told their parents reassuringly that they might not for a while.

"I keep wondering how that little girl is doing," Tom said sadly, thinking about her again as he sipped his coffee. "She might not have made it. We managed to stop the bleeding in the ambulance, but she'd already lost a lot."

"Do you know where they took her?" Valérie asked him.

"Necker."

"We can check on her tomorrow." She had new respect for him as a doctor and a man after seeing what he'd done, his race to save the child and the others he had helped when he got back from taking her to the hospital. He had been tireless on the scene, ingenious in the methods he used, highly skilled and dedicated. He had done every-thing he humanly could to save each child he worked on. He wasn't the buffoon she had thought him to be. She had seen not only his competent side, but the flood of compassion he had emanated. "You're a fantastic doctor," she said, as they finished their coffee. And the other three Americans had been impressive too, and the French medical teams as well. "I try to be a decent doctor," he replied. "But it's not always possible," he said simply, hoping the little girl he had run with didn't fall into the category of those he couldn't save.

He left Valérie at two in the morning, and didn't attempt to talk to her counselees or their parents. Valérie knew much better than he what to say to heartsick, broken parents. He went back to his apart-ment then, and didn't even bother to undress. He collapsed onto the bed, too exhausted to move, and just lay there and cried until he fell asleep.

They all came to the meeting the next morning, looking rough and ragged and worried. As was expected, they felt worse the next morn-ing. Four more children had died during the night, and one teacher. One hundred sixty-eight. It was now officially the worst incident of its kind that France had lived through, with the heaviest losses.

Valérie was at the meeting, but said she couldn't stay long. She had too many counseling sessions to organize, and programs and counselors to coordinate. She had met with Solange that morning at seven o'clock, who said she never wanted to go to school and face her peers again. But Valérie and her grandmother had convinced her to try it in a few days and see how she felt. There was much healing that had to happen, on all fronts, and Valérie was working hard to orchestrate it.

The entire team talked for hours about what had been handled perfectly, and what fell short. They each had valuable feedback for Marie-Laure, for another incident in the future. Had there been several gunmen, it would have been worse.

Afterward, they visited the hospitals where the victims had been taken. Some of the damage they had sustained was horrifying. And the team suspected that several would lose limbs, after the explosive damage of the shooter's ammunition. At Necker, Tom had a happy surprise. They inquired about the little girl, but it took them time to match her case up to his description and find her. They asked what color her hair was, but he wasn't sure because she had been covered with blood. Her parents were standing next to her bed when Tom walked in. They talked for a few minutes in his awful French, and they addressed their gratitude to him in halting English. No one could easily absorb what had happened, and yet they all had to find a way to live with it.

Tom was relieved when he'd seen the little girl he'd saved. She was heavily sedated and had had surgery the day before, but he could see that she was doing well and it was likely she would survive.

Tom met up with Valérie again at the end of the day, and they had a glass of wine at a bistro near her apartment on the rue du Bac. She looked tired, and their guard was down. The events of the day before had brought all of them closer to each other. Their merits and talents as physicians had shown, and Valérie had seen over the walls he surrounded himself with. They were walls of lighthearted fun and laughter but solid nonetheless, and she liked what she saw. He was a serious, good-hearted person, and she understood now what his colleagues in Oakland saw in him and why he was so respected.

"So what makes you do this kind of work?" she asked him directly, as they relaxed for a few minutes. She was going back that night to another school where counseling had been set up for the survivors.

"Moments like yesterday," he said quietly. "Being able to make a difference in a matter of seconds before it's too late." She suspected more than that, but he didn't volunteer it. They all had a personal stake in it, whether they admitted it or not. "What about you?"

"We lived in Lebanon for two years when I was growing up, during the war there. I lost some friends I was close to. And I thought maybe I could change something in the world. I wanted to be an obstetrician when I started medical school, but I got hooked on psychiatry. The human heart and mind intrigued me more than delivering babies. I think I made the right choice for me," she said peacefully and smiled at him. Tom didn't say anything to her for a minute and then she could see something open up as he looked into her eyes and knew he could trust her with the secrets of his past.

"I grew up in a rural area of Montana. I was in a car accident with my parents and brother when I was eleven. The paramedics took a long time to come because everything is so spread out there. I stood there with them, and watched them die. I wanted to help them and didn't know how. Everything and everyone I loved disappeared that night. I knew that if I'd been a doctor, I could have saved them. I knew after it happened that I wanted to be able to save people one day. I went to live with my aunt and uncle in Oklahoma. They weren't kind, but they took me in. They didn't have much money. They were simple people, and they used what my parents had left to pay for what I needed. There was enough for medical school when I finished college, so I went." What he told her explained everything to Valérie and her heart went out to him.

"Is that why you never married and don't want kids?"

"Probably. It's pretty classic. You can lose everyone you love in a matter of minutes. Destiny can take it all away. I think I decided early on not to take that chance, so I try to keep it light instead. No ties, no losses, no heartbreaks. You can't lose what you don't have and tell yourself you don't want. It seems to work for me." But beyond the fun and games it was a lonely life, and she could see it in his eyes. "And why don't you want marriage and kids?" He turned the tables on her and she smiled.

"My parents had a hateful marriage, it didn't look like fun to me. I was the weapon they used against each other, the child that neither of them ever wanted or loved. They felt obliged to stay together for me, and hated me for it. I had no desire to do that to a child, or to live a prison sentence like the one they imposed on themselves, for my sake. It seemed much too unpleasant and complicated to me. I've lived with two men in my life. The relationships eventually played out, and I never wanted their children. I think some people aren't cut out to be parents, and I'm one of them. But I turned what I learned in my childhood into something useful for other people, and a wonderful life for me."

"It's amazing how the past always gets us in the end, isn't it?" Tom said seriously.

"It doesn't have to," she said philosophically. "We've both turned ours into something positive. That's already a lot. You saved a child's life yesterday by your quick actions, and I'm sure that's not the first time you've done it. You've more than made up for the parents and brother you couldn't save. And I help some people with my work. It's a good way to exorcise the ghosts of our past, don't you think?" He nodded, thinking about it. She wasn't a bitter person, and he admired how free she seemed to be.

They talked about other things then, and she said she had to go back to work. She would be very busy for the next few weeks.

"Can we have dinner sometime?" he asked her simply and there was none of the Don Juan act that usually served him so well. He was a man who liked a woman, enormously, and felt deep respect for her. And she was drawn to the man she had discovered behind the games.

"I'd like that," she said easily. "Things will calm down a little in a few days. And we'll have time in San Francisco." He liked that idea. He kissed her on both cheeks when he walked her to the Metro. She smiled and waved at him, and then she disappeared to go back to work.

Their debriefings and analytical meetings continued throughout the week, and they were all feeling pressured by how insistent the press were, seeking interviews with anyone who would talk to them at the various offices that provided emergency services. They wanted to know what they felt went wrong, how the event could have been handled differently, and how did they explain that so many lives had been lost. One journalist in particular was dogged about it, Jacqueline Moutier. She tried to corner Bill when he left the office one night, and he was tired of it. She'd been hounding them all day. And the Americans had only been observers at the scene. All decisions had been made by the French police. But the reporter was clearly looking for dirt and officials to demonize.

She followed Bill to the Metro, and asked him if he felt any one person was to blame, and the question enraged him. Despite the enormous loss of life, everyone had worked so hard to get the best possible result both after the shooting and during the hostage crisis. She pointed out that one family had lost two daughters, and their son was still in critical condition and he might die too. It was one of the many tragedies that had occurred, but it was no one's fault except the man who had shot them, and it infuriated Bill that she wanted to pin it on someone else and make everyone involved look bad. She personified everything he hated about the press.

"Why do you want to make it worse than it is?" he said, stopping to answer her with his eyes blazing. "I think it was handled as close to perfectly as possible. I am in awe of how well every aspect of this tragedy was treated." She was known for making trouble and pointing fingers unfairly to make her articles sensational, no matter who they hurt. He had the utmost contempt for her. She had already said once in the paper she wrote for that the police had been too slow to go in, and if they'd gone in faster, many more lives could have been saved. It wasn't true. If they had gone in earlier, they would have been ill prepared, and many more lives might have been lost.

"What's the point of making grieving parents feel worse?" he asked her harshly. "How do you sleep at night?" He threw it at her but it didn't slow her down for a minute. The others had left the office a few minutes before he had. Stephanie had gone to have dinner with Gabriel. The trauma they'd all been through had brought the two of them closer, which wasn't necessarily a good thing, but gave them both comfort. Wendy was having dinner at Marie-Laure's, and Tom and Paul had gone out together. Bill wasn't in the mood to join them, and he had a lot of reading to do, so he was going home alone, and had been followed by this pitbull of a reporter who seemed to him like the worst of her breed. She asked him his name and he told her, and the name of the hospital he was affiliated with in San Francisco, and then she disappeared. He was irritated thinking about her all the way home, and then he put her out of his mind and relaxed when he got to his apartment and called his girls. He couldn't wait to see them again on Friday. After what he'd seen at the *lycée,* they were even more precious to him. It made him realize again how ephemeral life could be, a fact he knew only too well from the work he did. He didn't need harsh reminders, and the images of the wounded and dead children had haunted him all week. Making ordinary plans with his children for the weekend gave him a sense of peace. The concierge at Claridge's had texted him that they'd gotten three tickets to a new production of *Annie,* and seeing it with his daughters would be a welcome relief, in contrast to the tragedies he'd seen firsthand that week.

Gabriel took Stephanie to dinner at Le Voltaire that night and it was cheering to be in the elegant, intimate restaurant. They were both feeling drained and shaken by the events of the week, particularly Stephanie. Dealing with the victims of car accidents and random head injuries was very different from mass killings of the kind they had just experienced. It had made her anxious about her children all week. Deranged gunmen were common in the States now too. They were less frequently motivated by political issues than they were in France, and more commonly similar shootings were committed by troubled students on university campuses, or disgruntled people with psychiatric problems that had been left to smolder for too long. It seemed to be a world crisis in many ways, and the members of the COZ and the other groups had been discussing in minute detail the need for early detection systems that needed to be much more acute than what existed now. She and Gabriel were both tired of talking about it, and she was happy to be out with him away from work. He had been massively busy and after the school shooting had the perfect excuse not to go home, although he insisted that he no longer answered to his wife. They never went out socially together and hadn't in several years. Stephanie's situation was very different at home, she had a marriage she was still trying to maintain, or had been until now. After almost two weeks in Paris, she was no longer quite so sure, and Gabriel was doing all he could to put doubts in her mind about the validity of her marriage, and the things he said had brought up questions for her, none of which had easy answers.

They both relaxed as the evening went on. The delicious dinner and excellent service cast them into another world, which made the *lycée* tragedy seem more remote.

"We could have a wonderful life together," he said with a hand on hers after they finished the main course, and she sighed.

"I wish I'd met you ten years ago," she said honestly, but then she wouldn't have Aden and Ryan, and she wouldn't have changed that. She wondered now how well she and Andy were suited to each other.

After seven years of marriage, everything was so difficult. He had been upset that she had refused to come home ever since the shooting. He didn't understand what she and the others had been through together, how much the teamwork and shared experience meant to them, and that what they were doing in the aftermath was important. There was no way she was going to leave now, unless one of her kids got seriously ill. Anything less than that, he could handle until she got home. And now she had another reason to stay, what she and Gabriel were feeling for each other seemed important to her too. The attraction they both felt so strongly was impossible to ignore. What if he was the right man for her, and he was her future? She needed to find out if their feelings were real, and it was very new. She felt as though she had been swept away and deposited on distant shores.

They took a walk along the Seine after dinner, holding hands. The night was chilly, but Paris was lit up and so beautiful, and the Eiffel Tower sparkled on the hour. Flags all over the city were flying at half-mast to honor the victims of the shooting, but nothing could dim the beauty of Paris, and they stopped walking when he kissed her. After the tragedy they had seen, they needed each other, and their feelings were an affirmation of life. Suddenly, all she wanted was to be with him, and he came upstairs with her when he took her home. They walked into her tiny bedroom in the moonlight. She had never needed anyone as badly, and to feel safe in his arms, no matter the risk they were taking with their future lives. Neither of them cared about anything else as they fell into her bed, seized and blinded by their passion. She felt as though she had been swallowed by an ocean of their love. Everything had happened so quickly between them, and the shooting had pushed them together with such force that it dispelled all reason and swept away everything else. When they came it was like being born together and she knew she couldn't live without him after that moment, and didn't want to.

"I love you so much it hurts," she whispered to him as she lay in his arms, and he gently stroked her hair with loving hands and held her close. She could feel his heart beating, and her own.

"I will never let anything hurt you, Stephanie." She loved the way he said her name, and she believed what he said.

He spent the night with her and they made love again when they woke in the morning. And as far as she knew, he never texted his wife or called home, so he was as separate and unaccountable as he said. He was hers now, if she wanted him, and she had given herself to him. Her lovemaking had never been as passionate with Andy.

They left for work together on the rented bikes in the crisp cold air of a Paris morning. They were both smiling as they pedaled through the traffic, and stopped to kiss, and have coffee and croissants at a bakery close to the office. As she looked at him, in spite of all they'd seen and been through, and the dangers ahead, she had never been as happy in her life. She felt as though she belonged to Gabriel now. And San Francisco was on another planet a million miles away.

When Gabriel and Stephanie arrived at the office together, the others guessed that they had spent the night in each other's arms. Their intimacy was obvious. No one commented, and shortly after they arrived, Bruno Perliot, the police captain, came to see Marie-Laure. He looked serious. There was some official business he wanted to discuss with her, and he wanted to be sure she had survived the trauma without too much damage. Even for professionals, it had been a hard event to participate in, and Marie-Laure was in the front lines with him and his men. Valérie offered counseling for those that wanted it, but Marie-Laure hadn't had time.

Bruno was quiet as they discussed the aftermath of the incident in Marie-Laure's office, and the aggressive stance of the press. The event was being examined and analyzed under a microscope by journalists, always hungry for some slipup or sign of sloppiness or incompetence on the part of the professionals involved, especially the police. He was used to it, and so was she. The French were always quick to criticize everyone. The press had been interviewing bereaved parents, particularly Jacqueline Moutier, whom Bruno had detested for years. They had clashed publicly on numerous occasions.

"I see one of your Americans talked to her," Bruno said and Marie-Laure was surprised. She wasn't aware of it, and didn't look pleased.

"I asked them not to speak to the press," Marie-Laure said apologetically. She liked Bruno Perliot and thought he had done an excellent job, despite the number of deaths. He had been humane and compassionate, efficient, and as cautious as he could be in the circumstances, by not letting his men go into the school without adequate backup and preparation. She had no complaints about anything he'd done, and he was extremely respectful of her. She was surprised he had come to the office to see her, and thought him very kind.

"He spoke very eloquently on our behalf," Bruno said, looking pleased as he handed her the article from the morning paper. "It sounds like Moutier got under his skin, as much as she does mine. If I can ever get her fired, it will be the greatest pleasure of my career," he said wryly and she laughed, and read the article he gave her. Surprisingly, Moutier had quoted Bill liberally, in full support of the Paris authorities in charge of the school tragedy. As she read down the piece, she raised her eyebrows and glanced at Bruno.

"I had no idea that's who he is. I never made the connection with the name. He's very discreet and only interested in his work, and ours," she said in praise of Bill. She was impressed by what he'd said to Moutier too.

"I'm surprised he's not staying at the Ritz or the George V," Bruno said, smiling at her. Moutier had done her research well, and come up with some very interesting information about Bill. He was of "the" Browning Oil family, one of the two principal heirs of his generation, with a younger brother in New York. It said that Bill Browning was a physician specializing in trauma, with considerable experience, lived in San Francisco, worked at San Francisco General Hospital, and stood to inherit one of the largest fortunes in America, estimated at many billions of dollars, and she'd taken a wild guess at how much. It mentioned their major holdings, and the list was long. The article then said that he was divorced and had two children, and had been married to the daughter of a British lord. The article closed with one of his more passionate quotes in admiration of the Paris emergency teams. "At least she gave us a decent shake for once," the police captain said. "It won't last long. She'll be stirring up some other crap about all of us by dinnertime tonight. She can't stand favorable stories. I think she was just excited about who he is, and to have discovered it, since, as you say, he's discreet. He's going to have every woman in Paris chasing him after they read that article. Maybe she did it to annoy him," Bruno said, and stood up. He had to go back to work, and his real purpose in coming there that morning had been to check on Marie-Laure, and make sure she was all right.

She thanked him for coming, and after he left, she walked over to the desk Bill was using. "Thank you for all the nice things you said about us to the press," she said gently, as he looked up in surprise.

"Did that awful woman print them? She followed me to the Metro last night, and I lost my temper. I can't stand her, she's a muckraker, digging for dirt, at everyone's expense. I told her what I thought about it, and how great I thought you all were in the crisis, including the police. She didn't want to hear it, so I'm amazed she printed it."

"So am I," Marie-Laure admitted. "I can translate the piece for you if you want," she offered.

"My French is good enough to read it, even if I can't hold a decent conversation to save my life." He smiled at her. He followed her to her office so she could give it to him and went back to his desk to read it. They were going to be in meetings that afternoon about the aftermath of the *lycée* shootings, but the morning had been easy and unscheduled for the Americans for the first time. A moment later, when Marie-Laure glanced at him, she could see he was furious and very upset. He came back to her office and was nearly shaking with rage.

"What right does she have to print that? Who my family is has *nothing* to do with my professional life, nor what I'm allegedly going to inherit, that's nobody's business. I've been working for thirteen years as a doctor, and that has *never* come out. I was careful that it didn't. It's totally irrelevant, and all it can do is complicate my life. No one is going to take me seriously if they think I have that kind of money behind me, and I'll have every gold digger on the planet on my ass," he stormed at Marie-Laure although it wasn't her fault, and he looked like he was near tears. She could see how much it meant to him not to have anyone know who he was or how much he had, but it was too late now, thanks to Jacqueline Moutier. The secret was out. Marie-Laure tried to calm him down, but he was all wound up and left the office a few minutes later to take a walk and cool off.

The article circulated around the office after that, and everyone was startled to realize how wealthy he was. Gabriel commented reasonably that it was nice for him, but it really had nothing to do with the work they were doing together, or their dealings with Bill. He was still the same man, no better or worse than before they knew his family was Browning Oil. And for his part, Gabriel didn't care. The others didn't either, but it was something to talk about. Paul Martin said he thought he was lucky, and Gabriel said not necessarily, that it probably would draw the wrong people to him if word got out. He said that it changed how people felt about you, with that kind of fortune. Jealous people were out to trip you up and take something from you, or be nasty about you, and the greedy ones were out for what they could get. It was easier if people didn't know. In that sense, Bill was right.

Bill was still upset when he came back from his walk. No one paid attention to him, they had all read the article and were trying not to show it. If the piece got syndicated to the States, which it might because he was who he was, he dreaded everyone at SF General knowing about his tie to Browning Oil and their fortune. There was nothing good it could add to his life. Silence had been golden for all these years, but there was nothing he could do about the exposure now.

Wendy came across the room to talk to him as he sat at his desk, looking like a storm cloud. She decided to approach anyway and spoke in a low voice. "I know you're not happy about the piece, Bill, but they didn't say anything bad about you. It makes you seem serious and hardworking, and news dies eventually."

"Not that kind of news, they'll pull it up anytime anyone wants to write an article about me. It makes it sound like my only accomplishment is having a family with money. And that's no thanks to me."

"No, it doesn't," she said. "Those things are an accident of birth. It doesn't say your family made their money by being nuclear arms dealers, or selling immigrant women into sexual slavery. Your family is part of the establishment, and you're a conscientious doctor who lives below the radar. After the initial shock has worn off, it's not much of a story one way or the other."

"I don't want women pounding on my door because of it, or maniacs threatening to kidnap my children." He was grateful they didn't live in San Francisco if that was going to become an issue, and Athena's father had had security for her for years, since he had a vast fortune too. It was the only common point they'd shared, rich parents, so he hadn't needed to worry about her motives, they had had enough other problems without that. It wasn't something he wanted to worry about. It was just easier if no one knew what his family had and he would have one day. He had already inherited quite a bit at thirty and thirty-five, and stood to get another windfall in a few months at forty, but that was no one's business but his own. The way he lived and dressed, nothing showed. No one would have guessed how rich he was. He was modest and humble.

"I can understand your concerns," Wendy said kindly, sympathetic to him. "I grew up in New Hampshire, and my father was kind of a small-time operator in a small town. He and my uncle made some shady deals. Nothing too large scale, but enough to get them into trouble, and my father went to jail for tax evasion for three years. It was the most exciting thing that had happened in our town since Paul Revere rode through it and Thomas Jefferson once spent a night there. It was all over the local newspapers, and I thought I'd die every time someone mentioned it, which they did quite a lot for a while. It gets old, people forget. My father died two years ago, and I was worried about their dragging up old history in his obituary. He did a lot of good things for our town in his final years, and they gave him a hero's farewell, with not a word in his obit that he had ever gone to prison. And no, people won't forget what you come from, it's part of who you are, but if they know you, they won't care. Trust me, it's true." He was touched by what she said, and thanked her, and he was calmer when they left for their meetings that afternoon, but it was still major news, and the people he was working with liked him even better because he never was pompous, showed off, or acted as though he was enormously wealthy. They respected him even more than before.

Only Paul, the young firebrand in the group, dared to tease him about it, as they headed across town in the van to visit some of the injured victims of the *lycée* shooting. "Now that the secret is out, Bill, I was hoping you'd buy a Ferrari, so I could ride around in it with you and pick up women." His brazen irreverence made Bill laugh since he knew it was well intended and Paul was joking. But the others held their breath for a minute, waiting to see how Bill would take it. Marie-Laure had shared how upset he was, and they had seen it for the past few hours since he'd read the piece.

"I'll buy you one before I leave," Bill quipped back. "I'm planning to buy a Deux Chevaux for myself." It was the classic small model antiquated Citroën, the smallest they made, the kind poor students drove.

Paul rolled his eyes with a look of disgust. "Some people just don't know how to spend their money. You'll never get a decent woman with that pile of junk."

"That's exactly the kind of woman I want," Bill said, as the others laughed, and everyone relaxed. Paul had broken the ice, and after that, they all treated Bill as they had before, and not like the heir to Browning Oil. He hoped things would go as smoothly in San Francisco, if word got out there. And their reaction increased his respect and affection for his new friends.

On Friday, Bill left from the office to take the Eurostar to London to see his girls. They'd all had a hard week in Paris, and were hoping to get some downtime on the weekend. Marie-Laure and Wendy were planning to visit some of the injured children, and were going to have dinner afterward. Marie-Laure's mother was helping with her children for the weekend, which gave her some free time.

Valérie was meeting with various groups in the counseling program, and she wanted to visit Solange to see how she was. She hadn't been to school since the shooting, and her grandmother had told Valérie that she was very depressed about her father's death. Tom was trying to get Valérie to take an evening off and have a quiet dinner with him. He was worried about how hard she was working. She was running all the counseling programs, visiting victims, meeting with bereaved parents, and had been on TV twice that week in draining interviews about the shooting and the loss of so many children, a first in France. She had a lot of weight on her shoulders, and Tom wanted to help her as best he could. He put aside his own plans to be available to her, and she was grateful to him for it. A new man had emerged from the joker he'd been when he arrived.

It meant Paul was on his own to cruise the bars, but after what they'd been through that week, he wasn't in the mood anyway. No one was. There was a pall over the whole city, and all of France. Gabriel was planning to stay at the apartment with Stephanie. They were inseparable now. In less than two dizzying weeks, Gabriel had become her life.

# Chapter Ten

Valérie's weekend was as busy as her week had been, and after half a dozen phone calls and as many texts, she let Tom join her for part of it, particularly the visits to the injured children. He was great with them. She did her visits to the bereaved parents alone, which was more delicate and part of her job.

Her visit to Solange Blanchet was heartbreaking, and she told Tom about it afterward. The girl was going to be marked for life. She was wearing a heavy mantle of guilt for her father, which Valérie tried to lighten for her, but it would take time, and a lot of help. With Valérie's advice, she agreed to change schools, and she and her grandmother decided that she should start using her mother's maiden name, which was the same as her grandmother's. Her father's name was too hated now in France and throughout the world, a mass murderer of children and adults was too great a burden for Solange to bear. But Valérie knew these were only the first baby steps for Solange. She had a long road ahead of her to be free of the past. Possibly a life's work, maybe until she had a family of her own.

Valérie met up with Tom again after meeting with Solange, and they had dinner together that night. Inevitably, they talked about the injured children, and the extensive surgeries they would have after the damage of the Kalashnikovs to their limbs. They had grueling years ahead, which seemed incredibly unfair, but at least they were alive.

After dinner, they went for a long walk, which led them to the rue du Bac where she lived. He remembered how pleasant her apartment was from the night she'd had them all to dinner, but she didn't invite him upstairs, and was honest about why.

"I don't want either of us to make a mistake, in the aftermath of the shooting and all the emotions it lays bare. We experienced some terrible things together this week. It would be easy to fall into bed to comfort each other, and I'm sure it would be well worth it." She smiled at him. She had the feeling he would be an incredible lover, but she didn't want to find out yet. "I want to keep things real between us, if that's all right with you. Not a game, not a joke, not a crutch for both of us to use and then throw away. I have this crazy feeling now that we could be important to each other, and I don't want to spoil that, or waste it, or use it up too soon. I hope that doesn't sound frightening to you. I know you've never had a serious relationship and you're proud of it. And I don't want to be another notch on your belt. We're both too old for that," she said, and a tremor went down his spine as she said it.

"Maybe not as proud as you think. My pride in never having been in love is more of a cover for not having the guts to try." She knew that, and nodded at what he said. She loved that he was honest with her and Tom liked what she had said. Whatever they shared now, whether friendship or romance, he wanted it to be real too. It was what he liked best about her, that she was so real, and not afraid to be. He had been afraid to be that open all his life, except in his work, which was the serious part of him.

She allowed him to kiss her on the lips and they stood together for a long time, and then she smiled the mysterious smile that turned his insides to mush and vanished behind the heavy door. He walked home alone after that, thinking of everything she'd said.

And when he got to his apartment, he didn't call Paul, his bar buddy in Paris, to carouse with him. He didn't have a drink. He went straight to bed, with Valérie on his mind.

The weekend in London with Pip and Alex was exactly what Bill needed. He didn't see their mother when he picked them up. She and Rupert were away for the weekend. And he explained the school shooting in Paris to the girls as simply as he could, particularly to Pip, who asked him a lot of questions about it. They had talked about it in school. Alex knew of it too, but was still too young to say much on the subject. Bill was thoughtful and sad as he discussed it with them. He told them about the children they'd been able to save.

"You're a hero, Daddy!" Pip said, impressed and proud of him.

"No, I'm not," he denied it, thinking of all the children who had died. "Everyone worked really hard to save them. We were a team. There were a lot of heroes."

For the rest of the weekend, they turned their minds to other things. He took them to a children's art exhibit. They went ice skating, and the production of *Annie* was fantastic. The girls loved it and so did he. Being with his own children gave him back a sense of normalcy. They had a big room-service breakfast on Sunday, went for a long walk in the park, had a quick lunch at a pizza parlor they loved, and he took them home. The time always passed too quickly, but was well filled, with activities they all enjoyed. He was good at keeping them busy.

They were sad to see him leave on Sunday afternoon, but were looking forward to meeting him in Paris the following weekend. And Euro Disney was still the plan. He'd had some qualms about it being dangerous, if there were any copycat events by other madmen, which inevitably one thought about now. Anything was possible. But the security at Euro Disney in Paris was so extreme that he had decided it would still be safe to take his children there, as safe as any place was in today's world, where anything could happen, anywhere, at any time. Even Athena had agreed and said she wasn't worried.

He was peaceful and happy, as he always was after he saw them, on his way back to Paris on the train. He was back in the city at seven o'clock, and ran into Wendy as they walked into their building at the same time.

"How was London?" she asked him with a smile.

"Terrific. We went to a new singalong version of *Annie*. My girls knew all the words, and so did I." He looked mildly embarrassed when he said it, but it had been fun. "What did you do this weekend?" He chatted with her as they walked up the stairs side by side.

"I saw Marie-Laure, and then we went to her apartment and saw her kids. I was going to see Valérie, but she was swamped."

"I figured she would be, for a while." He felt somewhat exposed as he talked to Wendy, now that everyone in the group knew of his ties to Browning Oil. He had played "poor boy" all his life. His vast family fortune had always embarrassed him, and still did. It seemed so excessive. He lived comfortably, but not extravagantly. And as they reached her door, he gave her a warm look. "Do you want to have dinner down the street?" There were no romantic undercurrents between them, which made it easy to be with her. She just seemed like she'd make a good friend. She hesitated for a minute and then nodded. She had nothing better to do that night, except her nails and hair.

"I'd like that, thank you." She dropped off the milk, eggs, and baguette she'd just bought, while he put his suitcase in his apartment, and they headed back down the stairs a few minutes later. She told him about the Picasso exhibit she had gone to at Le Petit Palais, and that she'd gone to church at La Madeleine, where there was a special mass for the victims of the shooting.

She commented on how subdued the atmosphere in the city was, and how affected people were by the tragedy at the *lycée*. The funerals for the victims had begun that weekend. Many were at Père Lachaise cemetery, and other cemeteries around the city. It weighed heavily on the Parisians, and had shaken everyone around the world, because in each country people realized how vulnerable they were and how easily it could happen to them. Bill had thought about it with his girls that weekend at the play. He and Athena had exchanged emails earlier in the week, when he inquired about the security measures at their school, and he was satisfied by what she said. Things seemed somewhat tighter in Britain than they were in France, but the British had been dealing with similar issues for years, since the heated days with the IRA.

Wendy could tell that he was feeling better about the article in the paper earlier that week. All he said about it was that he hoped it wasn't syndicated to the *San Francisco Chronicle,* but he didn't dwell on it as he had when it came out. He asked if she had heard from her boyfriend and she looked startled, but said she hadn't. She didn't explain why.

Over a chocolate éclair they shared for dessert at their favorite bistro, he asked her if she wanted to go to Euro Disney the following weekend with his girls. They were planning to go on Saturday.

"I got nervous about that too," he confessed, "but I think the security is very tight. And the girls can't wait to go."

"I'd love it." She smiled at him. "I don't get to do things with children very often. It was a relief seeing Marie-Laure's boys this weekend. They're really sweet. They're five, eight, and eleven, which isn't easy without a father. She seems to manage them really well, although she says it's hard, and her mother helps."

"I wish I saw more of mine," he said wistfully, and she nodded. "We do a lot of different things when they're with me in San Francisco, and go camping a lot." They were still chatting easily when they wandered back to the apartment, and he left her at her door. They were halfway through their stay in Paris, which seemed hard to believe. They all felt as though they had been there for months. A lot had happened since they'd arrived. And their agenda was heavily scheduled until the end. On a personal level, romances had started,

Gabriel and Stephanie's passionate affair, and he and Wendy were becoming friends. It had been a very full two weeks!

After a lustful weekend with Stephanie, Gabriel decided to go home on Sunday night. His boys were busy but he said he liked to touch base with them on Sunday nights and have dinner at home. And Stephanie was exhausted by then anyway. They'd had a very full weekend, and made love every time they came back to the apartment, and several times a night. She'd never had a sex life like what she and Gabriel shared. He was a very sensual man and couldn't get enough of her. And he had mentioned on Sunday that when he came to San Francisco, he wanted her to stay at the hotel with him, which brought her up short and was a dose of reality. It made clear his expectations, which weren't realistic for her.

"Gabriel, I'm not in the same situation you are. I have a husband who expects me to come home and be his wife again." He didn't look happy when she said it over breakfast in her tiny kitchen. "My husband has no clue that anything has changed."

"You told me that things haven't been working between you, and he suggested a separation."

"That's true, he did, when he was angry at me. And things aren't working. But we haven't done anything about it, or come to any conclusions. I'm going to have to talk to him when I go back. We'll have a lot to work out, with two small children." She knew that Andy would be shocked and devastated. She wasn't looking forward to it. For now, it was incredibly romantic being in Paris, but when she went home, she'd have to face the music if she and Gabriel were going to take this further, and it was still very new. They both had marriages to unwind if this was more than an affair. She was somewhat afraid to rely on it and have it blow up in her face. "Are you sure you want to do this?" she asked him seriously, and he looked offended that she would even question it.

"I've waited for you all my life, Stephanie. I'm not going to let you go now. Are you having doubts?" He looked hurt.

"No, but this is a very big deal if we both leave our marriages," she said quietly.

"I want to, and I hope you do too," he said, and she nodded as she listened to him.

"Then you have to give me some time. I have to tell Andy, and I want to find the right time to do it."

"As soon as you get to San Francisco seems the right time to me," he said quickly. "Then you can stay with me when I arrive two weeks later." He was on a fast track, and she wasn't quite there yet. She was passionately in love with him, but there would be a lot of practical details to work out and discuss with Andy, like custody of their two very young children, particularly if she moved to France. She knew that would break Andy's heart. She could tell how hard it was for Bill from talking to him, and his girls were slightly older than Aden and Ryan. She couldn't imagine flying them back and forth to France, at least for a few years, and in today's world of security risks, it was a terrifying prospect to have them alone on a plane.

"I can't just breeze in and out and stay at the hotel with you while you're there," she said pensively. "It would be putting it right in Andy's face. We need to be more discreet than that."

Gabriel thought about it for a minute. "Then maybe you should tell him after I leave. That way, you can stay with me at the hotel, and tell him you're at the hospital, on call every night." It was dishonest but would postpone an explosive announcement while Gabriel was there.

"Not for a month," she said realistically. She had never lied to Andy before, and she didn't like the idea of starting now. But she might have to, to some degree, to keep the peace until after Gabriel left. She didn't want high drama and ugly scenes with Andy while Gabriel was in town. She wanted to avoid having her romance with Gabriel turn into a soap opera, a classic love triangle, with two small children in the middle. That sounded like a mess to her. She needed time to work it out. Gabriel turned to her then and slipped the robe she was wearing off her shoulders and put his lips to her breast. It distracted her from everything she'd been saying to him and he didn't want to hear. A moment later, her dressing gown was on the floor, and he had her backed up against the wall making love to her, engulfed by passion, with her legs wrapped around him, and from there he carried her to the couch, and they forgot everything but each other. She couldn't think clearly and didn't want to, and then they went to bed and made love again. He was a powerful man and an extraordinary lover.

She brought up the subject of Andy again that afternoon when they went for a walk. She had thought about it and made a decision. "I'll talk to him after you leave. If I do it before that, everything will be a mess for the month you're there, but I can't stay with you every night. I have to be with my children too. I'll stay with you as often as I can." It wasn't what he wanted, but it was the best she could do. And there was another subject they hadn't resolved. "What am I going to do about work if I move here with you?" In two weeks, they had leapt far ahead down the road and were already dealing with big issues much sooner than they would have otherwise. "How would I practice medicine in France?" she asked practically. "I'm not going to medical school all over again here."

"You wouldn't have to. You would have to present your academic and work records, take a test, and you'd have to learn French, but it's feasible eventually," he reassured her, which came as a surprise to her. So she wouldn't have to give up her career for him, just her marriage, which was a lot.

"And I could probably get you a consulting job while you wait to be certified." But it would still be an enormous adjustment practicing in another country and starting all over again. She needed to think about that too, or she might resent him one day. She didn't want that to happen, nor did he.

"Do you want more children?" he asked her. He hadn't thought of asking her before. She was young enough to have several more if she wanted to, but she shook her head. They had six between them, which seemed like more than enough for her, although the prospect of more children didn't frighten him, and appealed to him with her.

"I can hardly manage the two I have," she said honestly, it wasn't what she wanted. Her work was a big issue, and he wasn't going to give up his career and move to San Francisco. He had an important government position and all the prestige that went with it, and a pension he would lose if he quit now. At forty-three he was on a serious trajectory. He no longer had a medical practice, but he had a very important job with public health, which she knew now was a big deal in France. So she would have to make the move for him, and all the changes and adjustments that went with it. She wasn't refusing to do so, but she knew she had to give it serious thought, so it was a conscious decision, and not a mad impulse she'd regret.

"We'll work it out," he said gently as they walked home. He seemed totally confident that they would. He had an arm around her waist, and when they got back to the apartment, they made love again. It made everything else seem less important and the practical issues less acute. She felt drunk on love when he went home at six o'clock to see his children. She dozed after he left, and she called Andy and the boys when she woke up. They were going to his mother's house for the day. She was going to bake cookies with them. They sounded happy and busy, and she felt oddly disconnected from them now. They seemed so far away.

After she talked to the boys, the conversation with Andy seemed stilted. She knew what was coming and he didn't. She had to find a way to wait two months to tell him. The next two weeks in Paris, the first two weeks that she was home, and the month that Gabriel would be in San Francisco. She felt like the consummate liar that she was becoming. But she was in love with Gabriel now, not her husband. And she hoped that Gabriel was right, and it would all work out in the end.

# Chapter Eleven

Gabriel and Stephanie were already starving for each other when they met in the office on Monday morning after one night apart. It made her realize how difficult it was going to be not to spend every night together when he came to San Francisco. She would have to finesse it as best she could, and be discreet. She wanted no high drama with Andy while Gabriel was there. And if all remained on track, she would ask Andy for a divorce as soon as Gabriel went back to France. And she'd still have to deal with the issue of her medical career, and what she'd have to do to qualify to practice in France. She'd have to start taking French lessons immediately in order to pass the exam for the language requirement. But she couldn't have a life with Gabriel in Paris without practicing medicine too. Being a doctor was all-important to her. And she'd have to find a school for the boys too. There was so much to think about. This was going to be the biggest decision she had ever made.

\* \* \*

Marie-Laure looked tired after the previous week. She was still dealing with press issues stemming from the school shooting. She met with numerous politicians, went to the Élysée for a meeting with the president to respond to his questions personally, and was keeping in close touch with the families of the victims. She had two assistants handling only that. They had an all-day debriefing scheduled the following day with the police. She knew she would see Bruno there, but he dropped by on Monday anyway to check on her. He had been extremely responsive to any questions and problems she had, and she was impressed that he was so attentive.

He spent half an hour in her office, and to thank him for his kindness, she extended an invitation to him for dinner at her home on Sunday night. She had just invited the "Team of Eight," as they called themselves now. It was the Americans' last weekend in Paris, and she wanted to thank them for how wonderful they had been. She was going to do an informal Sunday night dinner, and Bruno was touched to be asked. He said he'd be delighted so she jotted down her address, and asked if he'd like to bring a girlfriend and he said he was on his own and didn't have one. She knew he was divorced and had three grown boys who were all studying in other cities. He was forty-nine years old. He told her he'd see her the next day at the debriefing. Valérie teased her about it when she walked into Marie-Laure's office a few minutes later.

"I see we're getting a lot of police protection these days," she said with some amusement, and Marie-Laure looked surprised.

"I think he's just a nice person and was worried about us," she said innocently, and Valérie laughed.

"How many cases have we worked on with the police, and how many police captains have showed up to see how we are, *several* times after an incident?"

Marie-Laure blushed at what Valérie said and seemed flustered. "This was a *very* major incident."

"True, but I think he likes you, more than just as the head of this office. If you were a man, he wouldn't be here. He seems like a good guy."

"Don't be silly. Besides, he's a lot older than I am," she said, trying to be dismissive.

"Do you care?"

"No," Marie-Laure said honestly. He'd told her he was forty-nine at some point, and she was thirty-three. "I just don't think he likes me that way."

"I'll bet he does," Valérie said smugly. "You should go out with him."

"He hasn't asked me," she said, determined not to take Valérie's assumptions seriously. She didn't have time for a boyfriend. She had a demanding job and three young kids to keep her busy at night.

"He will ask you out," Valérie said and drifted out of her office.

The next day, even Marie-Laure began to wonder. Bruno was very nice to her, and attentive after the lengthy debriefing, and made a point of saying he was looking forward to dinner at her house on Sunday. Valérie gave her a knowing look after he left.

It was a busy week for all of them. They had the administrative fallout to deal with after the school shooting the week before, and the press was still all over them at the office.

They were all tired and somewhat frazzled by the time Bill picked his girls up at the Eurostar on Friday night. He had taken two rooms for them at a small hotel on the Left Bank. There was no room for the girls in the apartment. Their hotel room had a big canopied bed, which they loved, and Wendy joined them at an Italian restaurant, so they would at least know each other when they left for Euro Disney the next day.

She was shy with them at first, but they were such easygoing, warm, well-mannered children that she felt at ease very quickly. Pip had asked their father if she was his girlfriend before Wendy arrived for dinner, and he had said no, they were just friends, which seemed to satisfy her. He said she was a trauma doctor too, and they had met on the trip to Paris, but they were good friends now. After dinner, both girls said they really liked her, and were happy she was coming with them the next day. Wendy had told them at dinner that she had never been to Disneyland in California either, nor Disney World in Florida, so they told her all about it, and Alex said she was going to love it, and explained all the Disney princesses to her. Wendy smiled as she listened, and glanced at Bill. She was enjoying herself immensely.

Alex had lost both her front teeth and looked incredibly cute as they described all the thrills they had in store.

They picked Wendy up at the apartment at nine o'clock the next morning in a car Bill had rented. The girls were wearing sneakers, pink sweaters, and warm jackets, while Wendy had worn running shoes, jeans, and a parka too. They were ready for their big adventure. They got to Euro Disney outside Paris an hour later and the fun began. The girls ran from one ride to the next, and got their picture taken with all their favorite Disney characters. They had Wendy join them for most of the photo ops, and their father was in every one. They bought silly hats and Minnie Mouse ears, which they put on immediately, and gave Wendy a pair she also put on, and then posed for a picture with Minnie. They ate popcorn and ice cream, and a big lunch at a buffet. They toured Sleeping Beauty's castle, flew with Peter Pan, went up in the sky on the Dumbo ride, and went on the boat ride at the Pirates of the Caribbean. Pip went on the roller coaster with her father, squealed with terror, and then talked him into doing it again. Alex sat on Wendy's lap on a bench while they waited for them, and Wendy realized what she'd been missing with no children in her life. They were the most endearing children she'd ever met.

They all had a wonderful day, and Bill got the girls the Minnie Mouse pajamas they loved, some T-shirts, and the Cinderella costume that Alex wanted desperately.

"No Cinderella costume for you?" Bill whispered to Wendy at the last stop.

"I'm fine with the Minnie Mouse ears. I think I'll wear them to work on Monday."

"They suit you," he teased her. "No glass slipper?" He had gotten those for Alex too, and both girls were tired but ecstatic as they left the park at eight o'clock after they ate fried chicken for dinner. It had been a magical day for all of them, and far exceeded Wendy's expectations. It made her wish she had children of her own, a feeling she had never had before, or hadn't let herself consider in several years. There was no room for children in her life with Jeff. And now it seemed too late to change that, and she didn't want to, but she hoped she would see Bill's kids again when they came to California.

Both girls were asleep before they left the parking lot. They had seen the parade down Main Street at six o'clock, and the girls thought it was funny that Minnie and Mickey spoke French here.

"This was the best day I've had in years," Wendy said in a soft voice so as not to wake the girls, smiling at him. They had been on their feet for ten hours, and she was tired but she felt like a child again, and the girls had included her in everything. Alex's favorite ride was the It's a Small World boat trip, where they sang the song. "You're so lucky to have these children," she said with feeling.

"I know I am. They're the best thing that ever happened to me." Athena hadn't been, but it didn't matter anymore.

"I wish I'd had kids when I was younger," she said wistfully.

"Most women don't have them now until your age, or older. We had a woman last year at General who was forty-eight and having triplets. She'd been in a car accident, and she delivered early, but she and the babies were fine. And you're a long way from there."

"Not that long. I'm thirty-seven," she volunteered.

"You're a baby. I take it your 'complicated' guy doesn't want to get married." She hesitated for a long time before she answered and then decided to tell him the truth. She trusted him. And after the day with his children, she felt like they were truly friends.

"He is married. And has four kids."

"That's a problem," Bill said in an even voice and glanced at her. "And you want to stay in it?"

"No, and yes. I don't want to spend the rest of my life being some-one's Wednesday night special. I finally realized before I came here that that's what I've become, and all I'll ever be to him. I need more than that. But my whole life has revolved around him for six years, it's hard to let go. He's on vacation in Aspen with his wife and kids right now. I was going to tell him it's over when I go home."

"Have you heard from him since you've been here?" Bill was curious and sorry for her. It seemed hard to believe that a woman with so much going for her had gotten herself into that situation. But he knew others it had happened to. Married men were a dangerous game, and a dead end.

"He called on the day of the shooting, to make sure I was okay. I'm only allowed to text him during office hours. I can't call and email." It was embarrassing to admit. Jeff called all the shots.

"Sounds like he's got a sweet deal, for him, and not for you. Well, you can come to Disneyland with us whenever you want." Bill smiled at her. "I hope you decide to give yourself a better chance than that. You deserve it," he said sincerely. She nodded and they chatted the rest of the way into the city, and they were all sorry when Bill dropped her off at her building. The girls were awake by then.

"We have a big bed with a roof on it at our hotel," Alex explained to her. "Do you want to have a sleepover with us?" Both children had British accents, which Wendy thought was very cute.

"I'd love that, but there might not be enough room for you in the bed with me too," Wendy said gently.

"I'm going to wear my Minnie Mouse pajamas tonight. You should have got some too," Alex told her.

"I will next time," Wendy said and kissed them both goodbye. And then she kissed Bill on the cheek too. "Thank you for a fantastic day . . . and some good advice," she added, and he knew what she meant, about Jeff. "I hope I see you soon, in California," she said to the girls as she got out. "You have to come to my house for a barbecue, and I have a pool." She waved as they drove off to their hotel, and she was smiling as she let herself into her apartment. For once, she didn't miss Jeff, and she wondered what she'd been doing with him for six years. This was what she had been missing, and it was better than the one night a week she shared with him. That told her what she needed to know.

She sent Bill a text when she took her coat off, thanking him for how much fun the day had been, and how nice they'd been to include her. She was going to tell him again when she saw him at Marie-Laure's for dinner the next day.

When she looked in the mirror, she saw that she was still wearing her Minnie Mouse ears, and she laughed out loud. She felt like a kid again.

Valérie had to catch up on paperwork in the office on Saturday. She'd been out so much following the counseling sessions that she had fallen behind on her reports. But she'd agreed to have dinner with Tom again that night. It was something to look forward to. She enjoyed their time together, and the man she had discovered behind the flirting and the jokes. He had a sense of humor she loved, but he was also serious with her, and he wasn't hiding anymore. She was the first woman who had ever seen through him, and understood who he was. He had revealed himself the day he had run past her to save the little girl at the *lycée*. And the look on his face when he ran with her, desperate to save the child, had won Valérie's heart. There was no turning back from that, and Tom knew it too. Valérie had removed his protective covering, and had helped him take down his walls. He had been a man in camouflage, in a full suit of armor, until then. He felt lighter now. And she looked happy to see him when he picked her up at the office. She kissed him on both cheeks when she got in the car. He was driving an Autolib', a short-term rental you could pick up on the streets, like the bikes.

"Where to?" he asked, smiling at her. He'd been excited about seeing her all day.

"Why don't we go to Le Bon Marché and pick up something to eat? I'll make dinner for you," she offered.

They spent an hour in the enormous food hall, picking vegetables and fruit, mushrooms, artichokes, anything that looked good to them. They bought some crab for dinner, truffled mushroom soup, an assortment of cheeses, some pastries Tom couldn't resist, and a box of chocolates to take to Marie-Laure for her dinner party the next day.

They set it all out in Valérie's cozy kitchen on the rue du Bac, and he poured a glass of the champagne he had bought. The crab was already cooked and looked delicious. They put it in the fridge, and went to sit in the living room. He built a fire in the fireplace, and then came to sit next to her on the couch, and she looked wistful for a minute.

"I'm going to miss you when you're gone," she said. They had gotten used to seeing each other every day. And they liked working side by side. The whole team had meshed perfectly, both the French and the American side. It had been a lucky assortment of people, and not a rotten apple in the bunch.

"I'm going to miss you too," he said quietly. Three weeks in Paris had changed him, partly because of everything that had happened, but Valérie was an important part of it. He wanted to be a better man for her. "I can't wait till you come to San Francisco. I actually live just outside the city, on the other side of the bridge. I want to take you to the Napa Valley while you're there. There are some great restaurants and it looks like Italy. Everything gets very green around the time you're coming." He was looking at her and touched her hand. "I feel like we've been through so much while I was here, with the shooting and everything. The three weeks have flown by." They had one week left, but he knew that would go quickly too. "I wish I could stay." She looked surprised when he said it, and he had even surprised himself. "It would be incredible working here."

"You could work for one of the emergency services if you want to get certified here. Or for one of the agencies like Gabriel and Marie-Laure," she said thoughtfully, but he shook his head.

"That's not what I do best. The administrative side isn't for me. It's been great while I was here. But my forte is saving lives once people get pretty badly banged up. I love seeing patients." She had seen him at work and knew he did. "I'm better on the clinical side. How are your post-traumatic stress patients doing?" He was referring to her counseling programs. The idea of his practicing in France seemed like a distant dream and not real to him. He loved his job at Alta Bates.

"It's going to be a long process for most of them. You don't recover quickly from something like that. The teachers are having the hardest time, feeling guilty about the kids they couldn't save. So many of them didn't have a chance. The surviving children will recover best in the end. They're in the early stages right now. And the parents of the survivors are badly shaken too. I want to get everything set up now, so there's no lapse in service while I'm away." She was extremely conscientious, as was he. He poured her another glass of champagne, as they sat and looked at the fire, and then he turned to her and kissed her. They had agreed not to rush anything, but it felt like the right time to him, and he was leaving in a week. He wanted her to know how much she meant to him when he left. She smiled after he kissed her, and then she set down her glass and slipped her arms around his neck.

"You're a very special man, Tom Wylie. Do you know that? . . . And very special to me." And with that she kissed him, and he felt pulled toward her like a magnet, and he couldn't stop kissing her. All he wanted was more, and she did too. Slowly everything had changed in the past three weeks of being together every day, and living through a tragedy together. It sped up time, and provided some kind of glue.

They lay down on the couch together, as he gently ran his hands down her long lean body, and then slipped them under her sweater and touched her breasts. She arched at his touch, and he pulled her sweater off and admired her. She had a beautiful body and he had never wanted a woman more in his life.

She was wearing a skirt that slipped easily down her legs and she didn't object when he took it off, and then gracefully she stood up and pulled him with her. She led the way to her bedroom and he followed her willingly, admiring her bottom in a black lace thong, which was the sexiest thing he'd ever seen. Everything about her excited him. She peeled away his clothes as he removed the rest of hers, a black lace bra and the thong, and she'd been wearing stockings with garters beneath her skirt, which he hadn't expected. She was a woman of surprises and mysteries, and at last they lay naked in her bed, and he couldn't keep himself away from her. He wanted her so desperately that he was inside her moments later, and she guided him expertly through what pleasured her and tantalized him to heights he'd never dreamed of until he couldn't stand it anymore, and he sounded like a lion when he came and she came with him. She lay in his arms afterward, sated and pleased.

"That was nice," she whispered to him and kissed him, and he looked amazed.

"Nice? You call that nice? Don't ever try 'fabulous' on me, it would kill me. . . . You're the sexiest, most fantastic woman in the world."

"I'm happy you think so. You're pretty unbelievable yourself." She lay pressed against him, and he was aroused again within minutes. And it was even better the second time. After that, she rolled out of bed and put on a pink silk dressing gown, and went out to the kitchen. He followed her there, naked, as she set out the crab and the rest of the food for him, and poured the last of the champagne into two glasses. She set out a feast for him on her kitchen table, and they ate and talked and laughed and kissed, and Tom had never been happier in his life, and neither had she.

Valérie and Tom stayed in bed at her apartment all day Sunday, until they had to dress for the dinner at Marie-Laure's. They were the last to arrive, with a suspiciously peaceful, love-dazed aura about them that the others noticed immediately.

Dinner at Marie-Laure's was casual and more chaotic than their welcome dinner at Valérie's, but Valérie had no children and had had time to get organized. Marie-Laure had been cooking all day, while keeping an eye on her children.

The atmosphere was warm and friendly, and Paul had fun playing with her sons. He was as big a child as they were playing video games. The Team of Eight was there, Gabriel had skipped Sunday dinner with his children to be there, and Bruno Perliot was happy in their midst. He helped Marie-Laure in the kitchen, mostly as an excuse to be with her. She was wearing tight jeans and high heels, and a white sweater that showed off her figure. She looked younger and much less serious than she did in the office, and Bruno was bowled over when he saw her. Everyone was in good spirits. Gabriel, Paul, and Bill had brought the wine, Stephanie and Wendy had brought dessert from Lenôtre, and Tom and Valérie brought the box of chocolates they had bought at Le Bon Marché the day before. Bruno had brought her an enormous bouquet of red roses.

Marie-Laure had fed the boys before the guests came and she put a movie on the TV in her bedroom for them after they roughhoused with Paul for a while and she introduced them to everyone. The children were a lively bunch, but they shook hands with everyone politely before they disappeared into her bedroom to watch the movie. Bruno could easily imagine how busy they kept her, as he remembered his own three boys when they were young. They'd been a handful for two parents, not just one. And Marie-Laure had said before that their father hardly ever saw them. He had taken a job at a hotel in Morocco and rarely came to Paris, only about once a year, and he had no time to have them visit him, so she managed on her own.

She had bought several roast chickens, and made pasta. There was bread and cheese and wine, and a casserole she had made. The food was plentiful and simple, less sophisticated than Valérie's *hachis parmentier,* but everyone had second helpings and the conversation was lively. Bill and Bruno spent some time talking while Bill told him about the hospital where he worked, and the problems they had with the gangs, which wasn't a phenomenon they encountered in Paris. But they had other problems. At regular intervals, Bruno went to check on Marie-Laure to see what he could do to help her.

Stephanie and Gabriel were glued to each other for most of the evening, and Wendy, Valérie, and Marie-Laure were worried about her. She had gotten very deep into the relationship, and they had each warned her of the dangers with married men in France who never got divorced. She would be giving up a marriage and radically relocating her career, and bringing two children with her, if she moved to France for him, as they both said she was going to. And custody of the boys might be complicated if Andy opposed their moving to France.

"Think it through carefully," Valérie warned her, as they put the cakes and pastries on platters. None of them wanted her to get hurt, or to dive into it blindly.

"I haven't said anything to my husband yet," she admitted. "I'm not going to until after Gabriel leaves San Francisco. I don't want any major drama while he's there." Valérie told her she thought it was a good decision. No one commented on the aura of intimacy between her and Tom. They were both single adults with no kids, and no commitment to anyone else, which was very different from Gabriel and Stephanie's situation, with spouses on both sides, two little boys on hers, Gabriel's four children and however they would react to it even though they were older, and Stephanie's medical career and all that practicing in France would entail. They were playing Russian roulette and inevitably someone would get hurt, even if only the spouses they were leaving. There was the potential for some real damage there, although they both seemed to be in denial about it. In Tom and Valérie's case they were free agents and the only people involved, with no great risks, although they had careers six thousand miles apart.

Paul and Wendy spent a long time talking that night about Doctors Without Borders, and it was obvious how much Paul had loved his time with them. Wendy found the stories fascinating. Bruno only had eyes for Marie-Laure that night, although he was very polite and talked to everyone, but it was obvious that she was the reason he had come.

The evening ended at midnight. They all had to work the next day. Bruno carried the two youngest boys to their beds for Marie-Laure before he left. Tom went home with Valérie. He was staying with her for the rest of the week. That afternoon he had invited her to stay with him in Oakland when she came to San Francisco, and she accepted. He warned her that the apartment was a little beaten up and not what she was used to, but she decided to take her chances. She liked the idea of being at his home with him for the month.

Their three weeks in Paris had brought all of them together with the speed and intensity of shipboard romances. Strong friendships had been formed, great passions and deep affections. Most of them hadn't known each other three weeks before, and now they were either lovers or fast friends. And surviving a tragedy together had forged memories and bonds they would never forget.

# Chapter Twelve

Everyone was in good spirits the day after Marie-Laure's dinner party. It was two weeks after the school shooting, all the victims had been buried, and the press had finally shifted their focus to other things, although the city and the world would never forget.

There were administrative meetings at the COZ that morning, and a new training film for hostage situations that they wanted to evaluate. But it looked like it was going to be an easy day, until eleven o'clock that morning, when Bruno called Marie-Laure on her cellphone and told her that there was a hostage situation in another school. It was exactly what they'd been afraid of, a copycat situation inspired by the first one. He told her the school and the address. The CRS and the SWAT teams were already on their way.

She reported it to the others, and two minutes later they were out the door and in the van. The school was in the fifteenth arrondissement, in an ordinary neighborhood, part commercial and part residential. All eight of them looked grim, thinking of the losses of two weeks ago, and now it was happening again. The wounds of the first one were still fresh.

They left the van a block away, walked to the scene, and stopped at a cluster of police who told them that Captain Perliot was waiting for them in the bus he used as a command post. Marie-Laure knew now that it was armored, and the windows were bulletproof. Bruno was somber as they hurried up the steps into the bus.

"We got a call telling us it was happening, and the phone lines are cut in the school. No one has heard gunshots, and we haven't been contacted again by the hostage taker. He said he has a bomb and he'll blow up the school if we go in. We don't have enough information yet to risk it." He was dreading another slaughter like two weeks before. They had brought even more troops this time. The street was already filling with ambulances and rescue vehicles when a call came in, patched through from the central police line. The caller sounded young and cocky, and Bill had the odd impression that he was drunk.

"Nice response, guys. I'm impressed. You had everybody out there in nine minutes. The kids are all okay. They're having a dance party in the gym. I scared the shit out of the teachers, but no one got hurt. I used to go to school here. The teachers are all jerks." And with that, he laughed and hung up. Someone waved from a window they believed to be in the gym, and suddenly they could hear music blaring as the face disappeared. Bruno looked like he was about to kill someone.

He sent the SWAT teams in with orders to hold their fire until they saw evidence of weapons or a shooter aiming at them, and then shoot to kill. In less than a minute, the building was swarming with police, the riot squad, and SWAT teams, as all the children and teachers were brought out unharmed, looking mystified. They had no knowledge of what had gone on, except that someone had announced over the PA system that there was no school today, and there was a dance party in the gym. And they'd discovered the phone lines were down. Loud music had gone on, there had been no evidence of guns or bombs. There were no hostages, and no one was harmed.

It was a prank, which the police had taken seriously. They couldn't do otherwise, given recent events. And the culprit had disappeared. No one was able to identify him. They hadn't seen him, only heard his voice on the PA system. There were five hundred students and seventy-five teachers milling around the street, while the SWAT teams continued to comb the school and found nothing except an empty bottle of wine and a vodka bottle in the gym.

Two hours later, the school was considered clean. The students had been sent home by then, and the press were having a field day with the embarrassment that an allegedly former student had made fools of the police.

At two o'clock, Bruno withdrew his troops, and everybody left. It was all over the news by that afternoon, and it set a dangerous example to others. Several youths in the area had been caught and brought in for questioning, but they turned up nothing.

"At least nobody was hurt and nobody got killed this time. I'd rather be made a fool of than go through the other nightmare again, when it was real," Bill said and they all agreed, but Bruno had been in a fierce mood when he left the scene. A joke like that cost the taxpayers a fortune and threw down a challenge that other idiots were likely to follow. And if they'd seen him and assumed he was about to fire on them or blow up the school, he might have been shot and killed. It had been a crazy, irresponsible thing to do, and it had jangled everyone's nerves.

They left the office early themselves. And Wendy and Stephanie started packing that afternoon. Wendy had to buy another suitcase for the things she'd bought while she was there. And Stephanie had bought a mountain of things for the boys, more than for herself.

They were still talking about the prank the next day when someone glanced at the TV they kept on in the office for breaking news, and Marie-Laure frowned as she saw a scene that caught her attention. A church had been blown up in Rome. No group had claimed responsibility for it yet, but it was believed to be the act of terrorists. A man had come into the church dressed as a priest, and had exploded a suicide vest, killing forty-seven people, injuring nineteen, and destroying one of the oldest churches in Rome. That one was not a prank, it was the real deal, and a reminder to them of the harsh dangers of the world they lived in.

They all stood listening to the news reports, and it was another wake-up call that they were fighting a war against an insidious unseen enemy who killed children, destroyed churches, and terrified citizens in every country. It was the new wave of how wars were fought. The Italian police were not sure yet if it was the work of one madman, like so many other similar incidents these days, or a planned attack by well-trained terrorists. Either way, people were dying in every country from incidents like this.

"At least it wasn't in France this time," Marie-Laure said, sounding tired. Bruno called her that afternoon and said the same thing to her. They still had no leads to who the prankster was the day before. No one had noticed him when he slipped into the school, and they didn't even know if he had left the building with the other students. He obviously was or looked like a kid himself and knew the school well. He'd gotten away with it, but it was a dangerous game to play, and people could have gotten killed or injured if Bruno had reacted hastily and ordered his men to storm the school. He was glad he hadn't or the press would have crucified him.

The rest of the week was uneventful, and on Thursday night, all eight had dinner together. Gabriel looked depressed that Stephanie was leaving, even though he was going to be with her again in two weeks, which seemed like an eternity to him. Stephanie was excited to see her boys, but nervous about facing Andy. For four weeks it was almost as though he didn't exist, and now she was going home to be his wife for six weeks until she told him that she was leaving him. And then she would have to start the process so that she could practice medicine in France. She had suggested to Gabriel that he meet with a lawyer and set his own divorce in motion, and he said he was going to wait until he came back from the States too, which made Valérie uneasy, even if Stephanie believed him.

Tom was unhappy to be leaving Valérie, but she had a lot to do in the next two weeks, to leave her PTSD counseling programs in good order. And Tom was going to do a major cleanup of his apartment to get it in decent shape for her. She suggested that an exorcist might be in order, and he said he was thinking about a bulldozer and a Dumpster. Either way, they both had work to do. And the Americans were all going back to their jobs for two weeks until the French team arrived and they were with them for another month of meetings and tours.

Bill was going to London the next day for a last weekend with his daughters, but after that, he wouldn't see them until July, which seemed like forever to him. His life was a wasteland when he was far from them, and the time in Paris had given him four wonderful weekends to share with them, but he'd have to live on the memory of that now. They would be lonely months for him until July.

And Wendy wanted to face her situation with Jeff, but she hadn't figured out how to do it, when, or what to say. She was afraid she would fall in love with him again as soon as she laid eyes on him, which was what had always happened before. She didn't know if she had the guts to leave him, but she wanted to try. She had gotten some perspective in Paris and was determined to act on it, if she could.

Marie-Laure was having dinner with Bruno the night they left. She had been startled when he asked her, and Valérie reminded her that she had been right. He was crazy about her.

Paul said Paris would be dead without their American friends. He reminded Tom to get ready to show him all the best bars and night-clubs in San Francisco. They were going to have a ball together, but Tom was considerably less enthused about the project a month after he'd first suggested it, now that Valérie would be living with him. Paul hadn't fully absorbed Tom's transformation yet, but the others had. They had all changed in the last four weeks, more than they could have imagined. It had been an extraordinary month, working with the French emergency services, and now they had a challenge to match when the four Parisians came to San Francisco. It was hard to imagine that they could provide as much for them to do in their own city, it wasn't Paris, but they promised to try.

When the flight took off from Charles de Gaulle Airport on Saturday morning, they left with heavy hearts, and looked down at the city they had come to love that had given them so much, and thought of the friends they'd left behind.

And on Sunday, Bill fought back tears when he said goodbye to Pip and Alex. He promised to call them every day, as he always did. They clung to him and when his flight left Heathrow three hours later for San Francisco, he was already counting the days until July.

# Chapter Thirteen

As soon as they came through Customs in San Francisco, reality hit Stephanie right between the eyes. Andy was standing there, looking tall and handsome in jeans and a sweatshirt, and as usual, he hadn't shaved, but somehow it looked right on him. Ryan and Aden were jumping up and down next to him, so excited they could hardly contain themselves, holding signs they had made for her. Aden's read "Welcome Home, Mom," and Ryan's "We love you, Mommy." Her heart did a flip and she had tears in her eyes as they flew into her arms, and she picked them both up, one by one, careful not to crush their signs. Seeing them brought home to her how long she'd been gone. Everything at home had seemed so unreal to her in Paris. She felt so far away, like a different person there, and she had to be the old person, or pretend to be, now that she was home. She could hardly remember who that person was. She'd been focused on a new life in Paris, and now she had landed squarely in her old life with both feet.

When she set both boys back down on the ground, she looked up at Andy and tried to read what she saw in his eyes. Fear, distrust, resentment, pain, longing. She wasn't sure what he felt for her anymore, or what she did, as she put her arms around him, and kissed his cheek.

"How was your flight?" he asked her.

"Long" was all she could think of to answer, as they walked along with her bags on a cart. Wendy watched her as she and Tom followed at a distance. She wondered how Stephanie was going to handle the complicated currents that lay ahead. She and Tom were walking to the cab stand together, and Tom whispered to her.

"I'm glad I'm not him. He's got a nasty surprise ahead." Stephanie's affair with Gabriel was no secret to them. Only Andy didn't know what was in store. It made them both feel awkward when they said goodbye to her. She introduced them to Andy, who nodded and smiled and asked them how they'd enjoyed Paris, and they tried not to sound overly enthusiastic, as a compassionate gesture to him. Stephanie hugged Wendy and promised to call her, and kissed Tom on the cheek and wished him luck with his housekeeping and he laughed.

"You have no idea how much there is to do. I'll be scrubbing and throwing things in a Dumpster for the next two weeks. I should probably move."

They walked outside together, as Stephanie and Andy and the boys headed for the garage with her bags. She kept up a constant stream of conversation with Aden and Ryan but she and Andy had hardly spoken to each other since she arrived. She didn't know what to say and she was afraid he would see something in her eyes. She hated lying to him, but she felt she had no other choice. And worst of all, she felt loyal to Gabriel now, but seeing Andy, she realized that as his wife, she owed him a great deal too. She felt torn in half, and fell silent on the drive home, as the boys screamed and yelled and chortled in their car seats in the back seat, while Andy didn't say a word. She wondered if he knew.

It took them forty minutes to get to their house, and as Stephanie walked in, she felt a tidal wave sweep over her, as though she'd been lost at sea for a month, and had just been washed back on shore at home. Yet part of her didn't want to be here, and wanted to be with Gabriel in Paris, not in San Francisco in the house in the Upper Haight.

Everything looked neat and tidy when she walked in, and Stephanie realized Andy had made a superhuman effort to get it all cleaned up for her. She was sure it hadn't looked that way while she was gone.

"The house looks great," she said to Andy with a smile.

"Thank you," he said quietly, and she was suddenly reminded of how cold and angry he had been when she left. Nothing seemed to have improved, and there was suddenly a chasm between them that she had no idea how to bridge, or if she should try. She didn't want to mislead him, nor tell him the truth in the next six weeks, and it was going to be a juggling act while Gabriel was there, trying to spend time with him. She had a knot in her stomach thinking about it, as she walked into their bedroom, and put down her purse and coat, while Andy carried in her two big bags, one of them mostly filled with toys and clothes for the boys. She had bought a sweater for Andy on sale, but nothing else. She had already divorced him in her mind while she was gone. And now she was back and he was real.

"Do you want something to eat?" Andy asked her, as though he didn't know what else to say to her. She shook her head.

"No, I'm fine. We ate a lot on the plane." It had taken eleven and a half hours to get home, and she'd been too nervous to sleep.

She opened one of the bags and took out what she'd bought for the boys and brought it to their room. They loved the toys, and she left the clothes on a chair, to hang them up later, and hugged them both again. They had grown in the past month. And then she went back to her room, took out the sweater for Andy, and laid it on the bed. It seemed a meager offering for his taking care of their two boys for the four weeks that she'd been gone. He walked into the room then, and she looked up at him, trying not to see the question in his eyes. Everything felt off between them, as though they were strangers living at the same address. She couldn't resurrect her feelings for him.

"The boys look great," she said quietly.

"Aden had a cold last week, but he's fine now." He had told her on the phone, but they were both groping for words in the awkwardness between them.

"It feels good to be home," she said, feeling like a liar, but she didn't know what else to say. She handed him the sweater and it was too small. He was taller and wider than she remembered. How could he become so unfamiliar in four short weeks? But she had filled them with another man.

He disappeared from the room then and left the sweater on the bed, while she unpacked her bags. She didn't see him for the next two hours, when he came back and said dinner was ready. The boys clattered downstairs from their room, where she could tell from the doorway they'd made a mess, and Andy had set the table and made hamburgers on the barbecue, with frozen French fries and a salad. The boys' favorite meal. It felt like she'd never left. Or like only her ghost had returned. She felt like a prisoner here. She couldn't even pretend that it was nice to be back. She missed the bistro down the street from the apartment, the friends she'd made in the last month, the streets and buildings of Paris, and Gabriel's arms around her while he told her everything would be fine. She had promised to text him when she arrived, but she hadn't yet. She'd been afraid to turn on her phone, and didn't want Andy to see his texts. She was going to read them later, and answer him when she was alone. She hadn't done it before dinner because she was afraid that Andy would walk in and ask her who she was texting. Just being in the house with him seemed like a lie. She had built a whole new life in Paris, or planned it, and now she had flown backward in time.

The boys provided ample conversation during dinner, and Stephanie helped Andy clean up afterward. He turned on the TV in the den, and watched a basketball game, and she went upstairs to give the boys their bath and put them to bed. Andy came up when she called him to kiss them good night, and then she found herself alone with him in their bedroom, with all the awkwardness between them, and he looked at her and closed the door so the boys wouldn't hear them.

"Something's wrong, Steph, isn't it? It feels weird between us now." She couldn't deny it, but she didn't want to admit it either. Not this soon. They had left each other on bad terms a month before, and nothing had changed between them. Only now she was in love with another man.

"I don't know, I guess four weeks is a long time. And things weren't great with us when I left. You didn't even say goodbye to me." But they had spoken on the phone since, though only about the boys.

"I was pissed. I didn't think you should go. You knew that and you went anyway." And as he said it, it suddenly hit her that she wasn't willing to give up a month in Paris for him, for her work, but she was willing to move her whole career to Paris for Gabriel. What was so different about them? Why was she willing to give up so much more for Gabriel than for her husband? But Gabriel made her feel loved. Andy made her feel guilty all the time, and now she really was.

"I thought the trip was important for my work," she said honestly. "It was an honor and an opportunity."

"And what I do is insignificant, is that it?" he asked, looking disappointed again, with the familiar angry edge to his voice.

"If you got a chance like that, I wouldn't stop you. And I know it was a long time."

"Did you have fun?" he asked. He looked like a kid who hadn't been invited to the party, and it made her feel sorry for him.

"Some of the time, yes, I did. Some of it was very hard, like the school shooting. It was heartbreaking, but I learned a lot."

"I was worried about you."

"I was never in any danger. It was just sad, so many people were killed, mostly children." He nodded.

"So what happens now? You go back to work? Business as usual?"

"I start on Monday at the hospital. The French crew arrives in two weeks, and I get leave for that. A lot of meetings and demonstrations, hospital tours, to show them our stuff here. It's an exchange."

"You'll be busy."

She nodded, and even more so with Gabriel. She could see that Andy felt left out, but there was no way to include him now, and she didn't want him and Gabriel to meet. That was too racy for her, and too stressful.

She went to take a shower then, and got into bed early. Andy was already in bed when she got there, and he didn't move closer to her when she got in. She turned off her light and slid down between the sheets. He read for a while, and turned off his own light. He didn't reach out for her or try to touch her, and then she heard his voice in the dark. He sounded scared.

"Did you fall in love with someone else while you were there, Steph?" She didn't answer for a beat, and then stiffened.

"No . . . it just feels weird between us now . . . like we've gotten disconnected somehow." He didn't answer for a long time. They'd been disconnected for months, or years.

"Let's give it time to get used to each other again," he said softly.

She nodded, grateful that he didn't want to make love to her. She had been afraid he would, and she didn't think she could do that. But maybe she'd have to. She didn't know how she would explain it to him so he didn't suspect anything, but for now she'd gotten a reprieve.

"I'm sorry," she said softly, and that time she meant it. Sorry that he was angry, that she had gone away, that she had cheated on him and fallen in love with someone else. And then the voice she used to love answered her in the dark and tore at her heart.

"It's okay."

Somehow they managed to get through Sunday. They both focused on the boys so they didn't have to focus on each other. On Monday, she went to work. She had gotten a dozen texts from Gabriel by then, telling her how much he loved her, how empty Paris was without her. He said everything she would have wanted him to say. He tried calling her on Sunday, and she didn't pick up. She was in the car with Andy and the boys, going to the park to take a walk and throw a ball around.

She called him from her car on her way to work on Monday morning, and he was just as passionate. It all came at her in a rush, and tears rolled down her face as she told him she loved him, but he couldn't tell that she was crying and she didn't want him to know. She was so confused, she didn't even know why she was crying.

When she got to UCSF in Mission Bay, it was a relief to get back to work. It was the one thing she knew how to do, no matter what else was happening. She could always work.

When Bill got back to his apartment on Sunday afternoon, it looked bleak and sterile. The lack of decor or paintings on the walls, the furniture he didn't care about when he bought it, suddenly seemed even more depressing. And he missed Pip and Alex so much, it physically hurt. He changed into shorts and running shoes, and went out for a run along the Embarcadero. But nothing helped. The apartment was just as empty when he got back. And he couldn't even call them. It was two in the morning in London.

He bought a salad at a deli on the way back from his run, and ate it in front of the TV. He thought about calling Wendy, just to hear a friendly voice, but called Tom instead. He sounded distracted and out of breath when he answered.

"Welcome back. I'm up shit creek. It's going to take me a year to get this place cleaned up. I should never have asked Valérie to stay here. I should just put the whole place in a Dumpster." Bill laughed at his distress, and suspected it was true.

"She's not going to care. She loves you."

"Not enough to live with this, unless she goes blind in the next two weeks."

"I should give you my place. It looks like a motel. I never bothered to decorate it or finish buying furniture. It's like living in an empty shoebox. It even has an echo."

"That's a lot better than this. I keep finding women's underwear under the bed."

"Don't tell me your sad stories." Bill laughed and was glad he'd called him. He'd gotten to like him a lot while they were in Paris. "The only underwear I find under my bed is my own."

"That's your own fault," Tom reminded him.

"True," Bill agreed with him. "When do you go back to work?"

"Not till Tuesday. I'm cleaning house all day tomorrow. I feel like someone's French maid."

"I'm on tomorrow. Do you want to have dinner this week?"

"I'd love to. You don't have a spare vacuum cleaner, do you? I think I gave mine away, or someone took it. Or maybe I never had one."

"It sounds like you need one of those services that cleans up crime scenes."

"That's not a bad idea. How's Wednesday? I'm working Tuesday night."

"Perfect." They agreed on a place near Bill's apartment that did good steaks and burgers, and had a busy bar.

Bill felt better after he called him. Going to Paris had been the right decision. He still missed Pip and Alex, but he had come home with seven new friends, three of them right in his own backyard.

When Wendy walked into her house in Palo Alto, it was spotless. Her cleaning woman came twice a week, and she could tell the pool cleaners had been there that day. Everything was in order, and there was enough food in the fridge to make breakfast, which was all she needed. The cleaner had left groceries for her.

She made herself unpack her bags before she texted Jeff, ignoring the rules he set for her about only texting him during office hours. She'd been gone a month, and she hadn't heard from him since his trip to Aspen. She wanted to see how he'd respond to her text. "Just got home. Paris was great. Nice to be back. Love, W." He didn't respond for several hours, and then sent "Welcome home. See you Wednesday. J." Not "I missed you. Can't wait to see you. Love, J." He didn't ask if Wednesday was convenient. He expected to find her at the same time, same place. She wished she had the courage to tell him she was busy, but she didn't. She had become a standard appointment, like a golf lesson or a massage. She wasn't a person to him anymore, she was a convenience. There was something so degrading about it, but only because she let it happen. She had a responsibility in this too. He couldn't use her if she didn't let him. She had allowed it to happen for six years. It actually wasn't like that in the beginning, but it had been for a long time. Once he stopped planning to leave his wife, she had become a weekly one-night stand on his terms.

He didn't stop by on Monday or Tuesday when she finished work, as he sometimes did. He didn't call her to see how she was, or say he was excited to see her.

He arrived at seven-thirty on Wednesday night, with a bottle of wine, as he always did, knowing that she would provide dinner. He didn't take her out anymore, in case someone saw them. Though he didn't admit it, she was his dirty secret. She didn't cost him a penny except for her birthday and Christmas. She saw it all so clearly now after being away for a month. She wasn't even his passion. They made love on Wednesday nights after dinner, but everything about their time together was orderly, scheduled, predictable, and as organized as he was. She suddenly realized what it would be like to be married to him. He controlled everything around him, and had the precision of a surgeon in all things. There was nothing spontaneous about him. She wondered how much fun Jane had with him, or if she was as cold and unemotional as he was. Maybe they made love on scheduled nights too.

He looked as handsome as ever when he parked his Mercedes in her driveway, and let himself into the house. He was wearing a suit, and she was wearing jeans and a lavender sweater she had bought in Paris. She usually dressed up for him, but this time she didn't. She had set the table and cooked dinner, and he smiled when he saw her. He didn't rush over to kiss her or tell her how much he'd missed her. Probably because he hadn't. She wondered if he ever did, and surely not the way she missed him for the six days a week she didn't see him over the last six years.

"You look great, Wendy," he said. "You cut your hair."

"Just a little." She smiled back, and felt all the same familiar pulls and tugs that broke her heart, or maybe this time it was her heart trying to set itself free from bondage.

He opened the wine he had brought, handed her a glass, and she took a sip. They talked about his work until dinner. He didn't ask her about Paris. By nine-thirty they were finished, and he went upstairs to shower and go to bed. He hadn't touched her yet or kissed her, and she realized that he never did. It hadn't shocked her before, but it did now. He hadn't seen her for a month, but she got the impression he hadn't missed her at all. He knew she'd be back. They talked about him during dinner, just as they always did.

He was already in bed, waiting for her, when she came out of her bathroom in a satin nightgown, dropped it on the floor, and slid into bed with him, and for an instant she hated herself for being so willing to sleep with him, no matter how little effort he made. But she saw it all so clearly now. She'd had a month to think about it, away from him.

He made love to her as he always did. He was an artful lover, but he never made her feel like he loved her, no matter how much she loved him. And afterward, he washed up and came back to bed, and ten minutes later he was asleep, without touching her again. She lay in bed looking at him, thinking that this was the last time she would lie next to him. She had given herself this one night so she could remember forever what it had been like and how little he gave her. And she wanted to be sure of what she was doing. Now she was.

She got up before he did, and was at the breakfast table when he came downstairs in his suit and a fresh white shirt he had brought in his briefcase. He looked impeccable, and she was disheveled and didn't care. He read the paper, and at exactly eight o'clock, he got up, smiled at her, and said, "See you Wednesday, if not before." And from there she veered off the script. She looked at him with sad eyes, and spoke softly.

"Actually, no, Jeff. I'm done. I'm sure you'll find another Wednesday night girl."

"What's that supposed to mean?" he asked, frowning at her. People didn't fire Jeff Hunter. He fired them.

"It means just what I said. I wanted to see you one more time, but this is it. We should have stopped a long time ago, and I finally realized it. Somehow, I kept stupidly hoping that one day you'd leave Jane and end up with me. That's never going to happen. It's all so clear to me now."

"I never said that's impossible, Wendy. In a few years . . ."

"In a few years, I'll be forty, and I'll have wasted nine years with you. I've decided to quit at six. You're never going to leave Jane, and I don't want to be your Wednesday night piece of ass for the rest of my life, or until you turn me in for a newer model."

"That's a disgusting thing to say." He looked furious, and for once he wasn't controlling what she did. He no longer could. She wouldn't let him.

"It was a disgusting thing to do to me, but I let you, so I'm as much to blame as you are. Take care, Jeff." She opened the kitchen door leading to her driveway and he stared at her and didn't move, which surprised her.

"This is ridiculous. Let's have dinner tonight, and we'll discuss it."

"What are we going to discuss? How many more years you'll stay married? We don't even go out anymore. You just come here once a week for dinner, get laid, and drop by for a glass of wine once in a while, when you feel like it. I deserve a hell of a lot more than that, I need a man who loves me, for starters. You haven't loved me in years, if you ever did. I'm just some kind of tune-up you give yourself once a week. I don't want to be your tune-up anymore."

"What happened to you in Paris?" he asked, genuinely upset.

"I woke up."

"Is this because of Aspen?"

"That and a lot of other things. It's the right decision for me." He walked toward her and tried to kiss her then, but she didn't let him. She couldn't. She knew that if she did, she'd be trapped again. And this time she wanted to be free. Somewhere out there was a man who would love her seven days a week, not just once a week and then go home to his wife.

He walked to the door with a bereft expression, and turned to look at her again. "If you wait long enough . . ." he started to say, and she shook her head.

"Nothing's going to change. We both know it." He walked out the door then, and she closed it behind him. She heard him drive away a few minutes later. And after he was gone, she realized that he hadn't told her he loved her for years while still trying to convince her to remain his mistress. She knew she had done the right thing, but she was suddenly panicked as she thought about what she'd done. What if she'd be alone forever? What if she never met anyone? What if she died all by herself one day? But it didn't matter. Whatever happened, it would be better than what she had with him. She had nothing with Jeff except loneliness and grief. And she had done it. It was finally over. She felt sadness, but most of all relief.

She felt whole again as she dressed for work, and proud of herself. And very brave. She was free.

# Chapter Fourteen

Tom Wylie looked slightly disheveled and arrived ten minutes late for his shift at Alta Bates on Tuesday. It was his first day back to work after the trip to Paris. He was as handsome as ever, as he stopped at the nurses' station and glanced at the admissions board, without noticing the nurses, which had never happened before.

"Well, look who's back!" the senior nurse at the desk said, happy to see him. They had missed his stories and light touch for the last month. "How was Paris?" He smiled in answer to the question with a dreamy expression.

"Fantastic. Much better than expected." He looked like a happy man. "What have we got in the house today?" he said, reading down the list of recent admissions, without a single lewd remark or inappropriate comment, which were his stock in trade, to the nurses. They all noticed it, and mentioned it to each other when he hurried off to the first room. He was back half an hour later, with the orders he wanted filled, and a list of tests the patient needed. He wanted him to have an EEG for a concussion and an MRI as soon as possible.

"What happened to you?" his favorite nurse, Maisie, asked him, looking disappointed. He usually propositioned her at least once a week. She was sixty years old and married with six grandchildren. He didn't mean it, and neither did she, but it was fun working with him. Maybe he was jet-lagged, but he seemed in good spirits and looked terrific. "How many hearts did you break in Paris?" He grinned at her when she asked.

"None. I met the woman of my dreams. I've spent the last two days cleaning my house because she'll be here in two weeks. Speaking of which, where do I buy a vacuum cleaner?"

She stared at him in disbelief. This was not the Tom Wylie she knew. "This sounds serious. A hardware store or a department store. Do you know how to use it?" She was laughing at him. The Great Tom Wylie had fallen. The women of Alta Bates were going to be heartbroken, but she was happy for him. He acted like a nervous kid with his first girlfriend. In fact, Valérie was the first woman he had loved. It was a whole new experience for him.

"Is there an art to using a vacuum cleaner?" He was worried. "Do I need lessons or a license for it? Don't I just plug it in and it does its job?" He was panicked.

"Yes, but there are different things it can do, depending on the attachments you use."

"Can it do dishes and sort through old laundry? I don't think I've cleaned my house since I moved in. Not seriously anyway. I buy new socks and underwear when I run out."

"That sounds frightening. You'd better check out what's under the bed." He appeared anxious when she said it. He'd only been kidding with Bill.

"Oh my God . . . good thought . . . probably the underwear of half the women on staff." He never ventured far for his dalliances, he didn't have to, they fell into his lap.

"We're going to have a lot of sad nurses and interns around here," she said, shaking her head. "So is the love of your life French?"

"Very much so, and the sexiest, most gorgeous woman you've ever seen."

"Twenty-two to twenty-five years old, I assume," she said, knowing him.

"Forty-two, never married and doesn't want to, no kids. She's a shrink with emergency services there."

"She sounds perfect for you. You'd better get that vacuum cleaner and learn how to use it, and check under the bed," she said as he nodded, grabbed another chart, and headed to the next room.

By the end of the day, word had spread, Tom Wylie had a girl-friend in Paris. Those who knew him well didn't take it seriously. He'd be on to the next one in five minutes, but the nurse he'd confided in disagreed, and said he was cleaning house for this woman. She suggested that the staff nurses in the ER had better claim their underwear before he threw it away. They all laughed at the idea, a few of them looked disappointed, but most of them didn't care. He was fun to be with, and he would always be around, even if he was momentarily off the market for some French girl. Whoever she was, they knew it wouldn't last.

That night, he did what Maisie had suggested and groaned as he pulled out a dozen forgotten thongs from under his bed. "Thank you,

God . . . and thank you, Maisie. . . ." He waited until midnight, and called Valérie on her cellphone. She was on her way to work.

"I miss you! I'm trying to get my apartment looking decent for you before you get here. We may have to stay at a hotel. I just bought a Super Duper Extravaganza All Purpose Robotic Vacuum Cleaner. It costs more than my car, and I need an engineering degree to run it." She laughed at the image of him cleaning house for her, and was sure it was a first.

"We'll do it together." The thought of that made him shudder, given what he had just found under his bed, along with dust balls the size of his fist.

They talked until she got to work, as he envisioned the office and missed it, and the people there. He wished her a good day, told her he loved her, and then they hung up, and he lay in bed smiling, and thinking of her. He couldn't wait for her to come, even though he had exchanged his role from hospital roué and menace to housekeeper in order to impress her, which was all he wanted to do.

He described his activities to Bill when he had dinner with him, and Bill couldn't stop laughing. "The nurses at Alta Bates must really be depressed," Bill said, happy to see him. They had a delicious steak dinner and talked about the cases they had, and agreed that it felt strange to be back in San Francisco. Paris had been great for both of them, although for different reasons.

Bill was missing his daughters fiercely, and he was looking forward to the distraction when the French team would arrive. The two men made a date to play tennis that weekend. Tom had a membership at a club in Berkeley and it sounded like a nice change to Bill.

Tom had fallen in love in Paris, but Bill had made a friend, several of them. He had thought of calling Wendy, but figured she was dealing with her difficult boyfriend, and knew he'd see her in two weeks. He didn't want to intrude. It was easier having dinner and playing tennis with Tom, although he liked Wendy too, and so had his girls. They'd asked about her several times, and he said he hadn't seen her since he got back. He had hit the ground running at SF General from the first day. Nothing had changed. And by the end of his first week home, Paris seemed like a dream.

The tension between Stephanie and Andy was palpable. She didn't know how to manage it or break through it, and neither did he. It was as if they no longer spoke the same language, and the dissent between them when she left had grown to massive proportions in four weeks. And she knew something he didn't. She had fallen in love with someone else. Andy's resentment about her work and the trip to Paris was like a shroud he was wearing and clinging to. It depressed her and made her angry at the same time.

She half ached to tell him she wanted out of the marriage and get it over with, and was half determined to avoid the drama now. And something else was holding her back, but she didn't know what it was. They both tried to be nice to each other, but most of the time it backfired, and one of them would start a fight. She was tired of his bitter resentment of everything she did, the disapproval, the comments, the guilt he tried to induce in her even when it wasn't warranted. She felt guilty enough about Gabriel without Andy making it worse, but he couldn't know that. Stephanie wanted to calm things down between them, but everything she did and said just increased the tension between them.

Once in a while, she saw glimpses of the old Andy, the one she had fallen in love with, when he did something nice for her, or tried to make peace, but within minutes one of them sparked the other, and they'd be locked in deadly battle again, with the boys watching them in dismay. Stephanie had no idea how to break the cycle, and neither did he. It was as if he was demonstrating to her all the reasons why their marriage no longer worked.

And Gabriel didn't make the situation any easier. She missed him terribly, but he was new in her life, and their affair had created a potentially explosive situation for her. She had a husband and children, and if they truly ended it, she wanted to make a graceful exit. She didn't want Andy to discover the affair. The affair had happened because their marriage wasn't working, the marriage wasn't falling apart because of the affair, although sometimes that was true too.

Gabriel was calling her a dozen times a day, to tell her that he loved her, or find out what she was doing. In Paris, it had seemed sexy and adorable. At home, with her husband two feet away from her and a child on her lap, it was stressful. Sometimes he sent her five or six texts one after the other, and Andy had asked who was texting her so insistently that she was running out of lies to cover it. She asked Gabriel several times to slow down, but he was ready and anxious to be out in the open. He thought Andy should know his time was up, and if it created a drama so be it. It seemed very French to her.

As soon as she went back to work, she realized how much she was going to miss it if she gave it up. The hierarchy and structure at UCSF had been so important to her, and still was. Without it, starting over in France, wherever she practiced she'd be a newcomer and outsider, and would have to rebuild her career from scratch in a foreign country. She would miss the stature and respect she had spent years to build at UCSF. She wondered if Gabriel truly realized what a sacrifice that was, or how affected her children would be by a divorce. His were older and had seen him and his wife lead separate lives for many years. For Aden and Ryan, divorced parents would be a tremendous loss and adjustment, not to mention moving to another country and hardly seeing their father at all. She remembered how pained Bill Browning had sounded in Paris about how little he saw his daughters, and now she would be doing that to Andy and their sons.

On the other hand, she didn't want to stay in a bad marriage forever. It was a lot to work out. She didn't want to end her relationship with Gabriel, far from it, but she needed to go more slowly, and she wanted to be sensitive to Andy's needs too, which Gabriel thought was unnecessary and ridiculous. According to him, it was over, and Andy just had to be a man, move on, and get out of the way. He seemed somewhat insensitive to other people's needs, and he told her she was being American whenever she talked to him about letting Andy down gently.

And just when she wanted Andy to be sensitive and reasonable, he wasn't and behaved like a jerk. And when she gave up on him completely, he did something sweet and reduced her to tears and intense guilt. It was all very bittersweet. She found a wedding picture of them in her closet and sat down on the bed holding it. Even at twenty-eight, they had looked like kids. They were *so* innocent and loved each other *so* much. He thought it was great that she was a doctor, and now it annoyed him every time she went to work, was on call, or stayed late. She could do nothing right, and the less well his freelance writing was going, the angrier he seemed to her.

"Things aren't going so great, are they?" he said in a soft voice one morning when he found her staring out the window with a sad expression. She turned to face him and there were tears in her eyes.

"No, I guess not." She wondered if the marriage would have been salvageable if she hadn't gone to Paris. Andy wouldn't have been as angry, and she wouldn't have met Gabriel. But the truth was that Andy had been growing increasingly resentful of her work for the past year or two, which didn't seem fair to her. They lived on what she made, which didn't bother him. But her working long hours did.

"What do you want to do about it?" he asked sadly and didn't approach her. There was a glass wall between them with no door on it. They could see each other, but they never touched anymore, nor did their hearts.

"I don't know yet." She was determined not to give him the bad news until after Gabriel left. "What do you think?"

"Counseling? A break? Divorce?" Hearing him say it out loud sounded extreme to her, but so was their situation, and the truth was that she wanted out. But she didn't want to say it yet.

"Maybe we should wait till the French emergency commission has been here. I'm going to be very busy with that for four weeks." They were due in a week. Her heart raced each time she thought of it. In seven days, Gabriel would be there.

"I could stay at my mom's," he suggested and that sounded pathetic to her too. "It might give us a breather." But they had just had a breather for four weeks when she was in Paris, and things were worse when she got home. But she'd been passionately involved with another man and she realized that skewed everything.

"Have you talked to your mom about it?" she asked, curious. He talked to her more than Stephanie talked to her parents, but he was an only child with a widowed mother, who liked to get into his business. Her parents were always careful not to get involved and to let their children work things out for themselves, since they were adults.

"She says we can work it out if we want to. It's up to us. I hope she's right, but to be honest, I don't see how. Things would have to change," he said, thinking about it, "if we want our marriage to work again."

"Change how?" She was curious about what he thought.

"Maybe I need to get a job so I don't feel so dependent on you. I hate to admit it, but I've been jealous of your work for the last year or two. You know what you want and what you're doing, and you're good at it. You go after your goals. I've been floundering. I don't even know if I can make it as a writer, and I don't want to work at a newspaper again. I feel lost," he said, with tears in his eyes, and she felt sorry for him. His admission that he was jealous of her career was huge. "I need to pursue my dreams again. You're going to be head of the department one day, and I'll be nothing." He sounded like a boy as he said it. But she needed him to be a man for her, not a child. Gabriel was an adult. And Andy's boyish charm had worn thin and just seemed immature. She knew she shouldn't, but she compared the two men constantly, and Andy was coming up short, and had for a while. It had left the door wide open for Gabriel to walk through and sweep her off her feet, just as he had. She had wanted to be faithful to Andy, but the lure of Gabriel was too great. Andy could sense that he had lost her, and he had a feeling that there was some-one else, but Stephanie kept saying there wasn't and he believed her. The constant calls and texts seemed suspicious to him.

She put on her white coat and had to leave for work then, so they didn't pursue the conversation, but it was clear that they both knew their situation was dire. Their marriage was on life support, and the only way out seemed to be to pull the plug.

Wendy called her that weekend to ask how things were going and Stephanie was honest with her.

"Pretty bad. It's been tense since I got home. And sad. We both know the marriage is dead."

"Does he know about Gabriel? Did you tell him?"

"I don't want to until Gabriel leaves. I don't want some awful French drama. After he goes, I'll tell Andy it's over. I just hope Ga-briel can keep a lid on it when he's here. He's been texting me a mil-lion times a day, Andy keeps asking me who's calling and texting me. I asked Gabriel to slow down, and he didn't like it. This is a mess," she sounded stressed and Wendy didn't envy her situation. "What about you? Did you see your guy?"

"I did," she said with a sigh. "I spent the night with him. I wanted to see him one more time. Being away for a month gave me some perspective. I was like a doll he took out of the closet to play with once a week, and then put back and went home to his wife. I don't think he knows who I am or cares. When he left, he said, 'See you next Wednesday' and I said, 'No.' I was done. He looked like he was in shock. I haven't heard from him since. Nothing. No begging, no texts, no calls. Maybe he was done too," or he just didn't love her. It seemed plausible to her now.

Stephanie was impressed that she'd done it. She didn't think Wendy would. "Do you miss him?"

"Less than I thought. I'm lonely, but I gave up a lot. I stopped seeing friends, or doing anything. I was always sitting around, hoping he'd show up. I need to get out and see people now. The French crew will do me good. And at least I don't feel like I've sold out, waiting for a guy who doesn't really love me and is never going to leave his wife." It scared Stephanie to listen to her. What if Gabriel did that to her after she left Andy, gave up her job, and moved to France? She'd be trapped. But at least she knew he loved her, for now anyway. She remembered Valérie and Marie-Laure's warnings, and even Wendy's, that French men don't get divorced, or not often, and according to Wendy, most Americans didn't leave their wives for their girlfriends either. They needed both women to make their marriage work, which was not how she felt about Andy and Gabriel. Having two men in her life and her head was driving her insane. She felt pulled in ten thousand directions, or two, which was worse.

"Let me know if you come to the city, and we'll have dinner," Stephanie said, missing her.

"I want to have everyone to my house for a barbecue the first weekend they're here," Wendy said, and Stephanie liked the idea. "Will you bring your husband?"

"No, he won't want to anyway. He's hostile about my work and everything related to it. He can stay with the kids. And that's too close for comfort, to have both of them there." It sounded stressful to Wendy too.

"I can't believe I'm free after six years," Wendy said, sounding a little dazed. Listening to her gave Stephanie the courage to do what she needed to. She dreaded telling Andy it was over. It was going to be a hard day, for him and their boys. And it would be even worse when she told him she was moving to France. She knew she had to see a lawyer, but wasn't ready to face it yet. That would make it all very real. "Well, I'll see you in a week," Wendy said. "Let's do a girls' night out with Valérie and Marie-Laure. That would be fun."

"We'll do it." Stephanie felt better after she hung up, it was a relief to talk to someone she could be honest with. She lied to Andy all the time now. Just being there with him was a lie. She was glad he hadn't tried to make love to her since she'd been back. She couldn't do it. They hadn't for a month before she left. It had been more than two months now. It was hard to understand how she could feel so distant and turned off by someone she had once loved so much, but it had been a while. Looking back, they had been drifting apart for two years, as his resentment of her grew.

Two days after Stephanie talked to Wendy, an invitation from the mayor's office came in the mail. It was for a reception for both the French and the American teams, given by the mayor and the San Francisco Department of Emergency Management, to honor all eight members of the joint commission. Their names were listed alphabetically, and Stephanie's was right above Gabriel's. The reception was to be held in the rotunda of City Hall. She stood staring at it, wondering what to do about Andy. He never wanted to do anything associated with her work, and he had been furious about her trip to Paris. It was easier not to tell him, so she was going to put the invitation away where he wouldn't see it, and that way she could go with Gabriel. She didn't want to be in one room with both men. Andy might instinctively sense something if he saw him. He was uncannily perceptive sometimes. It was a stress she didn't need, and she was about to put the invitation in her pocket when Andy walked in before she could. The invitation was white with a gold band around it, and crossed French and American flags at the top. It was very handsome, and caught his eye before she could hide it.

"What's that?" His antennae were up, as though he had radar, and she was annoyed that he'd seen it, although he didn't know what it was.

"Just an invitation, while the French crew is here. You'd hate it." He snatched it from her hand before she could stop him, and he looked at it, and then at her.

"They're honoring you, Steph. You weren't going to invite me?" He looked crushed and her heart was pounding. Being there with either man, if the other was there, would be a nightmare, and she had no idea how to handle it, and didn't want to.

"I didn't think you'd want to go. It's no big deal."

"Yes, it is. Of course I want to go." It was in the first few days they would be in town. If Andy figured it out then, it would make being with Gabriel even more difficult.

"Then we'll go," she said simply. There was nothing else she could say. She took the invitation, and put it in her pocket, hoping he'd forget.

"We're still married," he reminded her, as though she needed him to. She knew exactly who he was. She was now in a situation she had never thought could happen to her. She was a married woman with a lover. Gabriel was right. She needed to deal with it soon. And so did Gabriel. He still hadn't seen a lawyer. This was not who she wanted to be.

# Chapter Fifteen

As the plane touched down in San Francisco, Marie-Laure and Valérie were sitting next to each other, straining to look out the window as they flew low over the water and landed smoothly on the runway. It had been a very long flight, but they'd eaten, watched movies, and slept for several hours. It was ten P.M. in Paris and one P.M. in San Francisco but they were wide awake.

Paul and Gabriel were sitting together across the aisle. Paul couldn't wait to discover the nightlife of the city, although Tom had already warned him that he would be busy that weekend. He wanted to spend time with Valérie. He was picking her up at the airport, and taking her to Oakland. His apartment was as clean as he could get it, and he had gotten bright-colored Moroccan blankets to cover the old stains on the couch, new lamps, curtains, which he'd never had before, and a new rug from IKEA. He'd even bought new plates and glasses, since nothing he owned matched and the old ones were all chipped. He hoped she wouldn't run screaming out the door when she got there. And he had put flowers in vases on all of the tables, because he knew she loved them. The women he'd brought there in the past wouldn't have recognized it, and he felt like a kid again, as he waited for her outside Customs in a tweed blazer, jeans, a blue shirt, and brown suede shoes. He looked like a male model. Several women glanced at him as he stood there, but he didn't notice. His eyes were riveted on the door she would come through.

They had nothing to declare, and were there on business, so all four French doctors were processed quickly through Immigration, and came out into the terminal together, and were delighted to see Tom. He put his arms around Valérie and kissed her first. She managed to look as sexy and put together as she did in Paris, even after an eleven-hour flight, and he had an arm around her as he talked to the others. There was a van and driver waiting for them outside to take them to their hotel. They were staying at the Saint Francis in Union Square, and Tom had already told Paul to check out the bar nearby at the Clift hotel, which had a heavy pickup scene with a lot of hot young women in the lobby and bar. He had also suggested a number of other places, since he wouldn't be there to guide him.

Gabriel was planning to call Stephanie from the hotel, and she had promised to join him as soon as she could get away. Wendy was coming into the city to have dinner with Marie-Laure. She was going to show her the sights, in tamer fashion than Paul wanted to see them. They were all in good spirits and stood chatting for a few minutes, before Tom spirited Valérie away, and they got in their van. He kissed her as soon as they left the others, and all they both wanted to do was go to his place and go to bed. They had the same thing in mind, and she ran a hand inside his leg and kissed him on the neck as he drove.

"I'm going to drive off the bridge if you don't stop." They were on the Bay Bridge and didn't have far to go to where he lived, in the Temescal section of Oakland, which was a five-minute drive from where he worked.

They talked nonstop on the way there, and he carried her bag upstairs to his apartment, which had a view of a garden, and there were shops and restaurants all around them. The area was up and coming, and the new desirable neighborhood for young people. The building was old and no thing of beauty, but the rent was reasonable, and he had never cared what it looked like. But now he did, and he held his breath as they walked into his apartment and she looked around, smiled at him, and slid her arms around his neck. There was a quaint, charming quality to the place, which he had enhanced considerably with his new acquisitions, and she had the feeling that he had worked hard to improve it for her. She was touched. There was a large aerial photograph of the city over the fireplace that he had gotten at IKEA, and a similar one of Paris he had hung in his bedroom over the bed, so she'd feel at home. She immediately noticed the flowers around the room in vases. She kissed him longingly then.

"Thank you for making it beautiful for me, Tom." He was touched that she appreciated what he had done. She was observant and sensitive, and she began unbuttoning his shirt carefully, as he took off his jacket and threw it on the couch. They were in his bedroom naked within minutes, the decor forgotten. It didn't matter what city they were in, they were back together, and Tom was transported by her perfume, her body, her incredibly sensual ways. They lay exhausted and happy in each other's arms afterward, and he went to get her the champagne he had bought to celebrate her arrival. He walked out to the kitchen in all his naked glory, and she followed him as he handed her a glass. They toasted each other and went back to bed, and talked for a long time. She wanted to walk around the neighborhood to get a feeling for it, so he went to shower, while she lay on his bed looking unbearably sexy, and when he came out of the shower, she had a wisp of black lace balancing on her fingertip.

"Look what I found under the bed," she said with a mischievous look and his heart stopped. He thought he had gotten them all, but she had obviously discovered one more.

"Oh my God, I'm sorry . . . I checked everywhere . . . I'm sorry," he said remorsefully and she kissed him with a burst of laughter.

"Don't be, it's mine," she said, teasing him, as he grabbed it from her, and pushed her down on the bed.

"You rotten woman! I'm going to punish you for that. I even bought a new vacuum cleaner and cleaned under the bed myself, just for you."

"Good," she said as he kissed her, and a moment later he was making love to her again. She had nearly given him heart failure, thinking she had found further evidence of his dubious past.

"You are an evil, evil woman," he said as their lovemaking got increasingly serious, and he turned over as she sat astride him. She was a perfect match for him, and not so innocent herself, with a wicked sense of humor that he loved. He loved everything about her, and for once his fears of losing her hadn't stopped him. He was never going to let her go.

They finally did make it outside in the late afternoon. It was the last of a sunny day, and warm compared to Paris. She didn't wear a coat, and they wandered all over. Later, he drove her to the Berkeley campus, past all the hippie stores on Telegraph Avenue, and then he drove her past Alta Bates, where he worked. He was off for the duration of their conferences for four weeks, and was planning to be with her every minute.

They ate a burger at a small restaurant near his apartment, and then went back to his place and drank more champagne. He whispered to her, "Welcome home," to which she responded in her throaty voice, *"Merci, mon amour." Thank you, my love,* and his heart sang.

Gabriel called Stephanie on her cellphone as soon as he walked into his room at the Saint Francis. It was a perfectly decent businessman's hotel room with a city view downtown. He was distressed when she didn't pick up. She was having lunch with Andy and the boys, and she saw his number come up. He texted her two minutes later, and she responded.

"I'm here. When can I see you? Starving for you. *Je t'aime.* G." She repressed a smile as she read it, and felt the same thrill that went through her whenever she saw him or heard from him, especially knowing he had arrived and they were in the same city again.

"Soon. Call you in half an hour." Andy watched her as she answered with a serious expression.

"Work? I thought you were off today."

"I was. Head injury. I should go in. They want a consult." He pursed his lips and looked annoyed. They had no plans anyway. She had been careful not to make any, knowing Gabriel was coming in. She put the dishes in the sink, rinsed them, and then put them in the dishwasher. Andy was planning to take the boys to the park and throw some balls, and he didn't need her for that.

She went upstairs and got her bag and white coat, and was back down in two minutes. She was clearly in a hurry.

"I'll call you later," she said as she fished her car keys out of her bag. "Don't wait for me. It sounds bad. I may stay." Andy didn't react to it and nodded, as she kissed both boys and left.

It took her fifteen minutes to get to the hotel. He had texted her his room number, and she could feel her heart pounding as she rode up in the elevator. She had left her white doctor's coat in the car. She didn't even feel guilty for telling Andy a bold-faced lie. It was the only way she could get out of the house, and she was desperate to see Gabriel. Their two weeks apart felt like a hundred years.

She knocked on the door of his room, he opened it instantly, and pulled her into his arms in a single gesture and held her so tightly she could barely breathe.

"Oh my God, Stephanie, how I've missed you." He touched her hair and her face, and kissed her again, and ran his hands over her body, as she did the same to him. Their clothes were on the floor in minutes, as he pulled her toward the bed, and they made love until they thought they would die of pleasure. They had both lived for this moment. Everything else faded away, their worries and their plans and the people in their lives. They were alone on their own planet.

He made love to her again until they fell into a deep sleep, and it was dark when they woke up, feeling dazed and so happy to see each other and be together again.

They ordered room service, and she texted Andy and told him she'd had to stay, and would be home late. She kept it short, and Gabriel looked at her longingly and asked her to spend the night.

"I can't. Maybe I'll be able to figure it out at some point, but not the first night. I don't want to push our luck," she said soberly. She had a delicate balance to keep and Gabriel was disappointed.

"We only have four weeks, let's not waste a minute of it," he pleaded with her.

"If we're serious about this, we have the rest of our lives. I don't want to cause an explosion or arouse suspicion while you're here. We need to be careful," she said, kissing him, "I'm still married and living with my husband."

"Maybe you should have told him it's over before I got here," he said simply, not happy that she couldn't stay with him.

"That would have been worse. I would have been dealing with all the fallout from that now."

"Try to arrange it for at least some of our nights. Maybe we can go away for a weekend." She liked that idea, and she could claim to be going with the group, which wouldn't include spouses, since she was the only one who had one.

"We could go to the Napa Valley, there's a wonderful hotel there. We'll work it out," she reassured him, and felt very stressed.

They ate dinner naked in bed and she left him reluctantly at midnight after they'd made love again. She showered and dressed respectably. The whole group was meeting the next day for brunch at the Zuni Café, and Stephanie was excited about seeing them. Andy had already agreed to keep the boys, and was taking them to his mother's house for the day, so she knew they'd be busy. And Wendy had texted all of them about a barbecue at her house next Sunday night.

Andy was already in bed when she got home and appeared to be asleep. She had the feeling he wasn't, but he didn't say anything, and she didn't turn on the lights or speak to him. A few minutes after she got home, she slipped into bed beside him, thinking about the afternoon and evening she had spent with Gabriel. It was real, she was sure of that now. They were madly in love. But Andy lying next to her was real too.

Andy was already up when Stephanie awoke in the morning. He and the boys were downstairs, dressed and having breakfast. She went to sit with them, before they left for Orinda. She was leaving for brunch shortly after. Andy said very little. He didn't ask about the French team or their brunch meeting or their plans for the week. The only thing he knew about was the mayor's reception, which he was planning to attend and she wished that he wasn't. That was going to be dicey with Gabriel there too.

They were like a group of old friends when they met at noon at the Zuni Café. The food was European and American, with some California dishes, pasta, and fabulous oysters, which the French contingent were eager to try. They hugged and kissed when they met. Tom and Valérie looked peaceful and happy and exuded the aura of a couple as they joined the others, and Gabriel sat next to Stephanie and devoured her with his eyes. Bill was happy to see Wendy, she asked about Pip and Alex. Paul reported that he'd had a great night on the town. Marie-Laure had gone shopping in Union Square before having dinner with Wendy. They were all excited to be there, and would be touring SF General with Bill leading the way the next day, after the morning at the DEM, the Department of Emergency Management, and then they would be visiting the Emergency Operations Center the day after that. They had a busy week ahead. And Bill was eager to show them where he worked.

They were a boisterous group, talking and laughing in English and French, and Valérie asked Stephanie quietly how things were going with her unraveling marriage.

"Tense," Stephanie said, as she sat holding Gabriel's hand.

"Have you told him anything since you got back?"

"We agree that it's not working. I'll talk to him about it after you all leave. I didn't want to rock the boat too much while you're here. I'm sticking to that plan."

Someone mentioned the mayor's reception then, and they were excited about it. Stephanie used the opportunity to warn Gabriel that Andy was coming, and he was instantly upset.

"How did that happen? Did you invite him?" He was shocked.

"Of course not. He saw the invitation and grabbed it before I could stop him, and he insisted he wants to come. I don't know why this time, he never does. We'll just have to get through it and be discreet." Gabriel looked ruffled for a few minutes and then got drawn into conversation with the others and forgot about it. Tom told them about the trick Valérie had played on him, pretending she'd found a thong under the bed, when it was her own. "I nearly had a heart attack," he said, and she laughed. She was playful and naughty and sexy and he loved that about her too, as well as her serious, sensitive, loving, and smart side. She had all the qualities he'd ever dreamed of and never found in one woman.

"How are things working out with your situation?" Bill asked Wendy discreetly and she smiled.

"Done. I ended it when I got back." He looked surprised.

"I didn't think you'd do that, or not for a while. Married men are hard to get away from."

"It was time. It was long overdue, in fact, and I finally realized it. I'd been making a fool of myself for the last two or three years," she admitted.

"Welcome to the human race. I made an ass of myself for five, hating my ex-wife when we never should have been together in the first place. Some things take longer than others to get over. I'm proud of you," he said and they high-fived.

Valérie told the group then that Marie-Laure had had dinner with Captain Bruno Perliot twice in the last two weeks since they left. She looked embarrassed and shy, but pleased.

"He's very nice" was all she would say about him, but the American team were happy to hear it. He had seemed like a good man.

"Hopefully, we won't provide as much excitement as you gave us," Bill said solemnly, thinking of the school attack. "Just a lot of information, paperwork, and tours. The most dangerous location is at the hospital where I work tomorrow. Our patients shoot each other regularly if they haven't finished the job on the street." He insisted it was true. "The most challenging part of our job is dodging stray bullets while they kill each other and we try to save their lives. It's an interesting segment of society." He was joking but not entirely, and hand-guns were more common in the States than in France. "Very Wild West," Marie-Laure commented and they laughed.

They walked down Market Street to the Ferry Building afterward, through the food markets there, and then they walked along the Embarcadero by the bay. There were a lot of tourists. They walked far enough so they could see Alcatraz and the Golden Gate Bridge. Then they took cabs back to the hotel, and Tom and Valérie went to get his car. They left each other at five o'clock. Tom and Valérie went home to Oakland, and Stephanie went to the hotel with Gabriel, and they went up to his room. Marie-Laure, Wendy, and Bill had a drink at the bar, and Paul went back to the Clift, where he had liked the look of the girls the night before. He was doing fine without Tom as his guide, and just needed occasional advice about where to go.

Stephanie left Gabriel at eight o'clock, since she'd been gone all day, although he asked her again to stay at the hotel with him. He was persistent, but she said she had to see her boys. She wanted him to meet them, but not when Andy was around. She was going to try and arrange it sometime during his stay.

Andy had just put the boys to bed when she got home and she kissed them goodnight. They were already half asleep and had had a good day at their grandmother's.

"You got some sun today," Andy commented.

"We walked along the Embarcadero for miles. They want to see all the sights," she said blandly.

"Did you have fun?"

"They're a good group. You'll meet them on Wednesday." He nod-ded and didn't comment. She read the papers they'd been sent by the

DEM, and she was looking forward to seeing SF General with Bill. She hadn't been there in quite a while and heard wonderful things about their new facility. She was happy to be doing all of it with Gabriel. He texted her four times that night, and she had to tell him to stop, and then turned off her phone.

On Tuesday, they were going to be touring UCSF, with Stephanie as their guide. And suddenly, thinking about it made her sad. If she moved to France with Gabriel, she would be leaving UCSF soon. It was going to be like leaving home. The thought of giving up her job frightened her. Who would she be without her role at UCSF? It would be like losing a limb. And what if she didn't find a good job as a foreigner in France? There was so much to think about. She had nightmares about it that night.

# Chapter Sixteen

The administrative setup of San Francisco's emergency services was complicated but no more so than the elaborate system in France. Each country had their own way of dividing up vital services and deciding who should run them. In San Francisco, the Department of Emergency Management, the DEM, was responsible for planning, preparedness, communication, response, and recovery for daily emergencies and major disasters like the "multiple casualty incident" at the *lycée* in Paris. The DEM was the bridge between the public and first responders, and provided all the key coordination with city departments. It was originally known as the Office of Emergency Services, and other branches of emergency communications had merged with it, all under the umbrella of the DEM, which was run by an executive director and three deputy directors. When necessary, the DEM brought the Emergency Operations Center into action to support field operations and provide public information, among other functions. They had their own deputy director.

The DEM building was on Turk Street in the Tenderloin among the derelicts and drug addicts, not far from where the French team was staying in Union Square.

Marie-Laure, Paul, and Gabriel arrived together by cab at the DEM. Valérie came with Tom, and the American team met them there. Two out of three of the deputy directors had come. The executive director welcomed the French representatives and congratulated them on their handling of the *lycée* shooting, which had been a tragedy but could have been even worse, as the professionals knew, despite the rabble-rousing of the press and Jacqueline Moutier.

They discussed it for a few minutes, and each of the deputy directors spoke, explaining how the system of first responders worked, and what systems were in place for a major natural disaster like an earthquake, or a terrorist attack. Everything had been thought through with great care, equipment was state of the art, their approach was constantly updated, and manpower was strong. It was an efficient department and the French were impressed. It was a remarkably smooth operation that had been impeccably implemented. They also explained how the various hospitals in the Bay Area were used, and how triage was determined and by whom. They were scheduled to see the four most important hospitals in the next few weeks, as well as the Saint Francis Burn Center, which was a very important facility and had been crucial in the recent hotel fire in January.

The informational session continued until lunchtime, when the directors left them, and they were driven to a very good new restaurant South of Market, before moving on to SF General after lunch.

They were all fascinated by how different it was from France. It was more mechanized and systematized in the United States, in contrast to the many official protocols in France and the more traditional system there, run with less manpower, since they had less. The French system was very closely linked with the police and riot squads, since terrorism was unfortunately more common in France, although that could change, as one of the deputy directors pointed out. In the case of terrorism in the United States, the FBI and Homeland Security became involved. They had more departments to draw on and more staff.

"Everything is bigger in the United States," Gabriel commented, very impressed by what they'd seen so far. He conferred about it at length with Marie-Laure over lunch. Both cities and countries had much to learn from each other, which was the whole point of the exchange. They all felt enriched by what they'd heard.

After a delicious lunch, they headed for SF General, and Bill began the tour with one of the hospital's directors who joined them to add additional information.

The older part of the hospital was huge and rambling, and gloomy. It was in the area of Potrero Hill. They went in through the ambulance entrance, and took a lengthy tour through the bowels of the hospital, winding up in surgery and the various trauma units, which were of greatest interest to them. It was Bill's second home and he looked totally at ease. It was similar to the older hospitals in Paris, as the French members of the team commented. Their hospitals weren't light and airy either, but they were efficient, as was General. It was the best hospital in the city for acute trauma. They walked through the wards together and the French team was impressed at the broad range of severe cases they handled. They already respected Bill from their time with him in Paris, but even more so after the tour. His American colleagues were impressed too. Wendy had never been there, and Stephanie not for some time, and they were impressed by how severe the cases were. They all noticed that there were access codes on every door and armed security guards patrolled the halls. Their client base was potentially dangerous in the extreme. It reminded them of a prison hospital, and some of their patients belonged there or wound up there, which didn't seem to faze Bill. He was used to it, and moved through the halls and locked doors without feeling threatened. There were signs telling patients to remove their weapons, and metal detectors throughout.

"It really is like a war zone," Paul said to Bill respectfully.

They toured parts of the new facility of the hospital as well, which was in sharp contrast, with extraordinary new equipment. The French team were stunned to learn that the addition to the hospital had cost over nine hundred million to build, eight hundred million provided by the city, and another hundred in private donations. Bill gave them a brief tour of their elder care unit, which was beautiful. The tour ended at six, and had been very instructive.

Marie-Laure and Wendy admitted that they were exhausted, and Valérie wanted to go back with Bill another day to visit the extensive psych ward the hospital was very proud of. She was fascinated by everything they'd seen, and she and Tom were talking about it animatedly as they left. In a whisper, Gabriel asked Stephanie to come back to his hotel.

"I can't, I have to see my kids," she said softly. She knew that Andy would be upset if she didn't, even though he knew that she had busy days ahead for the next four weeks, and this was just the beginning.

"Can you meet me later?" Gabriel persisted, he was very determined and wanted to make love to her again.

"Not tonight. I need to spend one night at home or Andy will get suspicious, and he'll make a scene. When I'm not home, he takes care of the kids."

"Don't you have a nanny?" Gabriel was surprised as she shook her head.

"A housekeeper a few hours a day. The rest of the time, Andy does it. He works from home. On the weekend, we do it together or take turns if I have to work. Andy doesn't believe in childcare whenever we can do it ourselves. His mother was a full-time hands-on mom, and he thinks I should be too. And since I'm not around most of the time, he does the rest." Gabriel looked shocked.

"Men in France don't do that." But he understood better now why she had to go home, although he didn't like it. "Can't you hire a babysitter while I'm here?"

"Andy would wonder why. He likes taking care of our boys. But he expects me to show up when I can. It's hard when I'm on duty at the hospital. And then he expects me to come home and take care of the kids."

"You won't have to do that anymore, we can hire a nanny if you want," he said glibly. It was generous of him, but she felt uncomfortable when he said it.

In the end, Gabriel went back to the hotel with Paul and Marie-Laure and wasn't pleased about it. They were going to have dinner together, and Bill and Wendy were joining them. Tom and Valérie were going home to Oakland, to his new cozy, much cleaner apartment.

It was seven when Stephanie walked into the house. Andy was giving the boys their bath and she joined them, and sat down on the toilet to chat with them for a few minutes.

"Long day," Andy commented.

"We had orientation at the Department of Emergency Management this morning, and a tour of SF General this afternoon. They're keeping us busy. I'm doing the tour at UCSF tomorrow. It's interesting because each of our hospitals is so different." She tried to explain it while the boys splashed each other, and she helped Andy wash their hair.

She put them to bed while he cooked dinner. He had already fed the boys before their bath. Gabriel texted her three times while she was reading the boys a story. She texted him back when she finished, and then kissed the boys good night and headed downstairs to the kitchen. Andy told her he had eaten with Ryan and Aden, but he had made her an omelet and said there were leftovers for her. He didn't know if she'd be home for dinner so they hadn't waited for her. And he left her alone to eat in the kitchen. He hadn't sat down with her, and as soon as he left the room while she ate, Gabriel texted her again.

He wanted to know if she had changed her mind about spending the night. "I wish I could," she texted back. "I need to be here." He was silent after that for a while, pouting perhaps, and then texted her again.

"Tomorrow?"

"I'll try," she responded, feeling pressured by her responsibilities at home, Andy looming like a jailer, and the man who wanted to make love to her every minute of the day. She went to bed early that night, and Andy stayed downstairs to watch TV. He was keeping away from her, and she was grateful not to have to talk to him. She didn't know what to say. It was harder participating in the emergency services program here at home than it had been in Paris, where she had no responsibilities, and no husband and children to go home to at night. The juggling act she had to do in San Francisco was much more difficult, and the lies she had to tell made her feel guilty all the time.

The whole group met outside UCSF's new Mission Bay facility the next morning. It was state of the art in every aspect, and everyone who worked there was proud of it, and so was Stephanie. The new facility was a masterpiece of sorts. It had taken 1.52 billion dollars to build, ten years of construction, and another ten years of planning before that. It opened on schedule. A hospital administrator had joined them to complement what Stephanie had to say. The administrator filled in numbers and statistics, and Stephanie showed the team where she worked every day. She explained that they had started at the old facility on Parnassus, above the Haight, which was why she and Andy had bought their house there. In recent years, the hospital had moved several of their departments south and east, to Mission Bay, near the baseball stadium. The buildings were vast and robots traveled the halls delivering meals and equipment.

It had been an adjustment for the staff at first, because it was so much bigger, but Stephanie said she loved working there now, and didn't mind the drive down from her house. The working conditions were excellent. There were research facilities, a cancer hospital, a women's specialty hospital, and a 183-bed children's hospital. Every inch of the hospital was the most up-to-date possible, including a 207,000-square-foot outpatient building and a helipad. In Paris there was no hospital to compare to it, nor any that cost anything comparable to build. Stephanie said she felt lucky to work there. She was obviously proud as she showed them around, and Valérie watched her face carefully. She glowed when she talked about her work, and everyone in trauma and the ER knew her. It didn't go unnoticed, and Valérie and Marie-Laure exchanged a look. She would be giving up a lot for Gabriel, her whole familiar world and status, as well as her marriage.

They had lunch at a bar and restaurant South of Market with a pool table, and when the men went to shoot pool while they waited for lunch, Valérie again thanked Stephanie for the tour and then gazed at her thoughtfully.

"Do you really think you can give all that up, a job you love that much, and be happy practicing in France? You need to think about that carefully," Valérie said, concerned about her.

"What choice do I have?" Stephanie said. "If I want a life with Gabriel, I have to give this up." Wendy was listening to the conversation and was worried about her too. She knew she couldn't have given up her job for a man, and didn't want to.

"It's an enormous sacrifice," Valérie reminded her, "and you'd better be *very* sure he's going to leave his wife. You don't want to give all this up and then find yourself sitting in an apartment while he spends Christmas with his wife and children, and tells you he can't leave them yet. I know several women that has happened to. Right now he's madly in love with you, and I'm not saying he isn't going to get divorced, but when his wife asks him for half his savings, his pension, their summer house, and everything he has, it may be a different story. Living with her may not seem so bad. That's what French men do. Americans get divorced. Sometimes French guys don't, or damn few do."

"And not all Americans do either. Jeff used every excuse in the book. It was always a year or two or three away. I didn't have to give up anything to be with him, except my friends and my time. If I'd had to give up my job at Stanford, I'd have bailed a lot faster than I did. That would have been too much for me."

"He says he's going to take care of everything when he goes back, and call a lawyer."

"Maybe you should wait and see if he does, before you make a move. And I don't just mean your marriage. You trained for thirteen years for this job. You'd better be sure before you give it up." Stephanie felt sick as she listened, and nodded. She knew her father would have said the same thing about her job at UCSF. But she didn't want to lose Gabriel either. She felt torn. She was quiet when the men came back from playing pool and dug into the sandwiches they'd ordered. They were still talking about the medical facility they'd seen that morning.

"My poor hospital is going to look like nothing after that," Tom said sadly. "But we do a good job anyway." They had an excellent reputation and he liked working there. And they had built new additions too, just not on as grand a scale as UCSF, which was mammoth, or the new facility at SF General, which had government funds to use, and an enormous private donor.

They were scheduled to visit Alta Bates on Thursday, and Stanford on Friday, and then they were going to focus on emergency services operations thereafter, and drills similar to the one they'd participated in in Paris.

They had a lecture on terrorism, and another on natural disasters at the Emergency Operations Center that afternoon. An earthquake was the greatest potential threat to San Francisco, and the statistics and expected damage were terrifying if they had a big one.

Stephanie texted Andy after the lectures and told him they had a night meeting, and she went back to the hotel with Gabriel. He had hounded her all day, and she wanted to be with him too. She felt pulled by her responsibilities and her children, and her desire for him. She tried to explain it to Gabriel, but he was too hungry for her and their passion engulfed them as soon as they walked into the room. There was no time for conversation or reassurance, there was a sense of urgency now whenever they were together. It was starting to make her feel anxious. But after they made love, she was more relaxed and she tried not to think of the job and hospital she was giving up for him. There was too much to consider, too much to absorb. She didn't even realize how worried her friends were about her, or how stressed she looked. And Gabriel didn't see it either. All he saw was the woman he was so in love with, and wanted to take back to France, no matter what she had to give up to be with him.

She was exhausted when she went home that night, after arguing with Gabriel for an hour when he wanted her to stay.

The house was silent when she got home. Everyone was asleep. It was a relief not to have to talk to anyone. She felt peaceful in the silence.

They watched earthquake preparedness training films for all of the next day. And then a representative from the Fire Department explained NERT drills to them. They were Neighborhood Emergency Response Teams, which provided an ongoing framework for the city to deal with disasters, conduct rescue and medical triage, and transport victims to medical treatment facilities.

It gave them a break from on-site hospital tours, and they had the mayor's reception for them that night at seven. Stephanie wanted to be home at five to get dressed.

"How are you getting there?" Bill asked Wendy as they left the Emergency Operations Center.

"I told Marie-Laure I'd get dressed with her at her hotel and we'd go together, so I don't have to go back to Palo Alto. I think Paul is meeting us at City Hall. He's having a drink with some woman he met the other night." She smiled at Bill. Paul was the lovable bad boy in their midst now, and acted like a kid. It was a role Tom said he had played for twenty years, and had recently given up for more adult pursuits. But at thirty-four, Paul was a long way from there, and entitled to some fun.

"I'll pick you and Marie-Laure up at the hotel," Bill volunteered.

He offered Gabriel a ride too, since Stephanie had to go with Andy. Bill could see that Gabriel was unhappy about it. He and Stephanie had argued about it that afternoon and she said there was nothing she could do. Her husband had seen the invitation and announced he was coming, and for now, they were still married, as far as he knew anyway. So she couldn't tell Andy not to come. Gabriel said it would spoil the evening for him, which was a heavy weight on her.

Bill picked them up at the hotel at a quarter to seven. He and Gabriel were wearing suits, and Wendy and Marie-Laure were wearing short black cocktail dresses that showed off their figures. They were both pretty women.

They chatted on the way to City Hall, and Bill said he felt differently about the city having just seen the earthquake films. They reminded him of science fiction, but they were real. Some of the films were simulated, others were of real earthquakes in other parts of the world.

"I'm expecting the dome to fall in on us tonight," he said and the others laughed.

"I wouldn't like to be here in an earthquake," Marie-Laure admitted, and Gabriel sat staring out the window, brooding, thinking about Stephanie arriving with Andy.

Bill gave his car up to a valet parker, and they walked into the rotunda of City Hall. Three hundred people were expected at the reception, politicians, members of city government, and anyone involved in trauma and emergency services. And the mayor.

"Are you ready?" Andy asked Stephanie, as he walked into their bedroom. He'd been dressed for half an hour and was wearing a dark suit, white shirt, and navy tie. His hair was neat, he was freshly shaved, his shoes were shined, and she was startled for a minute. She had forgotten how handsome he was, or could be, when he made an effort. She hadn't seen him dressed that way in several years. She always saw him in jeans and sweatshirts or T-shirts now, with running shoes and five days of beard stubble on his face. But not tonight. He looked terrific and like the man she'd married and remembered from when he had a job.

She had tried on three dresses and didn't like any of them. Her hair was smoothed back in a long neat ponytail. She had makeup on, and she was wearing a white silk dress with a wide satin collar and a low back. It was sexy and elegant at the same time. She had on high heels and knew her feet would be killing her before the end of the evening, but the shoes looked great. She wanted to knock Gabriel's socks off when she walked into the room. And standing next to Andy, they made a dazzling couple as she caught sight of them in the mirror.

"We look pretty good together." She smiled at him, and he nodded. He hardly ever smiled these days. Even if she hadn't told him, he knew what was coming. Their marriage was in shambles, they never talked to each other, and divorce seemed inevitable, but he wanted to be there for her tonight. He was making the effort for her. He didn't care about her French friends. Their housekeeper had agreed to stay late, and they got in the car at ten to seven. They would only be a few minutes late. She was wearing a black fur jacket that was a hand-me-down from her mother over the white dress. Stephanie would never have bought it for herself.

There was silence in the car as they drove downtown, and Stephanie was thinking of Gabriel. She heard a text come in and glanced at it. "Where are you?"

"On my way," she answered.

"You get a lot of texts these days," Andy commented.

"One of the women on the French team wanted to know where I am," she said defensively, disgusted with herself. Lying again.

Andy didn't know what to expect when they got there, she hadn't told him anything about it, and didn't know much herself. The American and French teams were being honored, which she assumed meant a speech and some champagne.

They walked into City Hall together, past security and the metal detectors, and their names were checked off a list, and then they entered the rotunda, and Marie-Laure elbowed Valérie in the ribs when she saw them. Andy and Stephanie had just arrived and looked like movie stars.

"He looks like a Greek god," Marie-Laure whispered. "Why is she giving that up?" Gabriel was not nearly as attractive. He had a warm sexy manly quality to him, and was almost fatherly at times, but Andy looked like an actor or a model, and several heads turned as they walked in side by side. A photographer snapped their picture. Stephanie hadn't spotted Gabriel yet in the crowd, but he had seen them. Valérie glanced at him, and he seemed livid. Andy had upstaged him. Gabriel was not going to be able to show off with Stephanie tonight. Her handsome young American husband was very much in evidence.

Marie-Laure and Valérie approached Stephanie and Andy with Bill and Tom just behind them, and Stephanie introduced Andy. He was cool and aloof, and not very friendly. He appeared uncomfortable, and didn't make small talk with any of them. He didn't seem like a warm person, which explained more why she was attracted to Gabriel. Gabriel was full of emotion, passionate in his beliefs, and very French. He made up in personality for anything he lacked in appearance. He was a nice-looking man, but nothing like Andy who had the athletic, lean, powerful body of a man who went to the gym every day.

"He has nothing else to do," Marie-Laure said to Valérie. "He doesn't work."

"He takes care of the kids, she doesn't. She says it herself," Valérie defended him, even though she didn't know him. She felt sorry for him, he looked unhappy to be there, and they all knew something he didn't, that his wife was having an affair.

Wendy and Gabriel walked up to them then, and they all froze for a moment. Stephanie tried to appear calm while she introduced them, but she wasn't, her palms were soaking wet and she didn't meet Gabriel's eye. He shook hands with Andy with a stern expression as though he disapproved of him, almost as though he was pawing the ground, establishing his turf, as Stephanie stood by helplessly. An electric current passed between the two men as their eyes met and held. Andy seemed to grow taller, and Gabriel seemed more powerful, as Wendy disappeared into the crowd to find Paul. Stephanie felt like she was going to faint. Not a word passed between the two men, and an aide of the mayor's came to tell them that they were wanted at the steps in the center of the rotunda. They wanted all eight of the honorees lined up on the steps, so the mayor could begin his speech, and with that, the group moved forward. Stephanie told Andy she'd be back as soon as it was over, and they moved through the crowd as Stephanie tried to catch her breath. Her heart was pounding in her ears.

"Are you okay?" Valérie whispered to her. She was deathly pale, and Valérie could only imagine the stress she was experiencing with both men under one roof, and some instinct had warned each of them of danger.

"I think I'm going to throw up," she said, clutching Valérie's hand.

"You can't. You have to act perfectly normal, or your husband will figure it out. They both sense it, your husband just doesn't know it. Gabriel does, and he can barely keep himself in control." Valérie had seen it all. "You're quite a woman," Valérie teased her to lighten the moment, "to inspire that kind of feeling in two very attractive men. Your husband is gorgeous, by the way. But that's usually not enough, unfortunately." Valérie thought he looked boring, but he wasn't her kind of man. He wasn't interesting enough for her, or for Stephanie either. She was too bright for him. He seemed sour, restless, and bored. "Marie-Laure almost fainted when she saw him. She thinks you're betting on the wrong horse. But beauty isn't everything." Her patter had relaxed Stephanie a little, and the color had returned to her face. For a minute she had thought that one of the two men would hit the other, and there would be a brawl in the rotunda of City Hall because of her.

They had reached the steps by then, and were told by the mayor's aide where and how to line up. Stephanie felt numb, and the whole group stood expectantly while the mayor began his speech, listed the credentials of each member of the team, described the purpose of the exchange to benefit both cities, and commended all of them for their bravery during the recent school shooting in Paris, then he gave each of them a citation rolled up and tied with a gold ribbon. They thanked the mayor, then all posed for photographs with him, and a band began to play as hors d'oeuvres and champagne were passed on silver trays. It was a very nice reception and the French team were touched. And as soon as his speech was over, the mayor slipped away to his second event of the night.

Gabriel spoke to her in an undervoice as they left the steps.

"Stay with me tonight," he said urgently. "I need you."

"I need you too, but I can't. He senses something. This is going to turn into a mess if we're not careful. I can't tonight." He stared at her intensely, then stormed out of the building, but she couldn't do anything about it. At least he hadn't made a scene with Andy, and a few minutes later, Paul told them all that Gabriel had gone back to the hotel with a headache. And for once, he didn't text her. She went to find Andy then, and tried to include him in the group, but he had found someone he knew and was talking to him. Stephanie was more relaxed with only one of her men in the room, although she wished it could have been Gabriel and not Andy.

"Well, that was interesting," Bill said to Wendy. "For a minute there, I thought Gabriel was going to hit him, or maybe the other way around. I wouldn't have the nerves to be sleeping with someone else's wife, or want to. I'd be on Xanax all day long." She laughed. "That was intense."

"Yes, it was," she agreed.

"I like your dress by the way." It was short and tight, but not vulgar and she had the figure to wear it.

"I bought it for tonight."

"Lucky mayor," he said and she laughed.

"How are your girls?"

"They ask about you all the time. They want to go back to Euro Disney. So do I. That was fun. You were a good sport."

"I loved it," she said sincerely.

They all stayed for another hour, and the group wanted to go to dinner at a restaurant nearby. Andy said he was going home.

"I'll come with you," Stephanie said.

"Don't you want to go to dinner with your friends?" He seemed surprised.

"They'll be fine. I want to go home with you." She felt that she owed him something for coming. She didn't want to just dismiss him, even if she hadn't wanted him there. He had done it for her.

They left a few minutes later and drove home without saying a word. The boys were already asleep, and they let their housekeeper go home. Then he took off his coat, laid it on the couch, and looked at her.

"Did you have something going on with the guy I met, the one who shook my hand? I think his name was Gabriel something." He looked her squarely in the eye and she shook her head.

"No, I didn't," she lied to him. "We're all good friends." He nodded and didn't question her further. She didn't think he believed her, but he had the decency not to press the point.

"I thought he was going to take a swing at me for a minute," Andy added, as he watched her face. "There's only one reason a guy like him does that. It's a turf issue, between two men who both want the same woman. Maybe he's in love with you." Andy headed toward the stairs. "You looked very pretty tonight. I liked your dress." But he didn't approach her or tell her he loved her. He wasn't even sure if he did anymore, and he was sure she didn't love him. It was over. Their marriage was dead. And they'd have to bury it one of these days. He wondered if the French guy knew it, or sensed it, and was staking a claim. It felt like it to Andy.

# Chapter Seventeen

After the dignity of the mayor's reception at City Hall, and the tension of Andy and Gabriel's meeting, their tour of Alta Bates Summit Medical Center was easy and anticlimactic. Tom sang the hospital's praises, telling about their exceptionally good track record with cardiac surgery, neonatal intensive care, and obstetrics, and their outstanding emergency room facilities. He loved working there and they all noticed that nearly everyone in the hospital seemed to know him and said hello. Tom introduced the team, and the local staff were interested in what they were doing. The atmosphere was pleasant and welcoming and easygoing, and they could see why he loved it. And the emergency room was one of the best in the city. Valérie was proud of him as he showed them around.

They had lunch in the cafeteria because he said the food was so good, and everyone greeted him again. He took them to the doctors' lounge and all the little nooks and crannies where he hung out. They felt as though he was welcoming them into his home. Whereas San

Francisco General was a stern, imposing place, dealing with some of the city's most acute trauma cases, which was the challenge Bill loved, and Stephanie was proud of the extraordinary new facility where she worked, Tom was proud of the medicine they practiced at Alta Bates, providing outstanding care in a warm atmosphere that allowed him to be himself and have a strong rapport with patients and staff. In each case, the place where they practiced medicine suited them perfectly. They had each chosen the right venue for their talents.

Their tour of Stanford University Medical Center with Wendy on Friday was outstanding. They had an immensely impressive pediatric and adult trauma and critical care program. Their trauma center had been one of the best in the city for thirty years. And while Wendy was one of the most modest physicians in the group, her credentials, academic training, and history at Stanford shone the minute she walked into the building and started showing them around. Once she was in her own environment, they could see what a star she was. The administrator who joined them said she was one of the most valued physicians on the trauma team, and likely to be head of the department at some point. She looked embarrassed when he said it, but her extensive knowledge was obvious. They all listened to her raptly as she described what they did there, and the trauma services they provided as a matter of course. She was frequently a guest lecturer at the medical school, which she hadn't mentioned before. She was a very discreet person, and they all thanked her warmly after the tour.

It was difficult to decide which of the hospitals they'd seen was the most impressive. Although the teaching hospitals offered a broader range, each institution had a distinct personality and something special to offer.

Bill enjoyed talking to Wendy about it afterward since he'd done his residency there. He had been offered a job at SF General that he couldn't resist but he could see why she loved working at Stanford. She was typical of the high-quality physicians who practiced there. Her ex-lover Jeff was one of them too, in cardiac surgery. His surgical skills were what had won her admiration in the first place and the rest had come later. She was in love with her work and where she did it, and it showed.

She invited them all for a drink at her house after the tour, since it was close by. They were coming back on Sunday night for a barbecue, but they enjoyed a glass of wine sitting around her pool on Friday afternoon, and since they had a driver to bring them to Palo Alto, they could relax with a second glass. Valérie and Tom were sharing one of the lounge chairs, and Gabriel was sitting slightly apart from the group. He had been brooding and sulking for two days after meeting Andy, and Stephanie's refusal to spend the night with him afterward. He said that she had humiliated him. She had apologized profusely, but had explained repeatedly that if she had disappeared that night, Andy would have caught on that they were having an affair. Gabriel felt it was time for Andy to know, but he finally relaxed sitting at Wendy's pool on Friday afternoon, put his arm around Stephanie, and kissed her. They had had a busy and informative week, and she had promised to spend the night with him on Saturday. She was going to tell Andy that she had to work, to cover for someone who was sick. Friday night, they were having a girls' night, and the four men were going out together, which promised to be rowdy, and they'd have hangovers the next day.

The women were having dinner at Perbacco, an Italian restaurant downtown, and Stephanie was planning to join them for that too.

"I love your house, Wendy," Bill said warmly, as they sat in chairs side by side in the afternoon sun after the tour. She had decorated it in soothing muted colors, warm beiges and pastels, which suited her, with some paintings that she loved. "You inspire me. My place looks like a bomb shelter. It looks like the tenant has already moved out. But I like the view." She smiled at how he described it. But seeing where he worked and the long hours he put in, she could guess that he spent almost no time at home. "I have to do something with the girls' room before they come out this summer. I promised I'd paint it pink for them. Alex wants purple, but we compromised on pink." They exchanged a smile, thinking of his girls, now that she knew them. "Maybe you can help me pick the right shade. I'm not good with color. Or decorating." He had wanted to have the group over for dinner, but he didn't have enough chairs, or even plates and forks. And he only had four glasses. "I had a nice Victorian place when I was married. I never bothered after I sold it. I didn't care where I lived once Athena and the girls were gone." But he admired the fact that Wendy had a real home that looked like someone who loved it lived there.

"I could use a hand with the barbecue on Sunday," she said shyly. "I'm scared to light it."

"That's my forte. Ribs, chicken, and steaks. I'll come over in the afternoon, if you want."

"I'd like that." They exchanged a glance that stretched just beyond friends, but not too far. He'd been inching his way toward her since he'd heard that she had broken up with her married boyfriend, but he didn't want to scare her off if it was too soon.

"We should have dinner sometime," he suggested and she nodded. Valérie was watching them and smiling. She'd been hoping something would happen between them after Paris. She thought they were perfect for each other.

By the time they left, Gabriel had gotten over his two-day pout and forgiven Stephanie for bringing her husband to the party.

Valérie and Tom were talking about it on the way home in his car. The others had gone back to the hotel in the van. Valérie was worried about Stephanie. She thought Gabriel was putting too much pressure on her, and she already had a lot going on with two small children, a divorce in the offing, and a married lover who expected her to give up her job and move to France. "She's got so much on her plate." Tom nodded, and had thought the same thing.

As they headed toward Oakland, Valérie told him something offhandedly that startled him. "I'm having lunch on Monday with an old friend, by the way. He lives here."

"An old boyfriend?" Tom asked, suddenly worried.

"Not really."

"What does 'not really' mean? He was a boyfriend but lousy in bed?"

"Don't be silly. Just a friend," she said vaguely, and offered no further information. And as though to reassure himself and conquer her again, he made love to her when they got back to his apartment, before they both left for dinner. She could tell he was worried, but she liked to tease him at times, to keep him on his toes. She told Marie-Laure it was good for him, and that a man like Tom should never be totally sure of a woman, or he'd get bored. But there was nothing boring about her. He was still worried about her "old friend" when they shared a cab into the city and he dropped her off at Perbacco to meet the other women. He went to meet the men at the bar at the Big 4 on Nob Hill, which had a nice manly feel to it.

They all had fun that evening. The four women talked about what they'd been doing all week. Wendy told them they should come shopping at the Stanford mall in Palo Alto one weekend, and Valérie said that she and Tom were going to the Auberge du Soleil in the Napa Valley for a romantic weekend, and he was coming to France to go on vacation with her in July. And after her second glass of wine, Marie-Laure admitted that Bruno had called her twice that week, and they were having dinner when she went back.

"What about you and Bill?" Marie-Laure asked Wendy.

"We're just friends," she said firmly. "But I had a really nice time with him and his daughters at Euro Disney. They're adorable, really sweet kids."

"Just wait," Valérie said knowingly. "He looked very cozy with you this afternoon sitting by your pool."

"He's not interested. Honestly."

"I predict a romance in your future," Valérie said, pretending to read tea leaves, and they all laughed. It was an easy, relaxing evening. They went to the Fairmont for a drink afterward, and at midnight, they all went home. Stephanie texted Gabriel to see if he was at the hotel, but he answered that he wasn't back yet, so she went back to her house. She was staying with him on Saturday night, and had already set it up with Andy, with the story about working for a night, and then she was going to the barbecue with Gabriel at Wendy's on Sunday. He'd made reservations for them in Napa the following weekend too, at the same hotel where Valérie and Tom were staying. Marie-Laure was thinking of going skiing in Tahoe with Paul, if he didn't have a real date. She had been a ski champion when she was in school, and she wanted to try out the slopes in California before she went back, but didn't want to go alone. Wendy said she didn't ski anymore since she had a knee injury two years before.

It had been a perfect evening for the women, but the men weren't quite as restrained. They closed the bar at a pool hall South of Market at two A.M., near Bill's apartment, and the owner let them stay until three. They were all home by three-thirty, and Tom woke up with a massive headache the next day, and groaned when he got out of bed.

"Oh God, I'm dying." Valérie made him some evil brew with Jägermeister and an egg, and he actually felt better afterward.

"Where did you learn that?"

"In medical school," she said smugly.

"Must be French. They never taught us that here."

They spent a lazy day around his apartment and went to a movie that night. He was feeling better by then. He asked her again about the old friend she was having lunch with on Monday, and she ignored him and wouldn't answer. He was getting seriously worried. Valérie was the kind of woman you could never own, and he loved that about her. But he didn't like the idea of her having lunch with another man, which was the whole point, and why she'd told him, just to worry him a little, and keep him on his toes.

* * *

Stephanie left the house on Saturday afternoon, while Andy was at the park with the boys. She was at Gabriel's hotel by four, and they never left his hotel room. She didn't go home until noon on Sunday, and had lunch with Andy and the boys. She left again for Wendy's house at six, and had warned Andy that the team was having a working dinner, to get a jump-start on the week. Andy and the boys were watching a movie when she left, and Ryan had fallen asleep in front of the TV.

She picked Gabriel up at the hotel, and they drove to Palo Alto together in good spirits. They'd had an incredible time together the night before. The only thing she felt guilty about was that she hadn't spent much time with her children all weekend, except for lunch that day. But Andy had kept them busy.

She had a text from Andy as soon as they got to Wendy's. He said Ryan had woken up with a fever after the movie, and he had just thrown up. Andy couldn't find the thermometer and wanted to know where it was. She told him, and five minutes later, she got another text. "102.2. What do I do now?"

"Children's Tylenol." She told him how many drops and where it was. She was frowning while she texted him.

"Something wrong?" Gabriel asked her.

"Ryan has a fever. He gets them easily. But now Aden will get sick." It was inevitable with two kids.

Bill was busily working at the barbecue when they got there. He had the meat organized on trays and he and Wendy were doing an efficient job. The table was set in her big country kitchen, and they sat at the pool until dinnertime when it got chilly. The French crew loved that they were sitting outdoors in February in the sun, while it was freezing in Paris.

"I want to live here," Paul said.

"Don't we all," Valérie agreed, and Tom leaned over and kissed her.

"You're welcome to move here anytime." She smiled like a Cheshire cat in answer.

Stephanie called Andy before they sat down to dinner. He said Ryan seemed better, wasn't as hot, and was asleep again. She sat down to dinner, feeling relieved. And they had lively discussions and compared medical school experiences and pranks. Tom had some outrageous stories, and Valérie had a few herself. And Bill's skills at the barbecue were excellent. The dinner was delicious, and Wendy thanked him for doing all the cooking.

"I love it. I haven't done that in years." He had sold the barbecue with his house.

Everyone was relaxed and happy, they had become a tight circle of friends. They headed back to the city at ten-thirty and Bill stayed to help Wendy clean up. They'd had a wonderful relaxing evening to end the first week of the second part of their work together, and they were going to experience an earthquake drill that week, which sounded exciting. It was something entirely new and different for the French team.

When Stephanie dropped Gabriel off at the hotel, she went upstairs with him, but told him she could only stay a while. With Ryan sick, she wanted to go home. They made love again, and lay peacefully afterward, just enjoying being together. They had a long way to go, but she always felt safe and reassured when she was with him. She was sure he'd get divorced, and somehow they'd find their way.

She heard a text come in, and didn't want to answer as she dozed in his arms, but she felt guilty not reading it, so a few minutes later, she got up and took her cellphone out of her bag. It was from Andy. "Just had a seizure. 104.8. Going to ER at UC. Meet me there. Leaving Aden with the Sanchezes." She was wide awake as soon as she read it. The Sanchezes were their neighbors and had kids the same age. And Ryan was having febrile seizures. He'd had them as a baby. They weren't dangerous but they were scary as hell, and so was 104.8. She started climbing into her clothes without bothering to shower. She called Andy but he didn't answer, which panicked her.

"What's wrong?" She was moving at full speed, and she told Gabriel as she dressed. "I'll come with you," he said and started to dress too, which was the right reaction but not in this case.

"You can't. How would I explain it?" She was closer to UCSF than Andy was at home, and she knew she could get there before he did. Gabriel was gazing at her bleakly.

"I don't want you to go alone," he said gallantly with his pants on and no shirt.

"I have to," she said and hurried into the bathroom to comb her hair and clean up her makeup. She looked like she had just climbed out of bed. In two minutes, she appeared relatively civilized, put on her shoes, grabbed her coat off the chair, and kissed Gabriel.

"I'm sorry. Call me after you've seen him. I'm sure he'll be fine. My youngest son used to get them too." She nodded. "Let me know if you want me to come." But there was no way he could. He didn't belong there with Andy, not until everything was out in the open, or when they were married, but not now.

She left seconds later, ran to the elevator, got her car from the valet, and she was headed to UCSF in minutes. She tried calling Andy again, but he still didn't answer. She parked in her usual space in the garage, and was waiting in the ER when he got there. He was carrying Ryan, who was bright red and appeared to be unconscious. She felt him and he was blazing.

"Where were you?" Andy looked desperate, as they waited for a nurse to put them in an exam room. Stephanie had already registered while she was waiting for them.

"At dinner with the group. We had dinner in Palo Alto with the doc from Stanford. I just got back to the city," she said as though it mattered. She was staring at Ryan now and didn't like the way he looked. She told a nurse to get the pediatric attending in, and saw one of the nurses she knew at the desk, who came over to see her right away.

"What's up?" she said, looking at Ryan, and took a thermometer out of her pocket as Andy held him and slipped it in his ear. Ryan stirred and started to cry and said his neck hurt. Stephanie and the nurse exchanged a look, and she checked the thermometer. "It's 105.1. I'll get the attending down here right now." She went to use the phone, and had one of the nurses take him into an exam room. Andy had him wrapped in a blanket over his pajamas and his teeth were chattering.

"He felt sick when he woke up after you left, but he was nothing like this." She could see that Andy was panicked but so was she. She didn't like the way the symptoms were presenting, and she hoped the attending pediatrician didn't agree with her. It looked like meningitis to her, which moved like lightning in children his age, and could be fatal. This couldn't be happening to them. She and Andy glanced at each other as the pediatrician walked in and went straight to Ryan. He tried to move Ryan's head toward his chest and couldn't, and Ryan screamed and threw up. The nurse helped clean him up with a damp cloth and changed him into hospital pajamas while he shivered. Stephanie had already put the hospital bracelet on his wrist.

"You probably think the same thing I do," the pediatrician said, looking at Stephanie. He knew she was a physician.

"Meningitis?" Stephanie said, dreading the word and he nodded.

"Seems like it to me. I want to try and get the fever down, and get a lumbar puncture on him right away, and some bloodwork." The big question was whether it was bacterial or viral. If bacterial, the risk to Ryan was even greater. The nurse hurried out to call the lab, and ordered the spinal tap. He told Stephanie and Andy they'd put him under a light anesthesia to do it. He was sure of his diagnosis and so was Stephanie. The lab technician came in then, and drew several vials of blood while Andy held him and Ryan cried miserably. They got an IV line into his other arm for fluids, and an antibiotic. He was looking worse by the minute. "When did this start?" the doctor asked Stephanie and she turned to Andy.

"Maybe around six or seven," Andy said in a hoarse voice. Everything was moving so quickly. It was one-fifteen in the morning, so he'd been sick for seven hours. She knew that children his age often died six to twelve hours after the onset of symptoms. It was one of the fastest moving, most lethal illnesses children could get. They were playing "beat the clock," and Stephanie knew it as tears filled her eyes and she glanced at Andy. They took Ryan away five minutes later to do the spinal tap, and Stephanie asked to go with him, but the pediatrician wouldn't let her. Parents were not allowed, even if she was a doctor and worked in the ER.

"He'll be out from the anesthetic in a few minutes. We'll get him back to you as soon as we can. I want him in Peds ICU," he said firmly and she nodded.

"We'll meet you there." She squeezed Andy's hand as they watched Ryan wheeled away on a gurney. He suddenly looked tiny. If he had meningitis, she was afraid Aden would get it, although it wasn't certain he would. But worst case, they could lose both their children within hours. Mostly it was just terrible luck that Ryan had caught it, and unlikely lightning would strike twice.

"Is he going to be okay?" Andy asked her as they went to the elevator to go upstairs to the ICU.

"I don't know," she said honestly. "It's not good." She got a text from Gabriel then, wanting to know what was happening, but she didn't answer. This was her time with Andy and she didn't want to be distracted by anyone. They paced the halls together while they waited for Ryan, and didn't speak to each other. There was nothing to say.

"What do we do, Steph, if it is meningitis?" he finally had the courage to ask, and she shook her head.

"Nothing. We wait and we pray. We're already giving him an antibiotic. They'll give him steroids after the tap."

They brought him back forty minutes later, still groggy from the anesthetic. They rolled him into a room and put him on a bed. A nurse took his vital signs, and another one hooked him up to monitors. He was still blazing, and they tried to cool him with damp cloths and added something to his IV to bring the fever down.

The pediatrician came back to confirm what Stephanie already knew. Ryan had meningitis. It was viral, so he had a better chance of survival, but nothing was sure, especially at his age. He was dozing from the fever and the anesthetic, as Stephanie stood next to him stroking his hair. She couldn't bear the thought that he might die, but she was praying he'd survive it. He was too little and too sick, and when she looked up, Andy was crying, and she was too.

"How did this happen? He was fine this morning. And now he's . . ." Andy choked on the words.

"That's how this happens, especially in kids his age."

"Can they do something?"

"Not much," she said, wiping the tears from her cheeks.

The doctor came and went for the next hour, and they brought in an infectious disease specialist, who spoke to both of them. He basically told them that although viral meningitis was less serious than bacterial, he still might die in the next few hours and they needed to prepare themselves. Andy broke down in sobs, and she held him. They didn't leave Ryan for the next two hours. Stephanie wanted to be there if he died. She had seen patients die through her work, but this was her baby, her youngest child. It was unthinkable, but it was happening. And then his skin started coming up in boils.

"What is that?"

"It's from the fever. He's boiling inside," she explained.

They stayed there all night. And at eight in the morning he was still alive, but barely. It had been the worst night of her life. She had thought of everything she had done wrong, everything she wished she had done differently, the times she wasn't with them because she was working, the marriage that had gone so wrong, while Andy got bitter and she got bored and they lost each other somewhere in the process.

At ten o'clock, Ryan opened his eyes and smiled at them, and looked like an angel. She thought he was dying, but he sighed and went back to sleep and kept breathing. At noon he was still alive.

The fever was down to 102, but he was still fighting for his life. She texted Valérie and told her what had happened and where they were, so she could tell the others. Gabriel was texting her frantically, but she didn't have the heart to answer him. What if this was her punishment for having the affair with him? It all seemed so stupid and irrelevant now. She thought she loved Gabriel, and she was going to divorce Andy and move to France. But what difference did any of it make if Ryan died? It put everything into perspective.

One of the nurses suggested that they go to the waiting room and lie down for a while. There was no one else there, and they'd been on their feet all night. They hated to leave him even for a minute, but the nurse said she would get them right away if anything happened. They sat down in chairs next to each other and looked like they'd been shipwrecked. He had survived for eighteen hours, which wasn't enough.

Andy was staring at her as they sat there. "I just want to tell you that whatever happens, I love you, Steph. I know everything has gone to shit with us, and it's my fault. I got lost somewhere along the way, and jealous of you. You're a star, Steph. You have a right to everything you've earned. And whatever happens with us, I'm going to get a job. We can hire someone to take care of the kids." His eyes filled with tears as he said it and so did hers. Their marriage was over anyway. "I've been a shit husband, trying to hold you back. You have a right to all of it. I don't know what went wrong for us. I don't know what happened in Paris, and I don't want to know. If you want a divorce, you can have it, and I'll move out. But I don't want to lose you, I love you and our boys. If you give it another chance after this, I'll be better, I swear. You're an amazing woman." She was sobbing when she went to hug him, and they held each other for a long time, trying to face the reality that their child was dying. Stephanie just prayed that Aden didn't get it too. They couldn't lose them both. Or even one of them. She couldn't bear it. But Aden was fine when she called Mrs. Sanchez to check on him.

"I haven't been a great wife either," she said, as they sat holding hands. "It's hard to do both. I want to be the best doctor, but then I'm a lousy mom."

"You're not a lousy mom. And one day they'll respect you for what you do. Other kids have working parents, and they do fine." She nodded. That was what she had hoped but it was harder than she'd thought it would be. Someone was always getting short shrift, their marriage if not their kids. "I think I just gave up somewhere along the way. I was so busy feeling sorry for myself and being pissed at you. Do you want out, Steph?" It was a big question at the wrong time, but as she looked at him, she knew she didn't. If Ryan died, they would need each other. They would either way.

"No, I don't," she said in a voice raw with emotion, and knew she meant it.

"Let's try to make it work. I don't know if we can, but let's try. Not for them, for us. And they need us both."

They sat with his arm around her for a long time, and when Stephanie looked up, she saw Valérie and Tom in the doorway. They had come to check on them and sat down quietly next to them.

"How is he?" Tom asked Stephanie.

"Not good, but he's still alive." Tom nodded. They had brought some soup and sandwiches, and they only stayed a short time. They didn't want to intrude, and they said the others sent their love. They'd canceled their meetings for the day, and they'd all had lunch together. Valérie had postponed her mysterious lunch. And Gabriel was beside himself and said that Stephanie wouldn't answer his texts. But if her child was dying, she wouldn't. She and Andy needed this time alone with him, whatever they did after that. Valérie wasn't sure what was happening after she saw them, and she and Tom talked about it. He had the feeling that they were making peace, but it was hard to tell during the crisis.

They went back and sat with Ryan after Tom and Valérie left. He woke up a few times, and the fever was slowly coming down. They had him down to a hundred by that night, and in the morning his temperature was normal. They had had Aden seen by his pediatrician by then, and he was fine. And Ryan had survived for thirty-six hours, which seemed like a miracle given how sick he was. It was Tuesday. Andy looked at her as a nurse brought them coffee in the waiting room.

"Did you mean what you said, or was that just terror talking?" Andy asked her. He didn't want to hold her hostage, and he knew she was in love with someone else. He'd known it since she came back from France. "About our marriage, I mean."

"I want to try. That's all we can do. Let's give it a shot." She smiled at him. "I'm still me and you're still you, the good and the bad parts. We used to love each other, and we still do. Maybe we can figure out how to make it work again." He nodded. It was what they had to work with. It wasn't perfect, but it was worth another try before they gave up.

Andy went home that night and got Aden from the Sanchezes. He was fine. He wasn't sick, and probably wouldn't get sick now. She had promised to call Andy if anything happened and Ryan got worse again. He wasn't completely out of the woods yet, even with viral meningitis. With bacterial, he would have been dead by then. She slept in a chair in his room that night, and she stroked his hair and kissed him, and thanked God that he didn't die, and hopefully wouldn't now.

Andy relieved her in the morning, and she went home to shower and change, and then she called Gabriel. He sounded frantic when he picked up. They were continuing their meetings and had had the earthquake drill the day before.

"My God, I've been worried sick about you. How is he?"

"He's still very sick, but I think he's going to be okay. He has viral meningitis. Thank God it wasn't bacterial, but he's been very sick."

"I know, Valérie told us. She said you'd get in touch with me when you could. Thank you for calling me, my darling." He sounded near tears.

"I want to see you," she said quietly.

"Of course. Come to my room. I'll meet you there." She didn't want to do that. She didn't trust herself. She still loved him. But she loved Andy too. She knew that now. And it was too soon to let go and quit. If Ryan had survived and beat the odds, maybe they could too.

And she knew something else now. Whatever happened with Andy, she couldn't give up her job at UCSF. Not for Andy or Gabriel, or anyone. She couldn't move to France. She wanted to stay here and do what she was doing there. It was too much to give up. She couldn't give up her job any more than she could give up her kids. She didn't want to start over somewhere else. She needed to stay here.

"Let's take a walk," she suggested. "I need some air."

She met him at the Ferry Building and they walked along the Embarcadero while she told him what she had to do. She had to try again with Andy, even if it didn't work in the end, but it might. And she couldn't give up her job. She didn't want to. It meant too much to her. He cried when she told him and told her she had broken his heart. He said he was going to get divorced for her, and she wondered if it was true. If he were, he'd have called a lawyer when she left Paris before he came to the States, but he hadn't, and she might have ended up like Wendy, waiting years for him to leave his wife, if he ever did. She'd never know now. But the sacrifices would have been too great on her side anyway, a man, a marriage, a career that she had built for years and sacrificed for. She hoped that she and Andy could put the broken pieces back together. It was possible, but nothing was sure in life. She had almost lost her son in the last three days, almost left her marriage. She felt as though she had lost her mind for a while, and she had found it again. Whatever happened with Andy, she had found herself.

"I won't survive this," Gabriel said dramatically. "I'll go back to Paris tonight."

"Don't," she said simply. "We can do this. We're adults. I love you, but not enough to give up my whole life for you. And maybe you don't love me that much either. Stay, and finish what you came here to do."

"I can't, you've destroyed me," he said, and she tried not to smile. He sounded very theatrical and very French. Ryan almost dying made everything else seem very small in comparison. And if he had died, she wouldn't have been talking to Gabriel at all, she would have been with Andy, who would have needed her more than Gabriel then.

"Let's try to do this nicely," she said simply, but she wasn't sure he had it in him. She left him at the Embarcadero, and walked back to her car and drove to the hospital. She had called Valérie before she got there and told her what had happened, and asked if she thought Gabriel would be okay.

"He'll be fine, he's just being histrionic. We'll talk to him. You're right. He should stay. Things happen in life. Your boy almost dying is a big reminder of that. Things can change in the blink of an eye. And I'm not sure he would have gotten divorced. He's too used to the life he has with his wife. We'll never know now. But I think you did the right thing."

"So do I. However it works out. And I'm not giving up my work for anyone, and they shouldn't expect it of me. He didn't volunteer to move here, and he's not even practicing anymore, he has a government job."

"Good point." Valérie sounded happy for her, and most of all that Ryan had lived.

Ryan was smiling when Stephanie walked into the room. Andy was with him and she smiled at both of them.

"We have a young man here who wants ice cream," Andy said happily.

"I think that can be arranged," she said, and asked the nurse at the desk to have some sent up from the kitchen. A bowl of vanilla ice cream came up a few minutes later.

"That was fast," Andy said as she handed it to Ryan, and he dug into it. There were still marks from the boils on his skin, and he was still very pale, but the worst was over, and he was going to survive. Maybe they would too. She hoped so. The doctor had said he could go home at the end of the week. Andy was going to watch him, while she did the rest of the conference, she didn't want to miss it and Andy agreed. The housekeeper was going to sleep at the house to help with Ryan, while she was busy.

Andy didn't ask what she had worked out with Gabriel, but he could tell that she had. She seemed quiet and at peace, and she felt back in her right mind. She had gone crazy for a while. The school shooting, being in Paris, not having her husband or children around, their marriage being in trouble, but she had come back to earth and landed on her feet. It felt good to be her again. And Ryan was alive.

# Chapter Eighteen

Marie-Laure and Paul went to Squaw Valley that weekend to ski, with the understanding that they were both free agents. They were fabulous skiers and he had fun skiing with her, and prowling the local bars at night.

Valérie and Tom went to the Napa Valley for the weekend. He waited until they were at their hotel, standing on the balcony of their room, looking out over the valley, to ask her the question that had been tormenting him all week. He knew she had met up with her old friend on Thursday.

"So how was your lunch date with your old boyfriend?" Valérie was an independent woman, and he knew he would never control her and didn't want to try, but he didn't want to lose her either. And he had fantasized a gorgeous French boyfriend who might stir up old embers again and cause a spark.

"I'm sorry to disappoint you. He was never my boyfriend. We went to school together." She grinned at Tom and he wanted to shake her.

He'd been worried about it since she told him. "I just wanted to keep you interested."

"You have my interest, and my heart. You didn't need to torture me," he scolded her, and wondered if what she said was true. She was not above using feminine wiles, and she had on him. "So why did you have lunch with him?"

"I did a little exploring before I came over here," she said, gazing at the valley, and then at him. "Jean-Louis teaches at Stanford at the medical school. He married an American, and they live here. He suggested something to me a few years ago that I wasn't interested in then, but I might be now. It depends on you actually. He offered me a guest professorship, teaching psychiatry. I thought it was boring compared to what I was doing with the post-trauma programs. But they can run them without me now. Everything is in place, and the kind of situations we are seeing today take a lot out of you. They're ugly. The world is more savage than it used to be. I think I'd enjoy being a guest professor for a year or two, and it would give me time to write another book while I'm here. I wanted to know if the offer would still be open to me." Tom was listening to her, fascinated and holding his breath.

"And what did he say?"

"He said it would be," she said softly and smiled at Tom. "I didn't know how you'd feel about it. I wanted to ask him first. I can't practice medicine in this country, or if I could, it would be a long, complicated process and I don't want to do that now. But I can teach. I think I'd like that. I could start in September, if that seems like a good idea to you." She had been saving it until she knew for sure, and she was planning to tell him over the weekend.

"You are a busy little bee, aren't you, Dr. Florin. I think it's a fantastic idea. I've been trying to think of ways to get you over here, but you trumped me on this one."

"And I can get a work permit to go with it."

"You might have to marry me to get a green card," he teased her, but it sounded like she didn't need one. "So are you going to do it?"

"Do you want me here? It's not just my decision." He pulled her into his arms and held her tight.

"What do you think?"

"I think I love you, and you need an apartment with bigger closets."

"I think we could work that out." He was smiling at her and had never been happier in his life.

"You can come over to France for a holiday in July, the way we planned, and I'll come back with you at the beginning of August, and start teaching in September. I can give them a decent notice at the COZ when I go back. That gives them three months to replace me."

"I want you to do it, if you'll be happy teaching," he said seriously. She nodded. She liked the idea, and she was ready for something new. The savagery they were seeing in mass crimes in Europe was too disheartening, too cruel, and inhumane. She had wanted to leave it for a while, and now everything had fallen into place. "I love you," he said simply and kissed her. They looked at the valley together. She was full of surprises. She was the woman he had always wanted and needed and didn't even know it. He had found her at last.

When Stephanie joined the group again after Ryan got out of the hospital, there were two weeks left. She'd only been gone for a week, but it felt like a century. Ryan was doing well, but they were keeping him home for several weeks. And Andy didn't complain when she said she was going back to the team. He encouraged her to go.

The others had talked Gabriel into staying, and he put on a tragic face whenever Stephanie was around. He didn't speak to her, and avoided her whenever he could, which she understood. It was awkward for her too, but she tried to behave as normally as possible. He had a right to be upset. Ryan's illness had brought her to her senses and ended their affair.

Things weren't perfect with Andy but they were better. The terror of almost losing Ryan had woken them both up to how foolish they had been, how careless with their relationship, and about what mattered to both of them. They were heading in the right direction again and he was going to look for a job, which Andy realized he needed for his self-respect.

Valérie told them all that she was coming back to San Francisco in August to teach at Stanford, after she told Marie-Laure her plans. Marie-Laure said she was going to miss her, but she was happy for her. Their job had gotten harder and harder in recent years and the burnout rate was high. She knew Valérie had been approaching that point. And she knew Valérie wanted to write again, as well as teach.

The last two weeks flew by, and Wendy gave a farewell dinner for them at her house with Bill at the barbecue again. Neither of them said anything, but they all had the feeling that something was happening there. They were both very private people, but the way they spoke to each other had changed. Bill seemed very familiar with her house, and she was helping him decorate his apartment. They were talking about a summer trip to the Grand Canyon with his girls. She was happy that Valérie was coming back, and she admitted to her privately that she and Bill were seeing each other when they had time off.

"And to think I almost didn't accept the exchange," Wendy said thoughtfully. "Life is so odd. You think you're on a path, and then suddenly everything changes. It happened to all of us. We all woke up in one way or another since we've been together. Not one of us is the same as we were before." She said it with wonder in her eyes. They all stayed late at her house, talking and laughing, and drinking a lot of wine, because they had a driver to take them home. They promised to visit each other, and get together when they could. Tom was going to be in France with Valérie in July, helping her pack up her apartment. Bill and Wendy promised to go to Paris sometime with his girls. Stephanie wanted to go over in a year or two with Andy and the boys.

And Paul admitted to them that he had decided to go back to Doctors Without Borders. He said the tribal wars he had dealt with before were cleaner than the urban ones he had experienced since. He missed his work in Africa, and felt it was time to return there for a while.

Gabriel finally stopped playing wounded hero that night, and Stephanie found a quiet moment with him by the pool when the others drifted inside for dinner. He hadn't spoken to her since she'd rejoined the group, and she didn't want to leave it on an angry note.

"I'm sorry, Gabriel, I truly am. I didn't expect things to go this way. I really wanted to come to France with my kids." She had been sure they would get married, but she didn't rub it in. "I think whatever happened, it would have been wrong for me to give up my job here.

I love what I do. We all do. We're all married to our work in a way, sometimes more so than to the people we're with. We work hard for it, even if it's difficult at times. My father is still delivering babies at seventy-two. I wanted to do it for you but it was too big a leap, and when Ryan got sick, I realized that I owed it to Andy to give it another try. I don't know if it will work or not. Maybe it doesn't matter. But it wasn't the right time to quit yet. I thought it was, but it wasn't. It all happened too fast. I never meant to hurt you. I'm sorry for us that it turned out this way."

"I'm not sure if I could have done it either," he admitted to her. "Old habits die hard. I thought I could too. My wife and I don't have enough life in our marriage to revive it, and I don't think either of us wants that. But the way we live works for us. We're used to it." It was the most honest he had been with her, and with himself, since the beginning. She had given him time to think in the past two weeks, and he had come to his own conclusions. Their flame had burned too hot, and they both might have been wounded in the end. "Take care of yourself, Stephanie. You can always call me if I can help you in any way."

"Thank you." They walked back to the others then, and joined the merriment over dinner.

Wendy hosted the dinner on Thursday night, and they were all leaving on Saturday. They spent their last day doing final errands and shopping for friends. Valérie, Marie-Laure, and Wendy had met Stephanie's children by then. And Ryan was back to his old bouncy self by the time they left.

\* \* \*

Stephanie, Bill, Tom, and Wendy met them at the airport before their flight. It was a beautiful spring morning. Wendy and Bill were going to lie by her pool afterward. It was an emotional farewell. Tom didn't know how he would survive without Valérie for the next three months, except that he was looking for apartments and she had given him a list of all her requirements, a decent bathroom, lots of closets, a garden, at least one fireplace, high ceilings, and a view.

They all hugged and kissed, even Stephanie and Gabriel, and they both got tearful for a minute, thinking of what might have been. "We would have been wonderful together," he whispered, but she was no longer so sure. Valérie had a good point, he hadn't been willing to give up his job for her, and expected it of her. But it didn't matter anymore.

Their four French friends went through security waving and blowing kisses. Paul said he had fallen in love eleven times in four weeks, which was a record for him, and Valérie texted Tom while he stood there, his heart aching to see her go. He read the text, "Look under your bed," and laughed as he touched his heart and waved again.

And then they were gone, and the others went back to their cars and drove home. Andy and Stephanie were going to the beach with the boys, and she was on duty at the hospital that night. It was her first day back at work. She made no apology for it. She had learned that lesson now.

When he got home, Tom looked under his bed, as Valérie's text message had said, and all her underwear was there, the lacy thongs with matching bras, the garters. She had left it all for him in one place, and he sat there and laughed holding it. It was going to be a long three months without her, but they had good times in store.

\* \* \*

Marie-Laure and Valérie sat together on the flight. They talked about everything that had happened, the changes they'd been through in the past two and a half months since they'd met their American friends. Valérie's life had changed the most of all since she was moving to California. Paul was going back to Africa. Stephanie and Andy had come full circle but were in a better place. Tom had reformed. Bill had opened up and come alive again, and Wendy had shed a man who had wasted six years of her life, and would have wasted the rest if she'd let him. None of them were untouched. Even Gabriel was going back to his old life, but by choice not default. The only one whose life hadn't changed was Marie-Laure. "The office won't be the same without you," she said to Valérie.

"Yes, it will, it'll be better. You'll get some new young thing who'll come up with a bunch of bright ideas and get everyone scurrying in all directions and shake things up. That's what we all need. It's what we did for each other." Marie-Laure nodded, thinking about it, and a little while later, she fell asleep.

The flight attendant woke her when they were about to land at Charles de Gaulle, to tell her that her official police escort was waiting for her.

"Good Lord, are we having threats again? Welcome back to France," she grumbled to Valérie. "They've sent the police for me for protection. God knows what's going on now." They came to get Marie-Laure when they landed, and escorted her off first. As she looked up, expecting to see uniformed police officers or CRS with machine guns waiting to accompany her through the airport, instead she saw Bruno in his captain's uniform standing there.

"What are you doing here?" she said to him with a smile.

"I thought you deserved a police escort for your triumphant return. You were gone a long time. It's about time you came home. We need you here." She smiled as she listened to him, and looked up into his smiling face with the lines around his eyes.

He walked her into the terminal ahead of the others. He picked up her bag from the conveyor belt and walked it to his police car outside and turned on the flashing lights, but not the sirens.

"I missed you," he said, looking faintly embarrassed to have admitted it. "When are we having dinner?"

"Tonight? I have to pick up my boys tomorrow." He was pleased. He would have her to himself for tonight at least. And after that, who knew what would happen, what madness might turn their lives upside down.

She was smiling as they drove into the city, darting through traffic, blue lights flashing, and she laughed.

"This is fun," she said, as they glanced at each other warmly. She was happy he'd come to the airport, and so was he. Tomorrow she'd be back in her office, planning for emergencies, and he'd be responding to disasters. And at the end of the day, they would have whatever they created together. They had met in the midst of chaos, and something good and worthwhile had come of it for all of them. Suddenly she realized that her life and Bruno's had changed too. It would be whatever they chose to make of it. And whatever happened after that, destiny would decide. It had turned out well for all of them so far.

# SILENT NIGHT

*Sometimes the best things happen*
*when we think all is lost . . .*

Paige Watts is the ultimate stage mother. The daughter of Hollywood royalty, Paige channels her own acting dreams into making her daughter, Emma, a star. By the age of nine, Emma is playing a central role in a hit TV show. Then everything is shattered by unforeseeable tragedy.

Now Emma is living with her aunt Whitney, who had chosen a very different path from her sister's. Whitney was always the career-driven older sister, loving a no-strings relationship and hating the cult of celebrity that enveloped their childhood. But at a moment's notice, Whitney must change her life in every way.

*Available for pre-order*

PURE HEART. PURE STEEL.

R